Charles Reade

Good stories of man and other animals

Charles Reade

Good stories of man and other animals

ISBN/EAN: 9783744749176

Printed in Europe, USA, Canada, Australia, Japan

Cover: Foto ©Andreas Hilbeck / pixelio.de

More available books at **www.hansebooks.com**

E A Abbey

GOOD STORIES

OF

MAN AND OTHER ANIMALS

By CHARLES READE, D.C.L.

WITH ILLUSTRATIONS BY E. A. ABBEY, PERCY MACQUOID
AND JOSEPH NASH

London

CHATTO & WINDUS, PICCADILLY

1884

CONTENTS.

LIST OF ILLUSTRATIONS.

THE PICTURE.

PART I.

I AM now seventy, and learning something every day—
especially my ignorance. But fifty-two years ago I
knew everything, or nearly—I had finished my education. I knew a little Greek and Latin, a very little
vernacular, a little mathematics, and a little war:
could march a thousand men into a field, and even out
of it again—on paper. So I left Paris, and went home
to rest on my oars.

Months rolled on; I still rested on my oars—rested
on them so industriously that at last my mother, a
very superior woman, took fright at my assiduous inac-
tivity, and bundled me out of the boat.

She had an uncle who loved her, and, indeed, had
reared her as a child. She wrote to him, concealing
neither her maternal pride nor her maternal anxieties.
He replied, ‘ Send the boy here, and if he is anything
like you, he shall be my son and successor.’ He was a
notary, and had a good business.

In due course the diligence landed me far from
home, at a town in Provence. A boy and an ass were
waiting for me. On these beasts of burden I strapped
my effects, and the quadruped conducted us by a bridle-

B

road through groves and by purling streams to a range of hills at whose foot nestled my uncle's villa, lawn, garden, and vineyard. The contrast was admirable. The hills, with their rocky chasms, were bold, grand, and grim ; and the little house, clothed with flowering creepers, the velvet lawn, watered twice a day, and green as emerald, and the violet plums peeping among the olive-coloured leaves, were quietly enchanting. 'Oh,' thought I, 'what a bower for a hard notary!'

The hard notary met me with open arms, embraced me, held me out, gazed at me, said, in a broken voice, 'You are very like your darling mother,' and embraced me again. I was installed in a pretty bedroom with a bay-window, curtained outside by a magnolia in full bloom ; pigeons cooed outside every morning an hour before breakfast, leaves glistened with dew, and flowers diffused sweet smells.

Next day my uncle took me into the town to his office, and introduced me to his managing clerk as his partner and successor. He left me under charge of this worthy while he pursued his real vocation, *bric-à-brac.* He was so unfortunate as to pick up a great bargain, a vile old jug; he itched to be home with it; so I had no time to master my new business that day.

The good *curé* dined with us, and my uncle presented us both to him, jug and nephew—especially jug; but the *curé* was impartial, and took a gentle interest, real or fictitious, in us both ; he was a man of learning and piety, and had seen strange and terrible things in France ; had known great people and great vicissitudes, though now settled in a peaceful village—'post tot naufragia tutus.' He was a gentle, amiable soul, a severe judge of nothing but cruelty and deliberate vice, and a most interesting companion if you chose; by which I mean that he had neither the animal spirits nor the vanity which makes a man habitually fluent; but, if you could suspend your own volubility and question him, a well of knowledge.

My uncle had two servants—Catherine, a tall, gaunt woman; tanned, hollow-eyed, and wrinkled; and Suzon, a pretty, rosy, bright-eyed maid. Her my uncle ignored; Catherine was his favourite—a model of industry, fidelity, and skill; besides, she resembled antique mugs, etc., whereas little Suzon was more like modern porcelain, Provence roses, and such like ephemeral things. Suzon was always in the background, Catherine always to the fore. She cooked the dinner; yet she must put on au apron and a cap of the past and wait upon us, even when the *curé* or a stray advocate from Paris was our guest, and Suzon would have done us credit. Erelong this latter arrangement became grievous to me, for I fell in love; and this gaunt creature came between me and the delight of my eyes. It was my first attachment. I had seen a good many pretty girls, and danced with them; but I thought them frivolous, and they took me for a pedant. I was a poet, and aimed high. Accordingly I fell in love with a picture—or with the goddess it represented.

My uncle's dining-room combined the *salon* and the *salle à manger.* It was very long and broad, and the round table devoted to meals could be placed in any part of the room. Eight could dine at it, yet there was room for it in the great bay-window, and it ran smoothly upon little wheels instead of casters; so did all the chairs, ottomans. fauteuils, and sofas. Chinese vases five feet high, and always filled with flowers, guarded the four corners of the room; vast landscapes were painted on the walls, and framed in panels of mellow oak; many pieces of curious old plate glittered on the sideboard; a large door-way with no door, but an ample curtain of blue Utrecht velvet, led into a library of choice books splendidly bound, many of them by antique binders, the delight of connoisseurs. Over the mantel-piece of the dining-room hung a picture in an oval frame, massive, and carved with great skill and simplicity; this frame had been chipped in places, and there was a black-looking hole in the right border, and some foreign substance imbedded.

The picture was a portrait (life size) of a young lady, resplendent with youth and beauty, the face oval and forehead pure, the lips and peeping teeth exquisite, and the liquid gray eyes full of languor above and fire below that arrested and enchanted. The dress had, no doubt, been selected for pictorial effect; for the waist was long and of a natural size, and the noble bare arms adorned only with dark-blue velvet bands, which set off the satin skin.

Soft sensations and vague desires thrilled me as I gazed on this enchanting picture, and I longed and sighed for the original.

The gaunt Catherine at dinner-time kept getting between me and my goddess, and I hated the sight of her, and said she purposely interposed her hideousness between me and that divine beauty. But now, having had fifty years to consider the matter, I think she stood behind her master's chair whether there was a love-sick dreamer at the table or not, and was intent on her duties not my dreams.

After I had thoroughly absorbed this lovely creature's perfections, and satisfied myself that her character was as noble, arch, and loveable as her features, I found it difficult to go on living without ever hearing her enchanting voice, or kissing her hand, or, at all events, some portion or other of her dress. So I asked my uncle timidly for her name and address.

The answer was discouraging: 'How should I know? I bought her for the frame, you may be sure; it is what the fools call *rococo; that* means admirable.'

'And so it is, now I look at it,' said I; 'but oh, uncle, what is that compared with the divine effigy?'

'Divine fiddle-stick!' said he. 'Look at her little finger, all out of drawing.'

Here was a notary against whom it could not be urged, 'de minimis non curat lex.' Why, I could hardly help laughing in his face.

'Her little finger!' I cried. 'Look at her lips, her teeth, her eyes—brimful of heaven!'

'That inspection I leave to you, young man,' said my uncle, calmly; 'but I should like to know what that black mark *in the frame* is.'

'And so you shall, uncle,' said I, with the ready good-nature of youth; and thereupon I jumped on a chair, and from the chair alighted like a bird on the mantel-piece, and my uncle ejaculated and trembled— for the wood-work, not me. I examined the hole in the frame and found a substance imbedded. I took out my penknife, nearly fell on my uncle's head, recovered myself with a yell, cut a small slice off the substance, and reported, ' Uncle, it is lead—a bullet, a big one. There, now, O, base world! Ah, sovereign beauty, your charms have well-nigh cost your life. Some despairing lover, whom she esteemed but could not love, or, likelier still, some rival crushed under her charms, has committed this outrage. Oh! oh! oh! There are some golden hairs attached to the bullet. Horrible! horrible!'

' Malediction on the fools!' cried my uncle. ' Why could they not fire at the daub and spare the frame?' He added, more composedly, that evidently some mob had attacked the house during the troubles, and one of the savages had fired at it out of pure ruffianism.

'No, no,' said I; ' that does not account for these golden hairs. Oh, uncle, who is she? I will travel all France if necessary. Do but tell me where I can find her.'

' How can I tell what churchyard she lies in? Why, it is fifty years since such frames were made in this now tasteless country.'

' Cruel uncle, do not say so,' cried I, in piteous accents. ' Ah, no; they found a quaint old frame to act as a foil to her youth and beauty. I will copy her. I will make an etching of her; I am rather skilful in that way. I will send impressions all round France; I will solicit information. I shall find her. She is single; she has not found her peer in my sex. Is it likely she would? I will surround her with homage; I will tell her how I pined for her and sought her, and found her first because I loved her best; I will throw myself at her feet; I will kiss the hem of her sweet robe, I will— Gone!'

Gone he was, in mid-tirade, with his hands in his pockets; he escaped my juvenile eloquence, and I heard him whistling.

I loved her all the more, and lived for our first rapturous meeting.

In due course another idle attempt was made to refrigerate my immortal love; this one came from that old hag Catherine. I used to set my easel after breakfast, and work nearly all day reproducing the beloved features. One afternoon I could not stop for anything. Catherine came in and pottered· about, laying the cloth for dinner. That was hard, but I thought it harder when suddenly her voice jarred upon my amorous soul with a calm observation :

'Is not that a waste of time?'

I looked up, amazed at such an interference.

'I mean,' said she, 'that we do not need another picture of *her*.'

'*You* don't, I dare say; female beauty is not to your taste; but the world requires a great many pictures of this peerless creature; and the world shall have them, whether you like it or not.' Catherine shrugged her shoulders, and said the world could do very well without them. 'And for my part,' said she, 'I cannot think what you see so admirable in that face.'

'Look at it without envy, hatred, or malice, if you can, and then you will see.'

Thus brought to book, the grim creature folded her arms and gazed on the portrait in a dignified and attentive manner that surprised me. 'I find it is beautiful,' said she, calmly.

'What a discovery!'

'The beauty of youth and health, and rather good features.'

'What a concession!'

'But I search in vain for the beauty of the soul. With youth should go modesty and humility; but here I see vanity and self-sufficiency.'

'And I see only a noble pride, tempered with such sweetness and archness. There, instead of running her down to me, when you might as well blacken the morning star, I should be truly grateful to you if you would help me find out where she lives. Alive she is; my heart tells me so. Death, more merciful than envy, has spared those peerless features.'

Catherine stared. 'Who is she? why, what does that matter to you? She is old enough to be your grandmother; look at the frame.'

'Malediction on the frame! You are as bad as my uncle. He bought her for the frame. *She* is not old; she never will be old; such beauty is immortal. Now tell me, my good Catherine. I dare say you have lived in this district all your life—— Gone!'

It was too true; the servant, like the master, had escaped my enthusiasm, and left me to my theories. But I painted on and loved my idol in spite of them all, and held fast my determination to discover her by publishing her features from Havre to Marseilles.

One day my uncle received a very welcome letter. It announced a visit from an old fellow-collegian of his, a highly distinguished person, a statesman, an ambassador and peer of France—the Comte de Pontarlais. This thrilled me with excitement and curiosity. I had never sat at the same table with an ambassador. Only I feared our way of living would seem very humble, and worst of all, that Catherine would wait at table, and get between his excellency and our one peerless gem, the portrait of my divinity.

I was all in a flutter as the hour drew near, and looked out for a carriage with outriders, whence should emerge a figure striped with broad ribbon and emblazoned with orders.

Arrived with military precision an elderly gentleman on a mule, with a small valise carried by a peasant. He was well dressed, but simply; embraced my uncle affectionately; and they walked up and down the grass arm in arm, to be as near one another as possible, since they met so seldom. From the lawn they entered the library; and I was going thither somewhat shyly to be presented, when Suzon met me in wild distress.

'Oh, Monsieur Frédéric! what shall we do? Here's Catherine been ailing this three days and scarce able to get about, and the master ordered a great dinner, and she *would* cook it, and not fit to stand, and she fainted away, and now she is lying down on her bed more dead than alive.'

'Poor thing!' said I. 'Well, you must get a woman into the kitchen, and you put on your best cap and wait.'

'Since *you* order it,' said Suzon, demurely, and lowered her eyelashes. Now, this extreme deference had not been her habit hitherto.

Encouraged by this piece of flattery, I added, 'And please stand behind *my* chair to-day instead of my uncle's. It is not that I wish to give myself importance—'

'The idea!' said Suzon.

'But that—ahem!—his excellency—'

'I understand,' said Suzon; 'you wish *me* to have a good look at him—and so do I.'

So may a man's best motives be misinterpreted by shallow minds.

The next moment I entered the library, and was presented, blushing, to his excellency. He put me at my ease by his kindliness and quiet, genial manner. To be sure, such men have a different manner for different occasions. He had long studied with success the great art of pleasing. Under this charming surface, however, I could see a calm authority, and in those well-cut features Voltairian finesse.

By-and-by Suzon announced dinner, and I took that opportunity to say that poor Catherine was very ill, and his excellency would have much to excuse.

His excellency interrupted me— 'My young friend, trust to my experience. Company is spoiled by service; the fewer majestic and brainless figures stand behind our chairs, the better for *us*. The most delightful party I can remember, everything was on the table, or on a huge buffet, and we helped ourselves and helped each other. Why, the very circumstance loosened our tongues, that formality would have paralysed. We puffed all the dishes, to which we invited our fair *convives*, and told romantic stories about them, and not a word of truth.' Thus chatting, he entered the *salle à manger* and was about to take the seat my uncle waved him to, when he suddenly started back, with an ejaculation, not loud' but eloquent, and his eyes fixed upon the portrait of my idol.

The very next moment he turned them with a flash of keen and almost suspicious inquiry upon my uncle; then quietly seated himself at the table, and his host, good man, observed nothing.

For my part, I was trembling with curiosity all dinner-time, and longing to ask the great man if he had seen some living beauty who resembled that portrait; but I was too shy. My eyes kept travelling from him to the portrait and back, but I said nothing. However, his quick eye must have detected me, for, after dinner was over, and Suzon ordered to make the coffee, his excellency, who was peeling a pear very carefully looked steadily at *me*, and said, ' May I ask how that portrait came here ? '

' Oh, yes, monsieur le comte,' said I. ' My uncle bought it in a *bric-à-brac* shop.'

My uncle hastened to justify his conduct—it was the frame which had tempted him. ' However,' said he, ' the picture, incorrect as it is—just look at that little finger !—has found a rapturous admirer in my nephew there, who, you may have remarked, is very young.'

' It has,' said I, stoutly. ' It reflects her beauty and her expression, and no bad picture does that. I'd give the world to find out the artist, for then he would tell me where I can find the divine original.'

' That does not follow,' said the count, drily ; ' these fair creatures keep in one place during the sitting ; but in the course of the next forty years or so they consider themselves at liberty to move about like the rest of us.'

'Oh, of course,' said I; 'but such beauty must leave traces everywhere. I am sure, if I knew who painted the picture, I could find the original.'

'I will put that to the test,' said his excellency. 'Come, now—I painted the picture!'

I bounded off my chair with the vivacity of youth, and stood staring at our guest with all my eyes. 'You!' said I, panting.

'Astonishing!' said my uncle. Then, calmly, 'That accounts for the little finger.'

'For shame, uncle!' said I. 'It's a masterpiece. Ah, sir, you must have been inspired by— Who is she? Who was she?'

'She was my betrothed!'

PART II.

I STARED at the speaker, first stupidly, then incredulously, then with a growing conviction that the marvellous revelation was nevertheless true; then my uncle and I, by one impulse, turned round and looked at the picture with a fresh gush of wonder; then we turned back to the count again and glared, but found no words.

At last I managed to stammer out, 'Betrothed to *her*, and not married!'

'Strange, is it not?' said the count, with a satirical shrug. 'Permit me,' said he, with ironical meekness, ' to urge in my defence that I have not married any one else.'

I said I could well understand that.

'Pooh!' said my uncle; 'he has been taken up with affairs of state.'

'That is true,' said his excellency; 'yet, to be frank, my celibacy is partly due to that fair person. She administered a lesson at a time of life when instruction deeply engraved remains in the mind for ever.'

'Tell us all about it,' said my uncle, 'if it is not a sore subject.'

'Alas! my friend,' said Monsieur de Pontarlais, after forty years, that subject is too sore to handle? Even the tender poets versify their youthful groans. I will tell the whole story—not to you, on whom it will be comparatively wasted, but to my young friend opposite. He is evidently fascinated by my fair betrothed, and her eye enchains him—as it once did me.'

I blushed furiously at this keen old man's sagacity, but stood my ground, and avowed the rapturous interest I felt in a creature so peerless.

Then came to me a bewitching hour. An accomplished old man told us a thrilling passage of his youth, with every charm and grace that could adorn a spoken narrative. The facts struck so deep than I can reproduce them in order; but the tones, the glances, the subtle irony, the governed and well-bred emotion— where are they? They linger still like distant chimes in my memory, and must die with me.

'I was born,' said Monsieur de Pontarlais, 'when parents married their children, and the young people had hardly a voice. At ten years of age I was betrothed to Mademoiselle Irène, only daughter of the Marquis de Groucy, my father's fast friend. Between that period and my coming of age great changes took place in France, and a terrible revolution drew near. But my father made light of all plebeian notions, so did his friend; and, indeed, if they had listened to anything so absurd as the new cry of Liberty, Equality, and Fraternity seemed to them, it would not even then have occurred to them to depart from the rights of nature; and was it not one of those rights that parents should christen, educate, confirm, and marry their children when and how they thought proper?

'Accordingly, at twenty-one years of age, my parents sent me into this very province to marry and make acquaintance with Mademoiselle de Groucy. The marquis, a tall military figure, bronzed by the suns of Provence, met me with his gun slung at his back. He embraced me warmly, and his dogs barked round me with the ready cordiality of sporting dogs. I felt at home directly.

'The marquis and I dined *en tête-à-tête;* I was anxious to see my bride, but she did not appear. After dinner we adjourned to the *salon,* but she did not appear. I cast timid glances toward all the doors; the marquis observed, and rang a bell, and ordered coffee and his daughter. The coffee came directly, and while we were sipping it a female figure glided in at the great door, and seemed to traverse the parquet by some undulating movement which was quite noiseless, though everybody else clattered on the floor at that epoch.

'Instead of the high shoes, bare neck, and short, slight waist of the day, she was in rational shoes, and a loose dress of India muslin that moved every way with her serpentine figure, and veiled without hiding her noble arms and satin bust. As she drew nearer her loveliness dazzled me. I rose and bowed respectfully. Her father apologised for this model of symmetry and beauty.

'"Be pleased to excuse her dress," said he. "It is my fault; they came roaring at me with news of a wild boar, and I forgot to tell her who was coming to-day."

'I said I did not pretend to judge ladies' dresses, but thought the costume beautiful. I suppose my eyes conveyed that I knew where the beauty lay. The young lady edged quietly away, and put her father a little between us; but there was no tremor, nor painful, blushing shyness.

'Afterward, at her father's order, she poured me out a cup of coffee with the loveliest white hand I had ever seen, and though reserved, she was more self-possessed than I was.

'The marquis invited me to a game of piquet. I was off my guard, and consented. The beauty saw us fairly engaged, then glided out of the room, leaving me a little mortified with myself as a wooer; for at twenty-one years of age nature prevails over custom, and we desire to please our bride even before we marry her.

'Next day, M. de Groucy, who was a mighty sportsman, invited me to join him; but with some hesitation and confusion I said I was very desirous to pay respect to my *fiancée*, and to show her how much I admired her already.

'My host thanked me gracefully in his daughter's

name, intimated that in his day marriage used to come first, and then courtship, but said I was at liberty to reverse the order of things if I chose: it would all come to the same at the end.

'On this understanding I devoted myself to wooing my beautiful betrothed. She gave me no direct encouragement, but she did not avoid me. She was often in her own room; and out of it she was generally guarded by a stately *gouvernante*, one Mademoiselle Donon. But this lady had the discretion to keep guard a few yards off, and I treated her as a lay figure. These encounters soon destroyed my peace of mind, and filled all my veins with an ardent passion for the peerless creature whose dead likeness hangs there—and it really is a likeness; but where are the prismatic changes that illumined her mobile features? And all of them, even scorn and anger, were beautiful; but each softer sentiment divine.

'Unfortunately, while she set me on fire she remained quite cool; though she did not avoid me personally, her mind somehow evaded mine on nearly every topic that young people delight in. She listened with polite indifference to all my descriptions of Paris and its gaieties; and when I assured her she would be the acknowledged belle of that brilliant city, she said quietly that it would not compensate her for the loss of her beloved mountains; and she turned from me to the window and fixed a long, loving look upon them that set me yearning for one such glance.

'She rarely contradicted me, but that must have been pure indifference, for she never doubted about anything; I soon found out that trait in her character.

'One day a local newspaper related a popular outrage in our neighbourhood. The rude peasants, in their political ardour, had sacked and destroyed a noble chateau.

'"Where will this end?" said I. "Will revolutionary madness ever corrupt the simple, primitive people one meets about this chateau?"

'"Why, it is done already," said my host. "Emissaries from Paris, preachers of anarchy, are wriggling like weasels all through the nation, with books and pamphlets and discourses teaching the common people that all titles are an affront to the ignoble, and all hereditary property a theft from those who have no ancestors. (Wait till a peasant gets a landed estate, and then see if his son will resign it to the first beggar that covets it.) Why, I caught two of their inflammatory treatises in this very house. By the same token, I sent them to the executioner at Marseilles, with a request that he would burn them publicly, and charge me his usual fee for the extinction of vermin."

'During this tirade Irène changed colour, and seemed to glow with ire; but she merely said, or rather, ground out between her clenched teeth, "Nothing will stop the march of free opinion in France."

'"I am afraid not," said her father. "Still I have some little faith left in charges of cavalry and discharges of grape-shot."

'"A fine argument!" said she, haughtily.

'I was so unlucky as to suggest that it was one the virtuous citizens who had just sacked the neighbouring chateau would probably understand better than any other. The father laughed his approval, but the daughter turned on me with such a flash of furious resentment that I quailed under her eye: it glittered wickedly. Nothing more was said, but from that hour I learned that my glacier was inflammable.

'It was not long before I received another lesson of the same kind. I happened to remark one day that Mademoiselle Donon, the *gouvernante,* as I have called her, must have been a handsome woman in her day. " Handsome ? " said the marquis; " there was not such a figure and such a face in the country-side; and the late marquise used to urge her to marry, and offered her a handsome dowry to wed one of her rustic admirers ; and I offered to lick him into shape and employ him in the house ; but poor Donon, accustomed to good society and French, could never bring her mind to marry a rustic and patter *patois.*"

' " What blind vanity ! " said Irène. " Those rustics are free men, and she is a menial. Such a husband would have elevated her in time to his own level."

' " Ay," said the marquis; " this is the cant of the day. But learn, mademoiselle, that in such houses as ours a faithful domestic is not a menial, but a humble friend, respecting and respected. And Donon is an intelligent and educated woman ; she would have really descended in the scale of humanity if she had allied herself to one of these uneducated peasants."

' Mademoiselle de Groucy made no reply, but her whole frame quivered, and she turned white with wrath. White ! She was ghastly. I looked at her with surprise, and with a certain chill foreboding. I had seen red anger and black anger, but this white-hot ire, never ; and all about what ? Her theories contradicted somewhat roughly by her father; but theories which I concluded she could only have gathered from books, for she rarely went abroad except to mass, and never without her duenna. Looking at her pallid ire, and the white of her eye, which seemed to enlarge as she turned her head away from the marquis in her grim determination not to reply to him, I could not help saying to myself, "I'm not her father, and husbands are apt to provoke their wives; this fair creature will perhaps kill me some day." I felt all manner of vague alarms at a character so cold, so fiery, so profound, so unintelligible to me, and asked myself then and there whether it would not be wise to withdraw my claims to her.

'But I could not. Like the bird that flutters round the dazzling serpent, I was fascinated by the beautiful, dangerous creature, and neither able nor honestly willing to escape.

'Meantime the grand and simple character of my father-in-law won my heart, and I used now and then to go out shooting with him—for his company, not the sport. One day he shot a hare running by the edge of a precipice; she rolled over and lay in sight of us on a ledge of rock, but at a depth of eighty feet at least, and the descent almost perpendicular. The marquis ordered his dogs by name to go down and fetch up the hare. They ran eagerly to the edge to oblige him, and barked zealously, but did not like the commission. We were about to abandon our prey in despair, when suddenly there appeared on the scene a gigantic peasant, with a shock head of red hair so thick and stiff and high that his cap seemed to be perched on a bundle of carrots. Close at his heels, with nose inserted between his calves, came a ragged lurcher. This personage looked over the edge of the ravine, saw our difficulty, grinned, and with perfect *sang-froid* proceeded to risk his life and his cur's for our hare. He made an oblique descent with the help of certain projections and shrubs, the dog sliding down at his heels, and on an emergency fixing his teeth in the man's loose trousers, till they reached a part where the descent was easier. Then the lurcher started on his own account, and with great dexterity scrambled down to the hare, and scrambled up with her in his mouth back to his master.

'But now came a very serious question: How were they to get back again? I felt really anxious, and said so; but the marquis said, " Oh, don't be afraid; this fellow is the athlete of the district; wins all the prizes; they call him the champion. He will get out of it somehow." The man hesitated a moment for all that; but he soon hit upon his plan. He took the hare up, and held her by the skin of her back with teeth the size of ivory chess-pawns; then he put his dog before him, and slowly, carefully, driving the points of his thick boots into every crevice, and grasping with iron strength every ledge or tuft that offered, he effected the perilous ascent. But it was no child's play. The perspiration trickled down his face, and he panted a little.

'I offered him a three-franc piece (none of them left now), but he declined it rather cavalierly, and busied himself with putting the hare into the marquis's game-bag. He was so generous as to add a little wooden figure he took out of his bosom. But this contribution was not observed by the marquis—only by me

—and I was pleased, and still more amazed by this giant's simplicity.

'On our return we were met in the hall by Irène and her *gouvernante*; and the marquis, when he took the hare out of the game-bag, told her how it had been recovered for him by the champion and his dog.

'"What is the name of that colossus that wins all the prizes?"

'"Michel Flaubert," said the young lady.

'"Ay, Flaubert, that's his name—a *vaurien* that wrestles and dances and poaches, and won't work. No matter; he saved my hare, he and his cur. I will buy that cur if he will sell him. What have we here?" And he drew out the little wooden figure. We all inspected the crude image. "It is a sportsman," said the marquis, "leaning on his gun. He will blow his own head off some day."

'Mademoiselle Donon opined it was a saint, and begged the marquis not to part with it: it would bring him good-luck.

'"You are blind," said Irène; "it is a shepherd leaning on his staff." And she put out her white hand, took the hideous statuette, and put it into her pocket. I said she did it great honour.

'"No," said she, "I only do it justice. You, who despise the simple art of a self-taught man, what can you do that you have not been taught?"

'"I can love, for one thing," said I. And Mademoiselle de Groucy coloured high at that, but tossed her head. "And in the matter of art, if I cannot cut little dolls that resemble nothing in nature, I can paint a picture that shall resemble a creature whose loveliness none but the blind will dispute."

'"Oh, indeed," said she, satirically; "and pray what creature is that?"

'"It is yourself."

'"Me?"

'"Yes. Do me the honour to sit to me for your portrait, and I am quite content you shall compare my work with the sculpture of the illustrious Flaubert."

'"A fair challenge!" cried the marquis, joyously. "And I back the gentleman."

'"Oh, of course," said his daughter. "But the day is gone by for despising our fellow-creatures."

'"I despise no honest man," said I. "But so long as education and refined sentiments go with birth, you will be superior in my eyes to any peasant girl, and why not I to a peasant?"

'The marquis stopped me. "Why waste your time in combating moonshine? My daughter knows these rustics only in landscapes and revolutionary pamphlets. Oh, I forget! she has seen them in church; but she never heard them, far less smelled them. Ye gods! when that Flaubert toiled up the precipice and brought me my hare, it was like a kennel of foxes."

'At that Mademoiselle de Groucy left the room with queenly dignity. She was invincible. Her way of retiring put us both in the wrong, especially me, and I made a vow to connive at her theories in future. What did they matter, after all? But I had gained one great point this time—I was to paint her picture. I foresaw, as a lover, many advantages to be gained by that, and I lost no time in buying and preparing the canvas. The best lighted room for the purpose proved to be Irène's boudoir; so I was introduced into that sanctum, and for some hours every day had all the delight of a painter in love. I directed her superb poses; I had the right to gaze at her and enjoy all her prismatic changes. She was reserved, and full of defence, but not childishly shy. She could not be always on her guard, so ever and anon came happy moments when she seemed conscious only of her youth and her beauty. Then a tender light glowed through her limpid eyes, and she looked at me with that divine smile which my hand, inspired by love, has rendered better, perhaps, than a skilful artist would have done whose heart was not in the work. The picture advanced slowly, but surely. The marquis himself one day spared his partridges and sat with us. He was delighted, and said, "This portrait is mine, since I give you the original"; and he ordered a magnificent frame for it directly.

' The portrait was finished at last, and my courtship proceeded with a certain smoothness, only I made no very perceptible advances. I never contradicted her republican theories; indeed, I was so subdued by her grand beauty I dared not thwart her in any way. Yet somehow I could not find out her heart; it evaded me. Often she seemed to be looking over my head at some greater person or grander character. I remember once in particular that I sat by her side on the verandah. After many attempts on my part the conversation died, and I was content to sit a little behind her, and watch her grace and beauty. She leaned her swan-like neck softly forward, her white brow just touched the flowering creepers, and she seemed in a soft reverie. I, too, contemplated her in quiet ecstasy. Suddenly she blushed and quivered, and her lovely bosom rose and fell tumultuously. I started up, and looked over to see who or what it was that moved her so. Instinct then told me I had a rival, and that he was in sight.

'I looked far and near. I could see no rival. It was the usual sleepy landscape: a few washerwomen at the fountain hard by, a few peasants dispersed over the background.

'For all that my mind misgave me, and at last I opened my heart to my friend the marquis. I told him I was discouraged and unhappy; his daughter's heart seemed above my reach.

'"Fiddle-de-dee!" said he. "It all comes of this new system—courting young ladies before marriage spoils them. They don't know all they gain by marriage, so they give themselves airs."

'"Ay," said I; "but that is not all; I have watched her closely, and there is some one her heart beats for, though not for me."

'"Nonsense!" said he; "there is not a gentleman she would look at in the district. I know them all."

'"But, monsieur," said I, "perhaps some prince of the blood has passed this way, or some great general, or hero, or patriot, and she has given him her heart; for she looks above me, and does not disguise it."

'"She has seen no such personage," was the reply. "Ask Donon, who never leaves her."

'"Then," said I, "it must be some imaginary character too lofty for poor me to compete with, for an idol she has."

' " Humph ! " said the marquis. " That is possible."

' " She reads pernicious books," said I. " I found her reading the ' Nouvelle Héloïse,' in her boudoir."

' M. de Groucy lost his composure directly. " The ' Nouvelle Héloïse,' " said he ; " and did you not fling it out of the window ? "

' I confessed I dared not. I dared do nothing to offend her.

' The marquis bestowed a look of pity on me, and left the room all in a hurry, and I awaited his return in no little anxiety. He came back in about half an hour, which he must have spent in ransacking his daughter's library. He re-appeared with the " Nouvelle Héloïse," a philosophic History, by I forget whom, a discourse on Superstition (vulgarly called Religion), by D'Alembert, and one or two works tending to remove the false distinction civilization had invented between *meum* and *tuum* and the classes of society. The marquis showed me the books, and then invited me to follow him. He went first to the kitchen, and made the cook brand these *chef-d'œuvres* of modern senti-ment with a red-hot iron ; then he had them carefully packed in a box and sent to the executioner at Marseilles for public conflagration.

' Having thus eased his mind, he reviewed the situation more calmly. " My son," said he, " you have tried your new-fangled system, with the result that might have been expected. You approach the girl cap in hand, and she gives herself airs accordingly—now we will try ancestral wisdom. Next Sunday I shall publish your banns in the church, and this day week (Wednesday) you will marry her ; and on Thursday you will find her obliging; on Friday, affectionate; on Saturday, cajoling. Saturday *afternoon* she will probably make the usual attempt to be master—they all do. You will put that down with a high hand, and from that hour she will respect and love you with all the loyalty of her race."

'His confidence inspired me. His affection and partisanship affected me deeply. I threw myself into his arms, and I remember I said, "If she would only love me as much as I love you—" And then my tongue faltered.

'The marquis patted me tenderly on the head with his huge hand—he was a man of great stature—and said, "She shall adore you. Leave that to me."

'I am bound to admit that so much of the programme as depended on him was carried out to the letter. The very next Sunday we all went to mass in state; and after the service the priest read out from the altar with a loud voice:

'"Are betrothed this day, the high and excellent Seigneur Grégoire, Viscount of Pontarlais, and the high and excellent damsel Irène de Groucy," etc. There was an angry murmur from the crowd: they objected to our titles. The marquis shrugged his shoulders with unutterable scorn at that, and said, aloud, "Monsieur le Vicomte, do me the honour to give your hand to your bride, and pass out before the rest of us."

'I came forward with a beating heart. Mademoiselle de Groucy was pale, and trembled a little—she was evidently taken by surprise; but she put her hand in mine without a moment's hesitation, and we marched down the aisle, and through the western door. But once outside the place the people flocked round us, and there were some satirical murmurs, at which the marquis changed colour, and his eyes flashed contemptuous ire, but presently a band of about twelve broke through the mass, headed by that very peasant who had rescued our hare for us; and he came, cap in hand, and begged the marquis to preside at the wrestling and shooting for prizes which were to take place that afternoon.

'I think, had it been any other applicant, the offended gentleman would have refused; but he remembered his hare, and the fellow's good services, and gave a cold consent. Then we turned to go home, but the crowd once more embarrassed us, and it was not a friendly crowd. My blood got up, and taking my betrothed under my arm I prepared to force a passage; but she slipped from me like an eel, and said, imperiously, "Flaubert, clear the way." The giant, on this order, stepped in front of us, and shoved the other peasants out of the way, right and left, as if they had been so much dirt. As soon as we were clear, he turned on his heel with as utter a contempt for those who were not his *equals* in brute strength as ever a French noble showed for those who were not his equals in birth and breeding.

' We walked home, mademoiselle in front, haughtily, as one whom no such trifles could disturb, but the marquis sombre and agitated. He put his hand on my shoulder, and said, "We have almost been insulted. This will end in bloodshed. I shall prepare the defence of my castle. You said a good thing the other day: grape-shot is an argument the *canaille* can understand.

Meantime, we honour that village with no more visits. Your wedding will be celebrated in my private chapel."

'I looked anxiously to see how my betrothed received this. She said nothing, but somehow her whole body seemed to hear it. After breakfast I entered her boudoir, and found her trimming a scarf of many colours with gold lace. It was in the worst possible taste, but I dared not say so. I asked, with feigned admiration, whom it was to adorn.

'"You, if you can earn it," said she, drily. "It is for the victor in the sports: the swiftest runner, the strongest wrestler. You have only to eclipse these despised peasants in such manly exercises, and I shall have the honour of placing it on your shoulders."

'I saw she was bent on mortifying me, and perhaps drawing me into a quarrel, so I remembered Wednesday was near, and said, as pleasantly as I could, "Do not think I share your father's violent prejudices. I desire to be just to all men. There is much to admire in the hardy, honest sons of toil. But neither are the gentry fit subjects of wholesale contempt. The peasant who carves a figure which one critic takes for a shepherd, another for a sportsman, and another for a saint, could not paint your picture to save his life, and a polite duel with glittering rapiers demands more true manhood than a wrestling bout."

'My words, I knew, would not please her, so I made the tone so humble and conciliatory that she vouchsafed no reply.

'Then I sat down beside her, and asked her to forgive me if I esteemed a little too highly that class she belonged to and adorned. None the less should her *opinions* always be respected by me. Then I added, " Why should we waste our time on such subjects? For my part, I am too happy to dispute. Oh, if I was only more worthy of you! and if I but knew how to make you love me a little, now that you have accepted me publicly as your betrothed—"

' " Say ' *my espouser*,' " said she, calmly. Then I remembered that in Rousseau's volume of poison, that pedantic, sensual hussey applies this term to the two suitors she despises. I was stung with the scorpion jealousy, and my old suspicion revived and maddened me. " Ah!" said I, haughtily, " and who is the St. Preux for whom you mortify me so cruelly? If he is worthy of you, how comes it he is afraid to show his face? "

' " Be assured," said she, with sullen dignity, " I shall never marry any one of whom I am ashamed."

' " Of that I am sure," said I; " and if ever St. Preux appears, and comes between my betrothed and me, it will be an honour to me to cross steel with him, and a greater still to kill him, which I shall do as sure as heaven is above us." At that time I was an accomplished swordsman.

' " Oh," said she, " then you would marry me against my will? "

' " No," said I, staggered by so direct a blow; " but I would not go back from my troth plighted at the altar; would you? The conversation is taking such a turn that I think Monsieur the Marquis de Groucy is entitled to share in it."

' She turned pale, but recovered herself in a moment. " That is unnecessary," said she. " I am sorry if I have offended you." She drooped her head with infinite grace, and when she raised it she smiled on me and said, "I am flattered by your affection. You have the prejudices of your class but not their vices. Let us be friends." She held out her white hand. I fell on my knees and kissed it devotedly.

'"Oh, how I adore you!" I sighed; and my eyes filled with tenderness. Even hers seemed to dwell on me with a gentler expression than I had ever seen before in them.

'But just as I was making friends with her so sweetly, came a cruel interruption.'

These words were scarcely out of the narrator's mouth when what I thought a cruel interruption occurred. The *curé* came in, dripping. My hospitable uncle had his outer garment removed, and a pint of old Burgundy spiced and heated, and in his warm hospitality would have resigned the story altogether.

But that was intolerable to me. As soon as I could with decency I said, timidly, '*Monsieur le curé* loves a good story as well as anybody.'

'That I do,' said the *curé*, with such zeal that I could have hugged him. And in short, after a few polite speeches, and a reminder from me as to where he had left off, Monsieur de Pontarlais resumed; and it struck me at the time that he was not sorry to have one more intelligent and attentive auditor, for indeed the good *curé* seemed to drink in every word.

'Well, gentlemen, my courtship was interrupted by a summons to visit the sports. As to the running and the shooting, I remember only that it was nothing to boast of, and that the prize for the latter was won by that red-headed giant, and that he came to the marquis, cap in hand, and received a pewter mug.

'Then came the wrestling. Two rustics, naked to the waist, struggled together with more strength than skill. One was thrown, and retired crestfallen. Another came on, and threw the victor. Each bout occupied a long time. The sun began to sink, and your humble servant to yawn.

'My betrothed was all eyes and enthusiasm, though the sight was more monotonous than delicate; but the marquis pitied me, and said, " *You* are not bound to endure all this. The result is known beforehand. After two dozen encounters a victor will be declared, and then ' the champion' will throw *him* with considerable ease; the champion is that red-headed giant, Flaubert. He will come forward, and go down on one knee, and my daughter will bestow this scarf on him. Brought your smelling-bottle, child, I hope? Then, on other occasions, I used to feast them all; but after their insolence at the church-door—insolence to you, *monsieur mon gendre*—I shall admit only the champion Flaubert and his guard of honour, twelve in number. Pierre has his orders; if the rest try to force their way, he will let the portcullis down on their heads. They have all been told that, *and why.*"

'Well, I did not care to see my betrothed put that scarf upon the champion, so I strolled away, and wandered about the chateau. An irresistible curiosity led me to that part of the building in which Mademoiselle de Groucy slept. Her bedroom was in a large tower looking down upon the parterre, which was, like the hanging gardens of Babylon, full thirty feet above the plain the castle stood on ; for indeed it was a castle rather than a chateau.   I entered her bedroom with a tremor of curiosity and delight; it was large and lofty; the bed had no curtains, and was covered with a snowy sheet—nothing more. _Spartan simplicity was seen in every detail.   The picture, framed as you see it now, rested on two huge chairs; and at this my heart beat.   On a table by the side of the looking-glass I discovered the quaint little figure Flaubert had bestowed upon the marquis along with the famous hare.   "Well," thought I, looking at that monstrosity and at my picture, "that is a comparison she is welcome to make." I was ashamed of my curiosity, and soon retired.   I went and sat in her boudoir.   Her work was about; there were many signs of her presence ; a delicate perfume mingled with the scents of the flowers.   I sat at the open window.   Voices murmured in the chateau, but outside all was still.   Soft dreams of coming happiness possessed me ; I leaned my head out of window and drank the evening air, and thought of Wednesday, and the life of bliss to follow.   I was calm, and for the first time ineffably happy.

'The sun set ; the castle was still; no doubt even the limited number of visitors admitted by the marquis had retired ; still I remained there in a delicious reverie.   Presently, in the darkness, I thought I saw a figure pass along close to the wall, and stop at the tower a little while.   Then it suddenly disappeared, so that it was most likely a shadow.   Shadow or not, I was going to be jealous again, when my betrothed entered the room gaily and invited me to supper.

' "You must not abandon us altogether," said she,

and she beamed so, and her manner was so kind and caressing, that I was in the seventh heaven directly. She gave me her hand of her own accord, and I conducted her to the *salle à manger*.

' "Oh, you have found him, have you ?" said the marquis, gaily. "That is lucky, for I have the appetite of a wolf."

' A noble repast was served in honour of our betrothal, and we did honour to it. I forget what was said, but I remember that for the first time Irène allowed her gifts to appear. What animation ! what grace ! what sparkling wit without ill-nature ! what inimitable powers of pleasing, coupled for once with the desire to please ! Oh, marvellous inconsistency of woman !

' Her father was fascinated as well as I, and embraced her warmly when she retired, with a sweet, submissive apology to me, saying that the day, though delightful, had been a little fatiguing.

' Her father and I remained, and instead of our invariable piquet, were well content to sing her praises and congratulate ourselves.

' The subject was inexhaustible, and I am sure we had sat together more than an hour when a great murmur of voices was heard, and Mademoiselle Donon came in with a terrified air to say that there was a tumult outside.

' "More likely a serenade on this festive occasion," suggested the marquis. But at that moment the great bell of the church began to peal. It was the tocsin.

' "Are we on fire," cried the marquis, "and don't know it ?"

'I ran to the window, threw it open, and looked out. I saw flaming torches moving towards the castle from various parts, and heard angry murmurs.

' "Sir," said I, in no little agitation, "they are going to attack us, as they did that other chateau."

' De Groucy smiled grimly. "All the worse for them if they do. I had the drawbridge raised at dusk, and we have plenty of ammunition."

' Here a servant came in with a face of news.

' "What is the matter?" asked the marquis.

' "They have not the sense to say," replied the man. He was the master of the hounds. "I hailed them through the grating, and asked them to declare their grievance. But the fools kept roaring, 'The champion! the champion!' and not another word could I get out of them. Do they think we have taken the blackguard prisoner?"

' "Stuff!" said the marquis; "that is a blind. Load all the muskets with ounce bullets this instant."

' The man retired to execute this order.

' "But, sir," said I, "may not the champion have been shut in when you raised the drawbridge? I thought I saw a figure on the parterre, groping his way about in the dark."

' "No, no," said the marquis. "If any one had been shut in by accident, he would have come to the postern, and the janitor would have let him out. Any stick to beat a dog! any excuse to insult or pillage their betters!—that is the France we live in now. So be it. Not one of the *canaille* shall enter the place alive."

' "I am at your orders," said I, catching fire.

'All these, you must understand, were hurried words, spoken as we marched, the marquis leading the way up the great staircase. At the head of it, Pierre and Guillaume met him with the loaded muskets and ammunition, and he then said to me:

' "You wonder, perhaps, to see me so calm, with women under my charge and wild beasts howling outside. But I am a soldier and know what I am about. This castle is simply impregnable to foes of that kind except at one spot, the small postern, and that is bound with iron. Should they batter it down, the aperture is small; we three can kill them all, one at a time, and at daybreak I will hand the survivors over to Captain Beaumont, who will be here with a squadron of mounted carbineers. The worst of it is, vicomte, I must disturb your betrothed, for it is only from her window we can fire upon the postern."

'He led the way to his daughter's room, and we naturally drew back. In the passage adjoining a cold wind blew on us, and a small but massive door, with gigantic bolts, was found to be ajar.

'The marquis turned round on us, astonished, and for the first time showed anxiety. He said, in a low, unsteady voice:

' "Who has opened this passage?"

' "Does it lead to the parterre?" said I, and began to fear some strange mystery.

' "It did," said he, "but I condemned it ten years ago."

' "Full that, sir," said Pierre; " 'twas I nailed it up, by your orders. I wish I knew the traitor who has taken out the nails and drawn the bolts back."

'The marquis's cheek was pale and his eyes flashed. "To the portcullis, Pierre and Guillaume," said he; "and if any stranger comes to it from the house, kill him without a word. You and I, son-in-law, can defend the postern."

'Our forces thus separated, he went on to his daughter's room, and knocked gently; there was no reply. He knocked louder; there was no reply.

'"She is asleep," said he; "I will go in and prepare her."

'Then I drew back, out of delicacy.

'He took out a pass-key and opened the door.

'There was a man in his daughter's room.

'That man was "the champion."

'"The champion" stood motionless, and looked quite stupefied.

'Mademoiselle de Groucy, quick as he was slow, darted before him with extended arms to protect him, but the next moment cried, "Fly, fly, for your life!" The moment she made way for him to fly the marquis levelled his musket, and fired at his head with as little hesitation as he would at a wild boar.

'What I took to be the champion's brains flew horribly before the discharge; the air was all smoke; a heavy body rushed between the marquis and me and drove us apart, and the door of the condemned passage was slammed. M. de Groucy strode into the room; I followed him. The smoke began to clear, and all things were visible as in a mist; patches of hair floated about, mowed by the bullet off the champion's skull.

'Irène leaned against the mantel-piece, white as a ghost; but only her body crouched, and that not much;

her haughty head was erect, and her eyes faced us, shining supernaturally. The marquis, stout as he was, sank into a chair and trembled.

'"How did that man get in here?" said he, hoarsely.

'"I let him in by the condemned door," said she, pale but unflinching. "Cannot you see that I love him?"

'"You love that *canaille*?" groaned the marquis.

'"I love that young man because he is a man, and has all the virtues that belong to his humble condition. He earns his bread, and I shall be proud to earn mine with him. But it is you and this gentleman who have hastened things; you were forcing me and hurrying me into a marriage without love. No misery, no degradation, can equal that. That is why I called him to my aid. I placed myself under his protection."

'"I will kill him," said the marquis to me, with deadly calmness.

'She came forward directly and folded her arms before him. "Then you will kill my honour, for he is my lover; I belong to him."

'At that audacious avowal the marquis rose like a tower, and lifted his hand to fell her to the earth. But he did not strike her. Better for her, perhaps, if he had, for words can be more terrible than blows.

'"Since you can fall no lower," said he, "marry your peasant, and live on his dunghill with him. You are no child of mine. I banish you, and I disown you, and may God's curse light on you and him for ever!"

'Then for the first time her proud head drooped

upon her hand, and that hand upon the mantel-piece.
"You will forgive me one day," she murmured, faintly.

'"Forgive you!" said he, with unutterable scorn;
"I shall forget you. You are no more to me now than
the dirt I walk on. Come, my son, my only child."
He took my hand and drew me away. He never looked
back, but I cast one long, miserable glance on her
whom it was my misery to love and hate. Her white
wrist rested on a high chair, her head was bowed, yet
her fearless eyes did not turn from us. She was
beautiful as she stood there half cowed by a father's
curse; as beautiful as she had been in her scorn, in her
ire, and in her happy reveries, when her lips parted
with that happy smile, and a tender fire glowed in her
dewy eyes.'

While the narrator paused, and we sat silent, looking at the picture, Suzon came hurriedly in, with tears
in her eyes, and told the *curé* Catherine was very ill
indeed, and begging to see him. He rose directly and
accompanied her.

'You had better sleep here,' said my uncle; 'your
bed is always ready, you know.'

'With pleasure,' said he.

As soon as the door had closed on him, I remarked,
rather peevishly, that I never knew an interesting
story allowed to proceed without a whole system of
interruption.

The elders smiled at my impatience. M. de Pontarlais suggested that perhaps I felt those interruptions
more than others. My uncle said: 'We must take
good men as they are, and thank God for them. I have

known him fourteen years, yet never once to neglect a sick person for any personal gratification whatever.'

Then I remember I was half ashamed of myself, and said I venerated the good *curé* and loved him dearly, and if he would stay with Catherine, well and good; but he would be coming back in a few minutes, and it was this perpetual *va-et-vient* that was breaking my heart and the thread of the only beautiful story I had ever heard told by word of mouth.

'Calm yourself, my young friend,' said Monsieur de Pontarlais: 'my story is nearly ended.

'The marquis compelled me to leave him, after a while, and seek repose. I could not find it; I raged with fury; I sickened with despair; I loved and I hated. This is the world's hell.

'The first thing next morning Mademoiselle Donon came to the marquis and me in tears, and told us she had heard all, but implored us not to believe one word against Irène's honour. She could only, until that fatal night, have spoken to the man at the village fêtes, or from the balcony of the parterre, forty feet above the ground. "Poor, inexperienced girl," said she, "how should she measure her words? She did not know what she was saying."

'"The pupils of Rousseau have not much to learn," was the grim reply.

'The next minute Pierre came in and told us mademoiselle had left the house with a bundle in her hand, and dressed like a peasant girl. I started up, but the marquis laid a hand of iron on me. "Let her go," said he—"let her taint a peasant's home; she shall not dishonour mine. Her own mother should not

keep her if she were alive and went on her knees
to me."

'This was the end. I stayed that miserable day,
and then the marquis sent me home. I told him I
should tell my father our tempers were irreconcilable—
his daughter's and mine.

'"What! tell a lie about her?" said the iron noble.
"Tell the truth, my son, and retain *my* love."

'Well, that difficulty was solved for me. I reached
home in a high fever, and it soon settled on my brain,
and I was insensible for weeks.

'I recovered slowly, and it was many months ere I
could walk. Ah, fatal beauty! you nearly killed two
men: the blackguard you adored with all those queenly
airs of yours—a bullet grazed his skull and ploughed
his hair to the roots; and all through you the gentleman you despised lay at death's door many a day.'

Our friend the *curé* came in as these words were
spoken. He looked very grave, and said that he must
stay the night. Catherine was, he feared, a dying
woman. She was asleep just now, but a sleep of utter
exhaustion.

My uncle was much concerned. He got up directly
to go and see his faithful servant, and the story was interrupted again, as I had foreseen, and the conversation
turned on poor Catherine and her humble virtues till
my uncle returned, looking very glum. Then Suzon
came in, bearing a huge silver bowl, and this was
speedily filled with wine, sugar, lemon, and spices—a
delicious and fragrant compound.

It was ladled out into our glasses, and under its influence I took courage and implored the count to finish

the story. He consented at once, but said it would have little interest for me now, since the principal figure had disappeared.

'I lay a long time between life and death, and even when I was out of danger my mind was confused and troubled. However, by degrees I recovered a certain dogged calm of mind, and indeed since then I have observed in other victims of the tender passion that a brain fever from disappointed love either kills the body or cures the heart.

'My long and dangerous illness was followed by a period of bodily weakness, during which those about me seemed leagued together to know nothing about the family of De Groucy. No doubt they had their orders.

'At last, one day, being now stronger, I asked my father, with feigned composure, if he still corresponded with my dear friend the Marquis de Groucy.

'"Yes, my son," was his reply. "He is in England. He has sold his property and emigrated. He came here on his way and wept over you, but you did not know him." This made my tears flow. After a while I said, "Father she whom I loved so dearly—oh, father, I can bear anything now; tell me. Her own parent has abandoned her, but perhaps she has come to her senses, and only needs a friend to save her from that wretch."

'"Grégoire," said my father, firmly, "be a man; forget that woman. She is not worth a thought. She has chosen her dunghill, let her lie on it." Then, as I persisted in begging him to tell me something about her, he said, "I will tell you this much: you have no betrothed, my poor friend has no daughter, and his noble race is extinct."

'After that I maintained a sort of sad and gloomy silence, and all those who really loved me flattered themselves I had forgotten her; but now, after so many years, I own to you, Monsieur Frédéric, that her beauty and her voice, and the love I had given her, haunted me, and were an obstacle to marriage, until celibacy became too fixed a habit. Even now, in the decline of life, my old heart thrilled at the sudden sight of her shadow there—the life-like image of one I loved too well.'

This set us all gazing at the portrait, and the *curé* in particular got up and examined it very closely, and with a puzzled air.

But I still thirsted for more. 'Surely,' said I, 'in the course of all these years you must have heard something more about her?'

'Not a word.'

'Made some inquiries?'

'None.'

'At least, sir, you know whether she is alive or dead?'

'No, I do not.'

Then I began to bemoan my ill-fortune. 'Oh, sir,' said I, 'when you began your beautiful story I felt sure I should hear all about her, and where she is now; but you lost sight of her when she was no older than I am, and there you drop the curtain, and all is dark. It is all over now; nobody will ever tell me the story of her life; nobody knows anything about her.'

'You are mistaken,' said the *curé*, gravely. 'I know a great deal about her.'

'Is it possible?' I cried, wild with excitement. 'Oh, how fortunate! Ah, my dear friend, tell us all you know.'

'Not so, Monsieur Frédéric. I must not tell you what I know as her confessor and director, but I will tell you all that I have a right to tell. Alas! it is a short but terrible history.

'Well, then, for many years before I came here I had a cure on the other side of the mountains, and among my parishioners was a family of farmers called Flaubert. The head of it was a widow woman, who farmed a little freehold with great ability and keenness, and kept the house with strict economy. She had two sons and their wives under her roof.

'The elder took after her, was prudent, laborious, and married a young woman who had a piece of land and a bit of money, and was also a managing woman. She had two children, and no more. The other son was a young man spoiled early in life by his physical gifts. He was of colossal size, yet could run like a deer and dance like a fawn; a first-rate shot, a poacher, and the champion wrestler of the district. Indeed he was called the "champion" even in his own family, and they were proud of him three or four times a year, when he brought home prizes from the fairs; the rest of the time they blushed for him. This young man's wife was a person you could not fail to remark. Her figure was stately and erect; her carriage graceful. As to her face, it had not the bloom of youth and beauty which illumines that lovely picture. Seven years of peasant life and the hot sun of Provence had tanned her neck and arms, and a discontented mind, which never looked to religion for comfort, had embittered her very face. I remember that even then a deep line crossed her forehead, and her cheeks were hollow, compared with that plump beauty, and her throat was not a smooth column like that. But now I think of it, her hands, though brown with exposure, were shapely, and not like a peasant's, and her eyes and eye-brows were really superb, and her forehead and face were white and smooth as ivory. Yes, I can just believe that this picture was like her in the flower of her youth. Only, as I said before, when I first saw her she was hardened by labour, bronzed by the sun, withered, as I now learn, by a father's curse, and soured by in-fidelity.

'The Flaubert family lived a quarter of a league from the village, and I saw the wife of Michel about, more than once, before I spoke to her. Her appearance and carriage were so striking that I made inquiries about her of the villagers with whom I had already made acquaintance.

'"Oh! the fair peasant!" said one. "The countess!" said another, in coarse derision of her superior; and they told me she was the daughter of a red-hot aristo, who had fled to England because she married a peasant for love. They gave me plenty of details, and you would smile if you heard the vulgar romances each narrator constructed on her true story, which, nevertheless, was romantic enough.

'The widow and her eldest daughter attended Mass, and I conversed with them. In due course I asked the widow if she had not another daughter-in-law.

'The two women looked at each other and shrugged

their shoulders. "Yes, I have, sir," said the widow, "to my misfortune."

' "Shall I not see her at Mass?"

' "Let us hope not; for she would only come to yawn or to mock. She is a pagan, I believe, among her other qualities."

' " Perhaps she attends to the home while you are out?"

' "She attend to the home!" and both women laughed heartily at the idea—so heartily that the younger thought it necessary to make an apology. The elder chimed in and said, in the sly way of a Provençal peasant, "If her outside has interested M. le Curé, I can give him a picture of her at this moment. She is sitting over my fire, burning her petticoat, with her hands lolling by her sides, making useless embroidery, or else in a pure reverie. As for her household occupation, she is either letting the pot boil over or get cold. I could not swear which; but 'tis one or t'other."

' Of course I checked these remarks, and lectured upon Christian charity. My discourse was received with respectful silence, but my hearers seemed turned into wood.

' Some days after this I was caught in a heavy rain, and the nearest shelter was the farm-house of the Flauberts. I knocked at the door, no notice was taken; I knocked again; a light footstep, and the door was opened by Madame Michel. She did not receive me hospitably. She said, in broad Provençal, "There is nobody in the house," and she held the door in her hand. Then I tried her in French. " Madame," said

I, "I am wet through, and if I could, without incommoding you——"

' "Do me the honour to come in," said she, with perfect accent and the most graceful courtesy. She seated me by the fire, and we entered into conversation. I believe we conversed about trifles, and I could not help admiring her grace and courtesy, and the French language, the language of politeness, which had at once recalled her to her native good breeding. She spoke it exquisitely, notwithstanding the little use she now made of it.

'I forget all our small talk; but I remember at last that she fixed her eyes full upon mine and said, "Monsieur, why did you speak to me in French?"

'I answered her honestly, and with some emotion: "Because, madame, I know your story from others" (her pale cheek coloured at that), "and to be quite frank, I came here hoping, by my advice and authority, to make matters smoother and more pleasant in this house."

' " 'You would but waste your time," said she. "These people hate me with all their hearts, and I despise them with all my soul. Matters are come to such a pitch that we endure each other only because we are about to part. My husband is heir to a small sum of money, and he has purchased a cottage and a few acres that are sold very cheap, belonging to an *émigré*. We shall do very well when we are alone."

' "You have my best wishes," said I; "but I am afraid you are too little accustomed to the hard life of a working farmer; and even your husband has never learned to dig and mow and labour like his brother;

his tastes appear to be for pastimes and games
and——"

' " You need not mince the matter," said she ; " he
is lazy, and, worse still, he is fond of drinking and
gambling. But it is all his mother's fault, with her
weak indulgence; and now she encourages him to
desert his home out of her jealousy of me. Once I get
him away from this vile woman he will stay beside me,
and lead an honest, industrious life, as I shall for his
sake."

' I knew Michel was hardened in his ill habits, and
that love could not convert him without religion. I
thought it my duty to tell her so. The woman froze
directly, and when I urged my views she encountered
me with all the cold infidelity and satire of this unhappy age. She was armed at all points by Messieurs
Volney, D'Alembert, Voltaire, and others, and by her
own self-confidence. So I told her I would not argue
with her but pray for her.

' " Do you believe prayers are heard ? " said she,
ironically.

' I told her I thought earnest prayers were always
heard, and sometimes granted.

' " Well," said she, " the most earnest prayer I ever
heard was when my own father cursed me and my
husband. Will God grant that ? "

' " Not against your souls," said I.

' She shrugged her shoulders, as much as to say the
exception was of very little value ; and I left the house
defeated and sad.'

' And I answer for it you kept your word and prayed
for this perverse creature,' said my uncle.

'With all my heart and soul,' replied the good *curé.* He continued:

'The next time I saw her was one evening; the whole family was there except Michel. They all received me in a friendly manner, and gave me the place of honour at a long table, about which they were all seated, picking the shoots out of some damaged wheat for their own use.

'The eldest son entertained me with a voluble discourse about the markets, the price of grain; and all the time Michel's wife sat with her feet at the fire, and her arms folded, and her head against the wall, in an attitude of sleepy disdain.

'But presently there was a whistle heard in the yard, and she started up, all animation.

'"There he is!" she cried, and darted out of the door. She soon returned with "the champion," who greeted us all, in a loud, jovial voice, with blunt civility.

'"Daughter-in-law," said her mother, "serve your husband."

'Then she cut an enormous slice of bread, and ladled a large basinful of soup out of the great pot. Unfortunately, the pot had been taken off the fire to put on more wood, and the soup was lukewarm. The champion made a grimace.

'"Cold weather outside and cold soup within," said he. This was not said harshly, but his mother fired up directly.

'"Saints in paradise!" she cried, turning towards her obnoxious daughter-in-law. "Is it possible that a woman can reach your years and not learn to keep her man's soup hot against he comes home wet and hungry?"

'The young woman just turned two haughty eyes upon her, and said, "It's nobody's business if Michel does not complain." Then I, to make peace, said I feared that I was the person in fault, for I had moved the pot a little to warm my feet.

'The champion—a good-humoured fellow at bottom —stopped me, and said, "Don't let's make a mountain of a mole-hill. The soup's very good if it is a little cold, and it's going to a warm place anyway;" and with this he shovelled it rapidly down his throat. "The worst of it is," said he, "that my feet are wet through with the snow and the slush;" and he took off a pair of enormous shoes and threw them roughly towards his wife, and said, "There, wife, put all that right for me."

'The daughter of the Marquis de Groucy took her peasant lord's shoes, bowed her head meekly over them, scraped the clay from them with a piece of stick, then wiped them with a damp cloth, then put some hot cinders inside, shook them out again, and brought the shoes to her master. He received them without a word of thanks. This gave me some pain, and I soon after took my leave. Michel's wife, remembering, I suppose, the habits of her youth, accompanied me to the end of the court that lay before the door. I took this opportunity of saying that since she had learned to humble herself before a man, and do the duty of a wife so meekly, I felt sure she would some day learn to humble herself before God, who abaseth the proud and lifteth up the lowly.

'What think you was the answer I received from this keen spirit, nursed upon the wit of Messieurs Volney, D'Alembert, and Voltaire ?

' "Monsieur," says she, "there are *curés* who can only talk religion; there are some who can also talk reason; you are one of the happy few who can talk reason if you choose, for you have been a man of the world.　If it is all the same to you, pray, when you do me the honour to converse with me, don't talk religion, talk sense.'

' "I consent, madame," said I sorrowfully; "but you must permit me to pray for you."

' About a fortnight after this I met the champion. He was going to a neighbouring fair, dressed in his Sunday clothes.　I asked him if he was going to compete for the prize for wrestling, as usual.　He said, "No; this time it's more serious.　My mother has at last paid me the eight hundred francs she has long promised me, and I am going to buy a cottage and a bit of emigrant's land—house and farm.　There my wife and I shall keep house alone.　The truth is, Monsieur le Curé," said he, "that the women can't agree at home; my mother despises my wife, and my wife hates my mother.　We shall do better apart."

' I had my doubts on that point, and thought both husband and wife equally unfitted for the labour and self-denial that lay before them; but I kept that to myself, and all I did was to warn this confident young man against the temptations of the fair.

' "Have no fear," said he; and went away full of buoyant confidence.

' That very evening he called at my house, pale and agitated, and told me a different tale.　He had been induced to gamble for a small sum, in order, he said, to buy his wife a gold chain; he had lost it, and his wild endeavours to recover it by the same unlikely means had thrown away his little fortune. One virtue the poor fellow had—filial reverence. He told me with tears in his eyes of all his mother's goodness and self-denial, and he said that he couldn't face her and tell her he had wasted in a day what had cost her four years to save. He spoke of leaving the country, and begged me to carry her his penitence and shame. I said, "My son, I'll do better: I will take you to her, and show you the depth of a mother's love."

'Well, at last I prevailed on him to come with me to the house, but he couldn't be induced to come in until I had made his confession for him. As I expected, the mother said: "Poor foolish boy! Just tell him to come in to his supper; his mother's arms shall not be closed to him." So I brought him in. The others received him in grim silence, but the old woman merely said: "Why, Michel, it's a pity you had not more sense; but 'tis your own money you have lost, and no one else has a right to complain. This house is always open to you." Then, finding his wife dead silent and terribly pale, he went to her to make his peace with her; but she started back from him and said: "Don't you come near me, you vile prodigal and madman. You've condemned me to live all my life with these people, who hate me, and I hate them with all my heart." As an outrageous quarrel was clearly impending, I withdrew; but something—I know not what—induced me to wait at a little distance, and pray for the peace of this ill-assorted couple. Alas! I had better have stayed; for, as I learned from the others, that angry wife reproached him and taunted him in her fury till he actually raised his huge hand and struck her on the face.

'She was stunned at first, I heard, but soon uttered a wild cry of anguish and frenzy, and catching up, with a woman's strange intent, some embroidery she had been working upon, she turned round and cursed them all.

'"Rot on your dunghill, all of you!" she cried, and tore open the door and dashed out.

'Then the old woman cried, "Mind, Michel, she will disgrace you!" and he dashed after her.

'Unluckily, she stumbled over something in the yard, and I saw the swift-footed champion overtake her, and seize her, and drag her back toward the house. She screamed, she struggled, in vain; but at last, by a furious effort, she half freed herself for a moment, and I saw her lift her hand high, and then strike the man on the breast. At this moment I was coming forward to interfere.

'To my surprise the giant uttered a cry of dismay, and staggered away from her, and burst headlong into the house. To be sure, the blow was furious, but it was only a woman's hand that struck, and I saw no weapon in that hand. As for her, she rushed the other way, and I think would have passed me without notice but that I uttered an ejaculation of pity and concern; then she stopped and glared at me, and I must tell you that I then noticed something which Monsieur de Pontarlais has already drawn attention to—the whites of her eyes showed themselves to me in the moonlight with a strange and, I may say, a terrible expression—the expression of some infuriated wild animal. "He struck me!" she cried. "He struck me! the woman who gave up all for him, and braved a father's curse. My curse and my father's be on *him* and all his brood!" With that she darted past me and disappeared.

'After a moment's hesitation I felt it my duty to enter the house, and make some sort of endeavour, however hopeless, to repair the mischief; indeed, I was prepared to use all the authority my office gave me, and take part with great severity against this ruffian, and all the rest who, by their animosity, had paved the way for this abominable outrage.

'Well, I went in at the open door; I found the champion leaning with his back against the wall, rolling his eyes as if in pain, and groaning loudly. The situation seemed to amuse his brother; at least, that person was jeering him for not being able to bring his wife back by force. "You'll win no more prizes for wrestling at the fair."

'"No," said the colossus; "I'm done for;" and with that, still groaning, he seemed to sink half down by the wall, and his hands grasped wildly at his breast.

'Then I looked, and saw something that began to give me a terrible misgiving. Being in his gala dress, he had on a white shirt, and in the middle of his ample bosom was something that had first looked like a very large stud or breastpin made of mother-of-pearl.

'Round this thing was a thin circle of red, fine as a hair, and this red circle I saw enlarging. My experience in the army told me how serious this was, and

I cried, "Silence! the man is stabbed, and is bleeding internally." As these words left my lips, the poor champion sunk to the ground, and gasped out once more "*Je suis un homme perdu.*" In a moment they were all around him, and after a few hurried words, with his mother's consent I took on me to draw the weapon out from the wound. It was an instrument ladies used in that day for embroidery. I think they opened a passage for the needle with it. The whole instrument was not four inches long, and the steel portion of it scarcely three inches; but a woman's hand had driven it home so keenly that even a portion of the handle had entered the wound. . When I withdrew this insignificant but fatal weapon the champion gave a sigh of relief. He then ceased to bleed inwardly, but immediately the blood spurted and poured out of him through that small aperture. All attempts to staunch it were vain, and, indeed, were useless, for his fate was to bleed to death either inwardly with pain, or outwardly without pain. I told them all that very gravely, and as tenderly as I could. Then the poor wretches burst out into imprecations on the woman that had brought him to that. Then I put on for the first time the authority of the Church. I took out my crucifix, and I ordered them all, even the mother who bore him, from the room. That grand body, so full of blood, of strength, and youth, resisted long the fatal drain, and God gave me time to do His work. The dying man confessed his sins; he owned the justice of this fatal blow, since he had raised his hand against the weak creature he had vowed to protect and cherish; he blessed his mother and his brother, and forgave his wife. Then I gave him absolution with all my heart and conscience, and he died in peace.

' Ah, my friends, who that had seen this could pride himself on youth and superior strength ?   Here was the champion of all those parts lying on his own floor, surrounded by the jugs and mugs and plates he had won by conquering the other Samsons of the district, felled by a woman's hand armed with a bare bodkin.

' I spare you, my friends, the mother's agony and all the sorrow of the house—sorrow that didn't soften the hatred, and that you cannot wonder at. They set the emissaries of justice upon the culprit's track and she was easily found, for no sooner did she hear the fatal news than she gave herself up to the law. She was tried at Marseilles, and it's a wonder to me that my good friend here does not remember that trial, for it caused no little sensation at the time. The friends of the deceased, and the mother especially, urged the prosecution with the utmost bitterness. The old woman, indeed, said that nothing could console her for the loss of her son but to see the murderess's head roll in the basket of the executioner. I was at the trial, and I remember little of it except the few words spoken by the accused; those words seem somehow graven in my memory. She wore a peasant's dress, but her demeanour was that of a noble; she was depressed, but dignified and patient; never interrupted, and never complained. When her time came to speak in her defence, she said :

' " Citizens, the public accuser has told you I killed my husband, and that, alas! is too true; but he has told you I killed him maliciously, and there he is quite mistaken. My husband was my all. I gave up father,

friends, rank, wealth, everything for him, and I loved
him dearly. He gave me a bitter provocation, and I
reproached him cruelly. Then he struck me barbarously.
What did I do? Did I seize some deadly weapon and
strike him in return? No. I merely fled; and if he
had let me escape, this calamity would never have
occurred. But he caught me, and seized me, and was
dragging me back to a house where every man and
woman was my enemy. My passion was great, I admit,
but my fear was greater, and in fear I struck, not
malice. Did I seek some deadly weapon? No; I
struck with what was in my hand, scarcely knowing at
the time what was in my hand. I believe that when
the weak are attacked with overpowering strength they
are permitted to make matters equal with some weapon.
But can you call that puny instrument of woman's art
a weapon? Was ever a strong man slain with such a
thing before? My husband died by the finger of God;
I was the unhappy instrument: and I am his truest
mourner, and shall mourn him when all else have forgotten him. Even his mother has another son, but he
was my all in this world. I say these things because
they are the truth, not to avert punishment. How can
you punish me? Imprisonment cannot add to my
misery, and death would end it. Therefore I ask no
mercy: be just."

'Before these words, and their sad and noble
delivery, the charge of wilful homicide dissolved away.
The prisoner was condemned to two years' seclusion in
a religious house.

'I visited there many times, and found her a
changed woman. Her heart was broken and contrite;

she wept for hours together, and in time she found consolation. Great was now her humility. When she regained her liberty I became her director.

'The penance I inflicted was—obscurity. For many years she has gained her own living under another name, and never revealed the story of her life. Some people say, with a sneer, "The greater the sinner, the greater the saint." But there is truth in it. Men can go on sinning within certain bounds all their lives, and not feel themselves sinners; but when they commit a crime, the world helps them to undeceive themselves, and penitence enters when self-deception retires. That criminal has long been a truly pious woman, humble, industrious, faithful, self-denying, and full of Christian charity. On earth she is obscure by choice; but methinks her seat will be high in Heaven.'

The good *curé's* words melted us all; and now we all desired to know her in her humble condition and alleviate her lot.

But the *curé* would not hear of it. 'No,' said he. 'This is a secret of the confessional. She is vowed to obscurity, and she must persevere to the end. But if you, Monsieur de Pontarlais, can forgive her the pain she once caused you, that would be a comfort to her.'

'Ah, poor soul, with all my heart,' cried he, and put his handkerchief to his eyes.

After this narrative and these reflections, we none of us felt disposed for small talk, and we soon retired to bed, all but the good *curé*, who was summoned hastily to Catherine's bedside by Suzon. That night the house seemed to me strangely unquiet. I was awakened several times by hurrying to and fro. But sleep soon comes again to careless youth. In the morning I found Suzon in tears, and my uncle himself very sad: the faithful Catherine was dead.

After breakfast the *curé* requested us to witness the official document he had to prepare on that melancholy occasion. He handed it to us with this remark: 'The confessional has no secrets now.' Judge my surprise when I read these words: 'Died, the 10th day of July, 1821, of general prostration, Irène de Groucy, widow of Michel Flaubert.'

My uncle took the picture down. 'I prefer,' said he, 'to think of my poor faithful Catherine as she was.' I was of the same mind. But when my dear uncle died, and it became my own, I hung it again in a room I frequented but little.

Lately, in the decline of my own life, drawing near to that place where beautiful souls should be highest, I have given the once-loved picture a place of honour. Being so strange a reminiscence of my youth, I think sometimes of poor Catherine viewing her own picture with such grace, dignity, and pious humility; and I expect to find that white-robed saint more beautiful by far than the picture which so fascinated me.

REALITY.

Miss Sophia Jackson, in the State of Illinois, was a beautiful girl, and had a devoted lover, Ephraim Slade, a merchant's clerk. Their attachment was sullenly permitted by Miss Jackson's parents, but not encouraged; they thought she might look higher.

Sophia said, ' Why, la ! he was handsome and good, and loved her, and was not that enough ? '

They said, ' No ; to marry beauty a man ought to be rich.'

' Well,' said Sophy, ' he is on the way to it : be is in a merchant's office.'

' It is a long road, for he is only a clerk.'

The above is a fair specimen of the dialogue, and conveys as faint an idea of it as specimens generally do.

All this did not prevent Ephraim and Sophia from spending many happy hours together.

But presently another figure came on the scene— Mr. Jonathan Clarke. He took a fancy to Miss Jackson, and told her parents so, and that she was the wife for him, if she was disengaged. They said, ' Well, now, there was a young clerk after her, but the man was too poor to marry her.'

Now Mr. Jonathan Clarke was a wealthy speculator;

so, on that information, he felt superior, and courted
her briskly. She complained to Ephraim. 'The idea
of their encouraging that fat fool to think of me!'
said she. She called him old, though he was but
thirty, and turned his person and sentiments into ridi-
cule, though, in the opinion of sensible people, he was
a comely man, full of good sense and sagacity.

Mr. Clarke paid her compliments. Miss Jackson
laughed, and reported them to Slade in a way to make
him laugh too.

Mr. Clarke asked her to marry him. She said no;
she was too young to think of that. She told Ephraim
she had flatly refused him.

Mr. Clarke made her presents. She refused the
first, and blushed, but was prevailed on to accept. She
accepted the second and the third, without first refusing
them.

She did not trouble Ephraim Slade with any portion of this detail. She was afraid it might give him
pain.

Clarke wooed her so warmly that Ephraim got
jealous and unhappy. He remonstrated. Sophia cried,
and said it was all her parents' fault—forcing the man
upon her.

Clarke was there every day. Ephraim scolded.
Sophia was cross. They parted in anger. Sophia went
home and snubbed Clarke. Clarke laughed, and said :
'Take your time.' He stuck there four hours. She
came round, and was very civil.

Matters progressed. Ephraim always unhappy.
Clarke always jolly. Parents in the same mind.

Clarke urged her to name the day.

'Never!'

Urged her again.

'Next year.'

Urged her again before her parents. They put in their word. 'Sophy, don't trifle any longer. You are overdoing it.'

'There, there, do what you like with me,' said the girl; 'I am miserable!' and ran out crying.

Clarke and parents laughed, and stayed behind, and settled the day.

When Sophy found they had settled the day she sent for Ephraim, and told him with many tears. 'Oh!' said she, 'you little know what I have suffered this six months.'

'My poor girl!' said Ephraim. 'Let us elope and end it.'

'What! My parents would curse me.'

'Oh, they would forgive us in time.'

'Never! You don't know them. No, my poor Ephraim, we are unfortunate. We can never be happy together. We must bow. I should die if this went on much longer.'

'You are a fickle, faithless jade!' cried Ephraim, in agony.

'God forgive you, dear!' said she, and wept silently.

Then he tried to comfort her. Then she put her arm round his neck, and assured him she yielded to constraint, but her heart could never forget him; she was more unhappy than he, and always should be.

They parted, with many tears on both sides, and she married Clarke. At her earnest request Slade kept away from the ceremony; by that means she was not compelled to wear the air of a victim, but could fling the cloak of illusory happiness and gaiety over her aching heart; and she did it too. She was as gay a bride as had been seen for some years in those parts.

Ephraim Slade was very unhappy. However, after a bit he comprehended the character of Sophia Clarke, *née* Jackson, and even imitated her. She had gone in for money, and so did he—only on the square: a detail she had omitted. Years went on: he became a partner in the house, instead of a clerk. The girls set their caps at him, but he did not marry. Mrs. Clarke observed this, and secretly approved. Say she had married, that was no reason why *he* should. *Justice des femmes!*

Now you will observe that, by all the laws of fiction, Mrs. Clarke ought to have learned, to her cost, that money does not bring happiness, and ought to have been miserable—especially whenever she encountered the pale face of him whose love she valued too late.

Well, she broke all those laws, and went in for life as it is. She was happier than most wives. Her husband was kind, but not doting; a gentle master, but no slave; and she liked it. She had two beautiful children, and they helped fill her life. Her husband's gold smoothed her path, and his manly affection strewed it with flowers. She was not passionately devoted to him, but still, by the very laws of nature, the wife was fonder of Jonathan than the maid had ever been of Ephraim; not but what the latter remaining unmarried tickled her vanity, and so completed her content.

She passed six years in clover, and the clover in

full bloom all the time. Nevertheless, gilt happiness
is apt to get a rub sooner or later. Clarke had losses
one upon another, and at last told her he was done for.
He must go back to California and make another fortune. 'Lucky the old folks made me settle a good
lump on you,' said he. 'You are all right, and the
children.'

Away went stout-hearted Clarke, and left his wife
behind. He knew the country, and went at all in the
ring, and began to remake money fast.

His letters were not very frequent, nor models of
conjugal love, but they had good qualities; one was
their contents—a draft on New York.

Some mischievous person reported that he was
often seen about with the same lady; but Mrs. Clarke
did not believe that, the remittances being regular.

But presently both letters and remittances ceased.
Then she believed the worst, and sent a bitter remonstrance.

She received no reply.

Then she wrote a bitterer one, and, for the first
time since their union, cast Ephraim Slade in his
teeth. 'There he is,' said she, 'unmarried to this day,
for my sake.'

No reply even to this.

She went to her parents and told them how she was
used.

They said they had foreseen it—that being a lie
some people think it necessary to deliver themselves of
before going seriously into any question—and then,
after a few pros and cons, they bade her observe that
her old lover, Ephraim Slade, was a rich man, a man

unmarried, evidently for her sake, and if she was wise she would look that way, and get rid of a mock husband, who was probably either dead or false, and, in any case, had deserted her.

'But what am I to *do*?' said Mrs. Clarke, affecting not to know what they were driving at.

'Why, sue for a divorce.'

'Divorce Jonathan! Think of it! He is the father of my children, and he was a good husband to me all the time he was with me. It is all that nasty California.' And she began to cry.

The old people told her she must take people as they were, not as they had been; and it was no fault of hers, nor California's, if her husband was a changed man.

In short, they pressed her hard to sue for a divorce, and let Slade know she was going to do it.

But the woman was still handsome and under thirty, and was not without a certain pride and delicacy that grace her sex even when they lack the more solid virtues. 'No,' said she, 'I will never go begging to any man. I'll not let Ephraim Slade think I divorced my husband just to get him. I'll part with Jonathan, since he has parted with me, and after that I will take my chance. Ephraim Slade! he is not the only man in the world with eyes in his head.'

So she sued for a divorce, and got it quite easy. Divorce is beautifully easy in the West.

When she was free, she had no longer any scruple about Ephraim. He lived at a town seven miles from her. She had a friend in that town. She paid her a visit. She let the other lady into her plans, and

secured her co-operation. Mrs. X—— set it abroad
that Mrs. Clarke was a widow; and, from one to
another, Ephraim Slade was given to understand that a
visit from him would be agreeable.

'Will it?' said Ephraim. 'Then I'll go.'

He called on her, and was received with a sweet
pensive tenderness. 'Sit down, Ephraim—Mr. Slade,'
said she, softly and tremulously, and left the room.
She had scarcely cleared it when he heard her tell the
female servant, with a sharp, imperious tone, to admit
no other visitors. It did not seem the same voice.
She came back to him melodious. 'The sight of you
after so many years upset me,' said she. Then, after a
pause and a sigh, 'You look well.'

'Oh yes, I am all right. We are neither of us
quite so young as we were, you know.'

'No, indeed' (with another sigh). 'Well, dear
friend, I suppose you have heard. I am punished, you
see, for my want of courage and fidelity. I have always
been punished. But you could not know that. Perhaps,
after all, you have been the happier of the two. I am
sure I hope you have.'

'Well, I'll tell you, Mrs. Clarke——' said he, in
open, manly tones.

She stopped him. 'Please don't call me Mrs.
Clarke, when I have parted with the name for ever.'
(*Sotto voce*) 'Call me Sophia.'

''Well, then, Sophia, I'll tell you the truth. When
you jilted me——'

'Oh!'

'And married Cl—— Who shall I say? Well,

then, married *another*, because he had got more money
than I had——'

'No, no! Ephraim, it was all my parents. But I
will try and bear your reproaches. Go on.'

'Well, then, of course, I was awfully cut up. I was
wild. I got a six-shooter to kill you and—the other.'

'I wish you had,' said she. She didn't wish anything of the kind.

'I am very glad I didn't, then. I dropped the six-
shooter and took to the moping and crying line.'

'Poor Ephraim!'

'Oh, yes; I went through all the changes, and
ended as other men do.'

'And how is that?'

'Why, by getting over it.'

'What! you have got over it?'

'Lord, yes! long ago.'

'Oh, in-deed!' said she, bitterly. Then, with sly
incredulity, 'How is it you have never married?'

'Well, I'll tell you. When I found that money was
everything with you girls, I calculated to go in for
money too. So I speculated, like—the other, and
made money. But when I had once begun to taste
money-making, somehow I left off troubling about
women. And, besides, I know a great many people,
and I look coolly on, and what I see in every house has
set me against marriage. Most of my married friends
envy me, and say so. I don't envy any one of them,
and don't pretend to. Marriage! it is a bad institution.
You have got clear of it, I hear. All the better for you.
I mean to take a shorter road: I won't ever get into it.'

This churl, then, who had drowned hot passion in

the waves of time, and instead of nursing a passion for her all his days, had been hugging celibacy as man's choicest treasure, asked her coolly if there was anything he could do for her.   Could he be of service in finding out investments, etc., or could he place either of the boys in the road to wealth.   Instead of hating these poor children like a man, he seemed all the more inclined to serve them that their absent parent had secured him the sweets of celibacy.

She was bursting with ire, but had the self-restraint to thank him, though very coldly, and to postpone all discussion of that kind to a future time.   Then he shook hands with her and left her.

She was wounded to the core.   It would have been very hard to wound her heart as deeply as this interview wounded her pride.

She sat down and shed tears of mortification.

She was aroused from that condition by a letter in a well-known hand.   She opened it, all in a flutter:

'MY DEAR SOPHY,—You are a nice wife, you are! Here I have been slaving my life out for you, and shipwrecked, and nearly dead with a fever, and coming home rich again, and I asked you just to come from Chicago to New York to meet me, that have come all the way from China and San Francisco, and it is too much trouble.   Did you ever hear of Lunham's dog that was so lazy he leaned against the wall to bark?   It is very disheartening to a poor fellow that has played a man's part for you and the children.   Now be a good girl, and meet me at Chicago to-morrow evening at 6 P.M.   For if you don't, by thunder, I'll take the children and absquatulate with them to Paris, or somewhere! I find the drafts on New York I sent from China have never been presented. Reckon by that you never got them. Has that raised your dander? Well, it is not my fault; so put on your bonnet, and come and meet

'Your affectionate husband,

'JONATHAN CLARKE.

'I sent my first letter to your father's house. I send this to your friend Mrs. X——.'

Mrs. Clarke read this in such a tumult of emotions that her mind could not settle a moment on one thing. But when she had read it, the blood in her beating veins began to run cold.

What on earth should she do? Fall to the ground between two stools? No; that was a man's trick, and she was a woman, every inch.

She had not any time to lose; so she came to a rapid conclusion. Her acts will explain better than comments. She dressed, packed up one box, drove to the branch station, and got to Chicago. She bought an exquisite bonnet, took private apartments at a hotel, and employed an intelligent person to wait for her husband at the station, and call out his name, and give him a card, on which was written

'Mrs. Jonathan Clarke,
At the X—— Hotel.

This done, she gave her mind entirely to the decoration of her person.

The ancients, when they had done anything wrong and wanted to be forgiven, used to approach their judges with dishevelled hair and shabby clothes—*sordidis vestibus.*

This poor shallow woman, unenlightened by the wisdom of the ancients, thought the nicer a woman looked the likelier a man would be to' forgive her—no matter what. So she put on her best silk dress, and her new French hat, bought on purpose, and made her hair very neat, and gave her face a wash and a rub that added colour. She did not rouge, because she calculated she should have to cry before the end of the play, and crying hard over rouge makes channels.

When she was as nice as could be, she sat down to wait for her *divorcé*; she might be compared to a fair spider which has spread her web to catch a wasp, but is sorely afraid that, when he does come, he will dash it all to ribbons.

The time came and passed. An expected character is always as slow to come as a watched pot to boil.

At last there was a murmur on the stairs; then a loud, hearty voice; then a blow at the door—you could not call it a tap—and in burst Jonathan Clarke, brown as a berry, beard a foot long—genial and loud, open heart, Californian manners.

At sight of her he gave a hearty ' Ah ! ' and came at her with a rush to clasp her to his manly bosom, and knocked over a little cane chair, gilt.

The lady, quaking internally, and trembling from head to foot, received him like the awful Siddons, with one hand nobly extended, forbidding his profane advance. ' A word first, if you please, sir.'

Then Clarke stood transfixed, with one foot advanced, and his arms in the air, like Ixion, when Juno turned cloud.

'You have ordered me to come here, sir, and you have no longer any right to order me ; but I am come, you see, to tell you my mind. What! do you really think a wife is to be deserted and abandoned, most likely for some other woman, and then be whistled back into her place like a dog? No man shall use *me* so !'

'Why, what is the row ? has a mad dog bitten you, ye cantankerous critter ?'

'Not a letter for ten months, that is the matter!' cried Mrs. Clarke, loud and aggressive.

'That is not my fault. I wrote three from China, and sent you two drafts on New York.'

'It is easy to say so : I don't believe it.' (*Louder and aggressiver.*)

CLARKE (*bawling in his turn*). 'I don't care whether you believe it or not. Nobody but you calls Jony Clarke a liar.'

MRS. CLARKE (*competing in violence*). 'I believe one thing, that you were seen all about San Francisco with a lady. 'Twas to her you directed my letters and drafts : that is how I lost them. It is always the husband that is in fault, and not the post.' (*Very amicably all of a sudden*) 'How long were you in California after you came back from China ? '

'Two months.'

'How often did you write in that time ?' (*Sharply.*)

'Well, you see, I was always expecting to start for home.'

'You never wrote once.' (*Very loud.*)

'That was the reason.'

'That and the lady.' (*Screaming loud.*)

'Stuff! Give me a kiss, and no more nonsense.'

(*Solemnly*) 'That I shall never do again. Husbands must be taught not to trifle with their wives' affections in this cruel way.' (*Tenderly*) 'Oh, Jonathan, how could you abandon me? What could you expect? I am not old; I am not ugly.'

'D—n it all, if you have been playing any games' —and he felt instinctively for a bowie-knife.

'Sir!' said the lady, in an awful tone, that subjugated the monster directly.

'Well, then,' said he, sullenly, 'don't talk nonsense. Please remember we are man and wife.'

Mrs. Clarke (*very gravely*). 'Jonathan, we are not.'

'Damnation! what do you mean?'

'If you are going into a passion, I won't tell you anything; I hate to be frightened. What language the man has picked up—in California!'

'Well, that's neither here nor there. You go on.'

'Well, Jonathan, you know I have always been under the influence of my parents. It was at their wish I married you.'

'That is not what you told me at the time.'

'Oh, yes, I did; only you have forgotten. Well, when no word came from you for so many months, my parents were indignant, and they worked upon me so, and pestered me so—that—Jonathan, we are divorced.'

The actress thought this was a good point to cry at, and cried accordingly.

Jonathan started at the announcement, swore a

heartful, and then walked the room in rage and bitterness. 'So then,' said he, 'you leave the woman you love, and the children whose smiles are your heaven; you lead the life of a dog for them, and when you come back, by G—d, the wife of your bosom has divorced you, just because a letter or two miscarried! That outweighs all you have done and suffered for her. Oh, you are crying, are you? What, you have given up facing it out, and laying the blame on me, have you?'

'Yes, dear; I find you were not to blame; it was—my parents.'

'Your parents! Why, you are not a child, are you? You are the parent of my children, you little idiot; have you forgotten that?'

'No. Oh! oh! oh! I have acted hastily, and very, very wrong!'

'Come, that is a good deal for a pretty woman to own. There, dry your eyes, and let us order dinner.'

'What, dine with *you*?'

'Why, d—n it, it is not the first time by a few thousand.'

'La, Jonathan, I *should* like, but I *mustn't*.'

'Why not?'

'I should be compromised.'

'What, with me?'

'Yes, with any gentleman. Do try and realise the situation, dear. *I am a single woman.*'

Good Mr. Clarke—from California—delivered a string of curses so rapidly that they all ran into what Sir Walter calls a 'clishmaclaver,' even as when the ringers clash and jangle the church bells.

Mrs. Clarke gave him time; but as soon as he was

in a state to listen quietly, compelled him to realise *her* situation. 'You see,' said she, 'I am obliged to be very particular now. Delicacy demands it. You remember poor Ephraim Slade?'

'Your old sweetheart. Confound him! has he been after you again?'

'Why, Jonathan, ask yourself. He has remained unmarried ever since; and when he heard I was free, of course he entertained hopes; but I kept him at a distance, and so' (*tenderly and regretfully*) 'I must you. *I am a single woman.*'

'Look me in the face, Sophy. You won't dine with me?'

'I'd give the world; but I *mustn't*, dear.'

'Not if I twist your neck round, darling, if you don't?'

'No, dear. You shall kill me, if you please. But I am a respectable woman, and I will not brave the world. But I know I have acted rashly, foolishly, ungratefully, and deserve to be killed. *Kill me, dear!* you'll forgive me then.' With that she knelt down at his feet, crossed her hands over his knees, and looked up sweetly in his face with brimming eyes, waiting, yea, even requesting to be killed.

He looked at her with glistening eyes. 'You cunning hussey,' said he; 'you know I would not hurt a hair of your head. What is to be done? I tell you what it is, Sophy; I have lived three years without a wife, and that is enough. I won't live any longer so— no, not a day. It shall be you or somebody else. Ah! what is that?—a bell. I'll ring and order one. I've got lots of money. They are always to be had for that, you know.'

'Oh, Jonathan! don't talk so. It is scandalous. How can you get a wife all in a minute—by ringing?'

'If I can't, then the town-crier can. I'll hire him.'

'For shame!'

'How is it to be, then? You that are so smart at dividing couples, you don't seem to be very clever in bringing 'em together again.'

'It was my parents, Jonathan, not me. Well, dear, I always think when people are in a difficulty, the best thing is to go to some very *good* person for advice. Now the best people are the clergymen. There is one in this street, No. 18. Perhaps he could advise us.'

Jonathan listened gravely for a little while, before he saw what she was at; but the moment he caught the idea so slily conveyed, he slapped his thigh and shouted out, 'You are a sensible girl. Come on!' And he almost dragged her to the clergyman. Not but what he found time to order a good dinner in the hall as they went.

The clergyman was out, but soon found: he re-married them, and they dined together man and wife.

They never mentioned grievances that night; and Jonathan said, afterward, his second bridal was worth a dozen of his first; for the first time she was a child, and had to be courted uphill; but the second time she was a woman, and knew what to say to a fellow.

Next day Mr. and Mrs. Clarke went over to ——.

They drove about in an open carriage for some hours, and did a heap of shopping. They passed by Ephraim Slade's place of business much oftener than there was any need, and slower. It was Mrs. Clarke who drove. Jonathan sat and took it easy.

She drives to this day.

And Jonathan takes it easy.

TIT FOR TAT.

CHAPTER I.

It was a glaring afternoon in the short but fiery Russian summer. Two live pictures, one warm, one very cool, lay side by side.

A band of fifty peasant girls, in bright spotted tunics, snow-white leggings, and turban handkerchiefs, blue, crimson, or yellow, moved in line across the pale-green grass, and plied their white rakes with the free, broad, supple, and graceful movements of women whom no corset had ever confined and stiffened.

Close by this streak of vivid colour moving in afternoon haze of potable gold over gentle green stood a grove of ancient birch trees with great smooth silver stems; a cool brook babbled along in the deep shade, and on the carpet of green mosses, and among the silver columns, sat a lady, with noble but hardish features, in a grey dress and a dark-brown hood. Her attendant, a girl of thirteen, sparkled apart in pale blue, seated on the ground, nursing the lady's guitar.

This was the tamer picture of the two, yet, on paper, the more important, for the lady was, and is, a remarkable woman—Anna Petrovna Staropolsky, a true Russian aristocrat, ennobled, not by the breath of any modern ruler, but by antiquity, local sovereignty, and the land she and hers had held and governed for a thousand years.

It may throw some light upon her character to present her before and after the emancipation of her slaves.

Her family had never maltreated serfs within the memory of man, and she inherited their humanity.

For all that, she was very haughty. But then her towering pride was balanced by two virtues and one foible. She had a feminine detestation of violence— would not allow a horse to be whipped, far less a man or a woman. She was a wonderfully just woman, and, to come to her foible, she was *fanatica per la musica,* or, if aught so vulgar and strong as English may intrude into a joyous science whose terms are Italian, *music mad.*

This was so well known all over her vast estates that her serfs, if they wanted new isbahs—*alias* log-huts— a new peal of forty church bells, mounting by perfect gradation from a muffin man's up to a deaving dome of bell-metal, or, in short, any unusual favour, would get the priests or the deacons to versify their petition, and send it to the lady, with a solo, a quartette, and a little chorus. The following sequence of events could then be counted on. They would sing their prayer at her ; she would listen politely, with a few winces ; she would then ignore ' the verbiage,' as that intellectual oddity, the public singer, calls it, and fall tooth and nail upon the musical composition, correcting it a little peevishly. This done, she would proceed to their interpretation of their own music. ' Let us read it right, such as it is,' was her favourite formula.

When she had licked the thing into grammar and interpretation, her hard features used to mollify so she seemed another woman. Then a canny moujik, appointed beforehand to watch her countenance, would revert for a moment to ' the verbiage.'

' Oh, as to *that*—' the lady would say, and concede the substantial favour with comparative indifference.

When the edict of emancipation came, and disarmed cruel proprietors, but took no substantial benefit from *her* without a full equivalent, she made a progress through her estates, and convened her people. She read and explained the ukase, and the compensatory clauses, and showed them she could make the change difficult and disagreeable to them in detail. 'But,' said she, 'I shall do nothing of the kind. I shall exact no impossible purchases nor crippling compensations from *you*. Our father the Emperor takes nothing from me that I value, and he gives me good money, bearing five per cent., for indifferent land that brought me one per cent. clear. He has relieved me of your taxes, your lawsuits, and your empty cupboards, and given me a good bargain, you a bad one. So, let us settle matters beforehand. If you can make your fortunes with ten acres per house, in spite of taxes, increasing mouths, laziness, and your beloved cornbrandy, why, I give you leave to look down on Anna Petrovna, for she is your inferior in talent, and talent governs the world nowadays. But if you find Independence, and farms the size of my garden, mean Poverty now, and, when mouths multiply, Hunger, then you can come to Anna Petrovna, just as you used, and we will share the good Emperor's five per cents.'

She was as good as her word, and made the change easy by private contracts in the spirit of the enactment, but more lenient to the serfs than its literal clauses.

By these means, and the accumulated respect of ages, she retained all the power and influence she cared for, and this brings me fairly to my summer picture. Those fifty peasant girls were enfranchised serfs who would not have put their hands to a rake for any other proprietor thereabouts. Yet they were working with a good heart for Anna Petrovna at fourpence a day, and singing like mavises as they marched. Catinka Kusminoff sang on the left of the band, Daria Solovieff on the right.

They were now commencing the last drift of the whole field, and would soon sweep the edge of the grove, where Madame Staropolsky — as we English should call her—sat pale and listless. She was a widow, and her only son had betrayed symptoms of heart-disease. Sad reminiscences clouded those lofty but somewhat angular features, and she looked gloomy, hard, and severe.

But it so happened that as the band of women came alongside this grove, which bounded the garden from the fields, Daria Solovieff took up the song with marvellous power and sweetness. She was all unconscious of a refined listener; it was out-of-doors, she was leading the whole band, and she sang *out* from a chest and frame whose free play had never been confined by stays, and with a superb voice, all power, volume, roundness, sweetness, bell-like clearness, and that sympathetic eloquence which pierces and thrills the heart.

In most parts of Europe this superb organ would have sung out in church, and been famous for miles around. But the Russians are still in some things Oriental; only men and boys must sing their anthems; so the greatest voice in the district was unknown to the greatest musician. She stood up from her seat and actually trembled—for she was Daria's counterpart, organised as finely to hear and feel as Daria to sing. The lady's lofty but hardish features seemed to soften all their outlines as she listened, a complacent, mild, and rapt expression overspread them, her clear gray eyes moistened, melted, and deepened, and lo! she was beautiful.

She crept along the grove listening, and when the sound retired, directed her little servant to follow the band and invite Daria to come and help her prune roses next day.

The invitation was accepted with joy, for the work was pleasant, and the remuneration for working in Anna Petrovna's garden was not money, but some article of female dress or ornament. It might be only a ribbon or a cotton handkerchief, but even then it would be worth more than a woman's wage, and please her ten times more; the contemplation of a chiffon is a sacred joy, the feel of fourpence a mere human satisfaction.

So the next day came Daria, a tall, lithe, broad-shouldered lass, very fair, with hair like a new sovereign —pardon, O race Sclavonic, my British similes!— marvellous white skin, and colour like a delicate rose, eyes of deep violet, and teeth incredibly white and even.

G

When she went among the flowers she just seemed
to be one of them.

The lady of the house came out to her with gauntlets and scissors, and a servant and a gig umbrella,
whereat the child of nature smiled, and revealed much
ivory.

Madame snipped off dead roses along with her for
nearly half an hour, then observed: 'This is a waste of
time. Come under that tree with me. Now sing me
that song you sang yesterday in the field.'

The fair cheek was dyed with blushes directly. 'Me
sing before you, Anna Petrovna!'

'Why not? Come, Daria, do not be afraid of one
old woman who loves music, and can appreciate you
better than most. Sing to me, my little pigeon.'

The timid dove, thus encouraged, fixed her eyes
steadily on the ground and cooed a little song.

The tears stood in the lady's eyes. 'You are
frightened still,' said she; 'but why? See, I do not
praise you; and I weep. That is the best comment.
You will not always be afraid of me.'

'Oh no; you are so kind.'

Daria's shyness was soon overcome, and every other
day she had to come and play at gardening a bit, then
work at music.

When the winter came her patroness could not do
without her. She sent to old Kyril, Daria's father,
and offered to adopt her. He did not seem charmed;
said she was his only daughter, and he should miss
her.

'Why, you will marry her, and so lose her,' said
madame.

He admitted that was the custom. 'The go-between arranges a match, and one daughter after another leaves the nest. But I have only this one, and she is industrious and a song-bird; and I have forbidden the house to all these old women who yoke couples together blindfold. To be sure, there is a young fellow, a cousin of mine, comes over from the town on Sundays and brings Daria flowers and me a flask of vodka.'

'Then he is welcome to one of you?'

'As snow to sledge-horses; but Daria gives him little encouragement. She puts up with him, that is all.'

'You would not like a good house, and fifty acres more than the ten a bountiful state bestows on you, rent free for ever?'

'Forgive me for contradicting you, Anna Petrovna; I should like them extremely.'

'And I should like to adopt Daria.'

The tender father altered his tone directly. 'Anna Petrovna, it is not our custom to refuse you any-thing.'

'And it is not your custom to lose anything by obliging me.'

'That is well known.'

After this, of course, the parties soon came to an understanding.

Daria was to be adopted, and some land and a house made over to her and her father as joint proprietors during his lifetime, to Daria after his decease.

Daria, during her father's lifetime, was to live with

Madame Staropolsky as a sort of humble but valued companion.

When it was all settled, the only one of the three who had a misgiving was the promoter.

'This song-bird,' said she to herself, ' has already too much power over me.   How will it be when she is a woman?   Her voice bewitches me.   She has no need to sing; if she but speaks she enchants me.   Have I brought my mistress into the house?'   This presentiment flashed through her mind, but did not abide at that time.

One Sunday she saw Daria strolling along the road with a young man.   He parted with her at the door, but was a long time doing it, and gave her some flowers, and lingered and looked after her.

Anna Petrovna felt a twinge, and the next moment blushed for herself.   'What! jealous!' said she,   ' The girl has certainly bewitched me.'

She asked Daria, carelessly, who the young man was.   Daria made no secret of the matter.   'It is only Ivan Ulitch Koscko, who comes many miles every Sunday.'

'To court you?'

'I suppose it is.'

'Does he love you?'

'He says so.'

'Do you love him?'

'Not much: but he is very good.'

'Is he to marry you?'

'I do not know.   I would rather be as I am.'

'I wonder which you love best—that young man or me?'

'I could never love a young man as I love you, Anna Petrovna. It is quite different.'

Madame Staropolsky looked keenly at her to see whether this was audacious humbug or pure innocence, and it appeared to be the latter; so she embraced her warmly. Then Daria, who did not lack intelligence, said, 'If you wish it, I will ask Ivan Ulitch not to come again.'

This would have been agreeable to Madame Staropolsky, but her sense of justice stepped in. 'No,' said she; 'I will interfere with no prior claims.'

This lady played the violin in tune; the violoncello sonorously, not snorously; the piano finely; and the harp to perfection.

She soon enlarged her pupil's musical knowledge greatly, but was careful not to alter her style, which, indeed, was wonderfully natural and full of genius. She also instructed her in history, languages, and arithmetic, and seemed to grow younger now she had something young to teach.

Christmas came, and her son Alexis was expected, his education at St. Petersburg being finished. Until this year he had not visited these parts for some time. His mother used to go to the capital to spend the winter vacation with him there: the summer at Tsarskoe. But there was a famous portrait of him at seven years of age—a lovely boy, with hair like new-burnished copper, but wonderful dark eyes and brows, his dress a tunic and trousers of purple silk, the latter tucked into Wellington boots, purple cap with a short peacock's feather. We have Gainsborough's blue boy, but, really, this might be called the Russian purple boy. A wonder-striking picture of a beautiful original.

Daria had often stood before this purple boy, and wondered at his beauty. She even thought it was a pity such an angel should ever grow up, and deteriorate into a man.

The sledge was sent ten miles to meet Alexis, and while he was yet three miles distant the tinkling of the bells announced him. On he came, at the rate of fifteen miles an hour, with three horses—a powerful black trotter in the middle, and two galloping bays, one on each side, all three with tails to stuff a sofa and manes like lions. Everybody in the village turned out to welcome him; every dog left his occupation, and followed him on the spot; the sledge dashed up to the front verandah, the ready doors flew open, the family were all in the hall, ready with a loving welcome; and the thirty village dogs, having been now and then flogged for their hospitality, stood aloof in a semi-circle, and were blissful with excitement, and barked sympathetic and loud. When the mother locked the son in her arms the tears stood in Daria's eyes; but she was disappointed in his looks, after the picture; to be sure, he was muffled to the nose in furs, and his breath, frozen flying, had turned his moustache and eyebrows into snow. Beard he had none, or he might have passed for Father Christmas—and he was only twenty.

But in the evening he was half as big and three times as handsome.

His mother made Daria sing to him, and he was enraptured.

He gazed on her all the time with two glorious

black eyes, and stealing a glance at him, as women will, she found him, like his mother, beautified by her own enchantment, and he seemed to resemble his portrait more and more.

From that first night he could hardly take his eyes off her. These grand orbs, always dwelling on her, troubled her heart and her senses, and by degrees elicited timid glances in return. These and the seductions of her voice completed his conquest, and he fell passionately in love with her. She saw and returned his love, but tried innocent artifices to conceal it. Her heart was in a tumult. Hitherto she had been as cool as a cucumber with Ivan and every other young man, and wondered what young women could see so attractive in them. Now she was caught herself, and fluttered like a wild bird suddenly caged.

Ivan Ulitch Koscko, who could not make her love him, used to console himself for her coolness by saying it was her nature—a cool affection and moderate esteem was all she had to give to any man. So many an endured lover talks; but suddenly the right man comes, and straightway the icy Hecla reveals her infinite fires.

Alexis soon found an opportunity to tell Daria he adored her.

She panted with happiness first, and hid her blushing face; but the next moment she quivered with alarms.

'Oh, no, no!' she murmured, 'you must not. What have I done? Your mother—she would never forgive me. It was not to steal her son's heart she brought me here.' And the innocent girl was all misgivings, and began to cry.

Alexis consoled her and kissed her tears away, and would not part with her till she smiled again, and interchanged vows of love and constancy with him.

Under love's potent influence she left him radiant.

But when she thought it all over, and him no longer there to overpower her, her misgivings grew, and she was terrified. She had an insight into character, and saw beneath the surface of Anna Petrovna. That lady loved her, but would hate her if she stole the affections of her son, her idol.

Daria's deep eyes fixed themselves all of a sudden on the future. 'Misfortune is coming here,' she said.

Then she crossed herself, bowed her head piously in that attitude, and prayed long and earnestly.

Then she rose, and went straight to Anna Petrovna. She found her knitting mittens for Alexis.

She sat at her feet, and said, wearily, 'Anna Petrovna, I ask leave to go home.'

'Why? what is the matter?'

'My father.'

'Is he unwell?'

'No. But he has not seen me for some time.'

'Is it for long?'

'Not very long.'

Anna Petrovna eyed her steadily. 'Perhaps you are like me, of a jealous disposition in your little quiet way. Tell the truth now, my pigeon; you are jealous of Alosha.'

'Me jealous of Alexis?'

'Oh, jealousy spares neither age nor sex. Come, you are—just a little. Confess now.'

Daria was surprised; but she was silent at first;

and then, being terribly afraid lest one so shrewd should discover her real sentiments, she had the tact and the self-defensive subtlety to defend herself so tamely against this charge that she left the impression but little disturbed.

Anna Petrovna determined to cure her by kindness, so she said: 'Well, you shall go next week. But to-day we expect our cousin, Vladimir Alexéitch Plutitzin, on a short visit. He is musical, and I cannot afford to part with you while he is here.'

Then Daria's heart bounded with delight. She had tried to go away, but was forcibly detained in paradise.

Vladimir Alexéitch Plutitzin arrived—a keen, dark gentleman, forty years old, and a thorough man of the world; a gamester and a *roué*—bully or parasite, whichever suited his purpose; but most agreeable on the surface, and welcome to Madame Staropolsky on that account and his relationship. He seemed so shallow she had never taken the trouble to look deep into him.

His principal object in this visit was to borrow money, and as he could not do that all in a moment, he looked forward to a tedious visit.

But this fair singer made all the difference. He was charmed with her, and began to pay her attentions in the drollest way, half spooney, half condescending. He was very pertinacious, and Daria was rather offended and a little disgusted. But all she showed was complete coolness and civil apathy.

Vladimir Alexéitch, having plenty of vanity and experience, did not accept this as Ivan did. 'This cucumber is in love with somebody,' said he; and he looked out very sharp. He saw at once that Alexis was wrapped up in her, but that she was rather shy of him, and on her guard. That puzzled him a little. However, one Sunday he detected her talking with a young man under the front verandah. It was not love-making after the manner of Vladimir Alexéitch, but they seemed familiar and confidential: clearly he was the man.

Vladimir burned with spite, and he wreaked it. He went into the drawing-room, and there he found Alexis and his mother, seated apart. So he began upon Alexis. He said to him, too low for his mother to hear, ' So our cantatrice has a lover.'

Alexis stared, then changed colour. ' Daria a lover —who ? ' He thought at first his own passion had been discovered by this shrewd person.

' Oh, that is more than I can tell you. Some fellow of her own class though. He is courting her at this moment.'

Alexis turned ashy pale, and his lips blue. ' I'll believe that when I see it,' said he, stoutly.

' See it, then, in the verandah,' was the calm reply.

With that the serpent glided on to the mother.

Alexis waited a moment, and then sauntered out, with a ghastly attempt at indifference.

Once in the hall, he darted to the door, opened it, and found Daria and her faithful Ivan in calm conversation. The sight of the young man was enough for Alexis. He said, angrily, ' Daria, my mother wants you immediately.'

' Farewell, then, Ivan,' said Daria submissively, and entered the house at once. Alexis stood and cast a haughty stare on Ivan; and the poor fellow, who had walked ten miles for a word or two with Daria, returned disappointed.

CHAPTER II.

MEANTIME, Anna Petrovna asked Vladimir Alexéitch what he had said to Alexis. 'Oh, nothing particular; only that our fair cantatrice had a lover.'

'Why, that is no news,' said the lady. 'But indeed he is not much of a lover, and I hope it will come to nothing. That is very selfish, for he is an old friend and a faithful one to her. His mother kept the district school at Griasansk, and taught Daria to read and write and work. Her son is a notary's clerk, and assisted her in her learning. Let me tell you she is a very fair scholar, not an ignorant savage like the rest of these girls. To be sure, her father has a head on his shoulders, and had sent her to school, contrary to the custom of the country.'

That favourite topic of hers, the praises of her *protégée,* was cut unnaturally short by Daria in person. She came in, and, gliding up to her patroness with a sweet inclination of her whole body, said, 'You sent for me, Anna Petrovna. Alexis Pavlovitch told me.'

'Indeed! Then he divined my thought. But I did not send for you; I heard your friend was with you.'

'He was.'

'What have you done with him?'

'I told him to go.'

'That you might come to me?'

'Certainly.'

'That was rather hard upon him.'

'It does not matter,' said Daria, composedly.

'Not to you, Daria; that is evident.'

Alexis came in and flung himself into a chair, manifestly discomposed. Daria cast a swift glance at him, then looked down.

Anna Petrovna surprised this lightning glance and looked at her son, and then at Vladimir; then she turned her eyes inward, mystified and inquiring, and from that hour seemed to brood occasionally, and her features to stiffen.

Vladimir watched his poison work. Some days afterwards he joked Alexis about his passion for a girl who was already provided with a lover, but found him inaccessible to jealousy. The truth is, he and Daria had come to an explanation. 'She loves nobody but me,' said the young man, proudly; 'and no other man but me shall ever have her; not even you, my clever cousin.'

'Oh, I make way for the head of the house, as in duty bound,' said sneering Vladimir. 'But when you have got her all to yourself, what do you mean to do with her? I am afraid, Alexis, she will get you into trouble. Her people are respectable. Your mother's morals are severe. She is attached to the girl. What on earth can you do with her?'

'I mean to marry her, if she will have me.'

'Do what?'

'Marry her, man. What else can I do?'

Vladimir was incredulous and amused at first; then

taking a survey of the young man's face, he saw there the iron resolution that he had observed in the boy's mother. He looked aghast. Alexis marry this blooming peasant—a woman of another race, a child of nature! She would fill that sterile house with children, and *he* would die the beggar that he was. Vladimir did not speak all at once. At last he said, 'You cannot; you are not of age.'

'I shall be soon.'

'Your mother would never consent.

'I fear not.'

'Well, then——'

'I shall marry Daria.'

When Alexis said this, and looked him full in the face, Vladimir turned his cold pale Tartar eye away, and desperate thoughts flashed across him. Indeed, he felt capable of assassination. But prudence and the cunning of his breed suggested crafty measures first.

He controlled himself with a powerful effort, and said, quietly, 'Such a marriage would break your mother's heart; and she has been a good friend to me. I cannot abet you in it. But I am sorry I treated a serious matter with levity.'

Then he left him, and his brain went to work in earnest.

The truth is that a more dangerous man than Vladimir Alexévitch Plutitzin never entered an honest house. Crafty and selfish by nature, he was also by this time practically versed in wiles; and his great expectations, should Alexis die without issue, and his present ruin, made him think little of crime, though not of detection.

He was too cunning to go and tell Anna Petrovna all at once, and so reveal the mischief-maker to Alexis. He was silent days and days, but went into brown studies before Anna Petrovna, to attract her attention. He succeeded. She began to watch him as well as her son; and at last she said to him one day, 'There is something mysterious going on in this house, Vladimir.'

'Ah, you have discovered it!'

'I have discovered there is *something*. What is it, if you please?'

'I do not like to tell you; and yet I ought, for you have been a good friend to me, and if I do not warn you, you will perhaps doubt my regard. I don't know what to do.'

'Shall I help you? Alexis and Daria!'

'There, then, you have seen it,'

'I see he is *extasié* with her, and no wonder, since I am. Luckily she has too much good sense.'

'Anna Petrovna, my dear kinswoman and bene-factress, it is my duty to undeceive you. She is more timid and more discreet, because she is a woman; but she is just as much in love. It is a passionate attach-ment on both sides, and—how shall I tell you?—marriage is to be the end of it.'

'Marriage! My son—and my serf!'

'Serfs exist no more. We are all ladies and gentle-men, thanks to God and the Tsar.'

Anna Petrovna turned pale, and her features hard as iron. 'Viper,' said she, not violently, but sadly. Then her breath came short, and she could not speak.

But after a little while this just woman half recanted. 'No,' said she, 'I had no right to say that. She sought me not; *I* brought her into this house, and she was a treasure to me. *I* brought him into the house, and she saw her danger, and asked leave to go. But *I*, who ought to have been wiser than she, had no forethought. I have made my own trouble, and it is for me to mend it. There shall be no discussion on this subject. You must not let Alexis know you have spoken to me, nor shall I speak to him.'

Vladimir consented eagerly. It was not his game to quarrel with Alexis.

That very afternoon Madame Staropolsky said to Daria, 'Daria, my little soul, you were right and I was wrong; you shall visit your father this afternoon.'

Daria turned red and white by turns, and acquiesced, trembling at what this might mean. Two maids were sent to assist her in packing. That gave her no chance of delay.

In one hour a large sledge came round, filled with presents for her father. Anna Petrovna blessed her fervently, but with a feminine distinction kissed her coldly, enveloped her in rich furs, and packed her off *sans cérémonie*. She dashed over the hard snow for a mile or two, then through the village, sore envied, and followed by each cur, and at last landed triumphantly at her own farm and her father's, warmly welcomed, admired, and barked after; only the tears trickled down her cheeks from the door she quitted to the door she reached.

That evening the house looked blank. Everybody

missed Daria, and Alexis kept looking at the door for her. At last he asked, with indifference ill-feigned, what had become of her.

'Oh,' said his mother, 'she has gone home. She wished to go last month, but I detained her. I wished you so to hear her sing.'

She then turned the conversation adroitly and resolutely.

But Alexis as resolutely declined to utter anything but monosyllables. He could conceal neither his anger nor his unhappiness. He avoided the house except at meals, yawned in Vladimir's face, and even in his mother's; and once, when she asked tenderly why he was so dull, replied that the house had lost its sunshine and its music.

This was a cruel stab to Anna Petrovna. She replied, grimly, 'Then we will go to Petersburg earlier than usual, dear.'

One day he cleared up and became as charming as ever.

Anna Petrovna, whose mother's heart had yearned for him, was comforted, and said to Vladimir, 'Ah, youth soon forgets. Dear Alexis has come to his senses and recovered his spirits.'

'So I see,' was the reply. 'But I do not interpret that as you do. I take it for granted he sees the girl every day.'

'What,' said Madame Staropolsky, 'under her father's roof? He would not wrong me so, after all I have done for him. But I should like to know.'

Artful Vladimir took her hand tenderly. 'I don't

like spying on Alexis, but you have a right to know, and you shall know.'

She pressed his hand gratefully, then left him with a deep maternal sigh.

In a few days he made her his report. Alexis. rode straight to the farm every day, and spent hours with Daria. Her father encouraged him, and, indeed, ordered the girl to receive him as her betrothed lover.

The mother's features set themselves like iron, but she uttered no impatient word this time. She just directed her servants to pack for Petersburg.

When Alexis heard this he said he should prefer to stay behind until the full summer.

'No, my son,' said Madame Staropolsky, calmly; 'you must not abandon me altogether. If I have lost your affection, I retain my authority.'

'So be it; I must obey,' said he, doggedly. 'I am not of age. I shall be soon, though, thank Heaven!'

The iron pierced through the mother's heart. She winced, but she did not deign to speak.

That evening Alexis did not come home to dinner. He arrived about ten o'clock, with his eyes red and swollen, would take nothing but a glass of tea, and so to bed.

At the sight of his inoffensive sorrow the mother's bowels began to yearn over her son. 'Oh, my friend,' said she to her worst enemy, 'what shall I do? He will not live long.' Vladimir pricked up his ears at that. 'Aneurism of the heart—very slight at present, but progressive. Why poison his short life? She is virtuous. It is only her birth. I am a miserable mother.'

Her crafty counsellor trembled, but his cunning did not desert him.

'And I can't bear to see you weep,' said he. 'Yes, try the capital and its female attractions, and if they fail, let him marry his enfranchised serf, and found a plebeian line. I would rather endure that shame than see you and him really unhappy. But if you only knew how many of these unfortunate attachments I have seen cured, and the patient begin by hating and end by thanking his physician!'

'We will go to Petersburg to-morrow,' said the lady, firmly.

They made the journey accordingly. They took a house on the Krestoffsky Island, and by advice of Vladimir furnished both Alexis and himself with large funds, aided by which this Mentor set himself to corrupt his pupil.

Everything is to be bought in capitals, and the Russian capital contained women of good position who were easily tempted to feign attachment to this Adonis, and cajole him with superlative art, which, by the way, in one case became nature through the lovely baroness falling really in love with him. With the assistance of these charmers, and constant letters from Daria, which he took the precaution to receive at a post office, and post his own letters with his own hand, he passed three months rather gaily. He saw he was being cunningly dealt with, and being a Sclav himself, he kept demanding money for his pleasures and certain imaginary debts of honour, and hoarding it for a virtuous and imprudent purpose.

As for Vladimir, he became easy about his pupil,

and pushed his own interests with the aid of his grateful patroness. Her vast lands and her economy had made her prodigiously rich, and by consequence powerful, and, with her influence and the money she furnished, Vladimir got the promise of a police mastership in a town and district about seventy miles distant from Smirnovo.

But all of a sudden his complacency and the tranquillity of his patroness received a shock. Alexis disappeared, in spite of all the money invested to cure him of a virtuous attachment by pleasure, folly, and a little vice if the good work could not be achieved without it. For some days he was sought high and low in St. Petersburg, and the police reaped a harvest before they found out, or at all events before they revealed, that he had hired a travelling carriage, taken a *permis de voyage*, and gone south post-haste.

Anna Petrovna hurled Vladimir after him, and Vladimir, whose appointment was just signed, donned a uniform, and when he left the railway demanded posthorses anywhere in the name of the law, and achieved the journey to Smirnovo faster even than Alexis.

He dashed up to the door of the house. It flew open, as usual, without knock or ring.

'Alexis Pavlovitch?'

'Not here.'

'Has he not been here?'

'Yes; slept here one night about two days ago.'

Vladimir made no noise, but into his carriage again, and away to Daria's cottage.

Empty, all but an old woman, as deaf as a post, and put in charge for no other reason.

From her he could get nothing; from the neighbours only this, that the old man and his daughter and Alexis had set forth on a journey, and neither they nor the troika nor the horses had been heard of since.

Plutitzin returned crestfallen to headquarters, wrote to Anna Petrovna, and then went to bed for twenty-four hours.

Next day he put on his uniform, galloped about the country, and tried to learn the direction those three fugitives had taken.

He cajoled, he threatened. 'They mean marriage,' said he, 'and the man is a minor. His marriage will be annulled, and all who have aided and abetted him sent to Siberia.'

The simple country folk swallowed this brag, coming out of a uniform. They trembled and offered conjectures, having no facts, and then he swore at them and galloped elsewhere. But when he had ridden two horses lame, it struck him all of a sudden that he was acting like a fool. Why hunt these culprits in the neighbourhood they had left?

Within eighty miles—a mere step in Russia—was his new post, at Samara, and all the machinery of his office; here he was but a private person cased in an irrelevant uniform.

That very night he wrote to the municipal authorities of Samara, and let them know he should arrive at his official residence on the morning of next Thursday.

He gave just time for this missive to get ahead of him, and then started. But he made two days of it, and inquired at all the stages. Nor were these inquiries fruitless.

Thirty miles from home he struck the scent of the fugitives, and they seemed really to have anticipated his track; but then it was nearly three weeks ago.

At the last stage before Samara he donned his uniform and a glorious military decoration he had obtained before he left the army of his own accord, because he was threatened with an inquiry based on his neglect to pay debts at cards, and, thus resplendent, he drew near the scene of his future power and glory—stipend moderate, money to be obtained by bribes indefinite.

As he surmounted a rising ground three miles from the town a peal of musical church-bells broke out—one of the drollest and prettiest things in Russia, on account of the bells ranging over three octaves, and the curious skill of the ringers in sometimes running a series, sometimes leaping off treble lowers into profound wells of melody. Tinkle, tinkle, tinkle, b-o-m-e. Tinkle bome, tinkle, tinkle, tinkle, bome.

All this tintinnabulation and boomen gratified Vladimir's vanity. With what quick eyes had Adulation seen the coming magnate, and with what watchful fingers rung him into the town of Samara! so Vladimir read 'the bells.' He smiled, well pleased, and longed to be there; but he had another rise to surmount first, and as his jaded horses plodded up it, down glided an open calêche, with glossy and swift horses, and in it sat Alexis and Daria hand in hand; she with her cheek all love and blushes on his shoulder; he, seated erect and conscious, her protector and her lord.

The carriages passed each other rapidly, but in that moment Alexis drew himself higher, if possible, and his

black eye flashed a flame of unspeakable triumph on
his baffled pursuer.

Then there whirled through the brain of Vladimir
some such thoughts as these : 'Without her father—
church-bells—that look of triumph—useless to follow
them—let him have her—she will keep him from
marrying till he dies—this marriage illegal—I will
annul it on the spot—*quietly.*'   .

Revolving the details of this villainous scheme, he
entered the town of Samara.

CHAPTER III.

VLADIMIR went straight to the church. The priest's
office was vacant by bis recent decease. The deacon
was there. Vladimir terrified the simple man; told
him he had taken part in an illegal act—the marriage
of two minors, one of them under a false name. The
woman a lady of rank; the *soi-disant* Alexis an enfranchised serf, whose real name was Kusmin Petroff.

'Is it possible ? ' said the dismayed deacon. ' Why,
her father attended the ceremony.'

'Her father ! Did he look like a nobleman ? '

'No; more like a respectable peasant.'

'Of course. It was her major-domo,' said the
unblushing Vladimir, ' and it will cost him a trip to
Siberia; and, if you are wise, you will endeavour not
to accompany him.'

'My father,' said the poor man, ' it all seemed
honest; they sojourned here—more than a fortnight.

Their banns were published. You cannot suspect me of complicity. I implore you not to bring me into trouble.'

'Oh, as to that,' said the chief of police, 'all depends on your present conduct. Noble families do not love public scandal. If you place yourself under my orders now, I dare say I shall be able to protect you.'

These terms were eagerly accepted.

'Now, then,' said this grim functionary, 'is this sham marriage registered?'

'Only on a slip of paper, preparatory to my entering it on the register.'

'You will hand that paper to me.'

'Here it is, my father.'

'And the book of registration?'

'Yes,' said the deacon, faintly.

'A much higher authority than I care to name will decide whether there shall be a correct entry or none at all. While his Imperial Maj—while this grave matter is under consideration, make all future entries on loose paper *pro tem.*'

The book was handed over to the chief policeman, and returned in three weeks, with the remark that it had been to St. Petersburg in the interval.

The simple deacon received it with a genuflection. He thought that it had passed through the sacred hands of the father of his people.

Meantime Vladimir wrote to Anna Petrovna and told her all, addressed the letter, and burnt it. He remembered that she had wavered, and, besides, he recollected her character. She was too scrupulous to co-operate with him in his sinister views, and indeed had not the same temptation.

He wrote briefly, to say that Alexis and Daria were living together as man and wife, and it was even reported that he had deceived her with a form of marriage; but that might be untrue.

Anna Petrovna wrote back to say she should return to Smirnovo at once, and summoned him to her side, 'for,' said she, 'I am alone in the world.'

Instead of melting into tears at the sad words, Vladimir's eyes flashed with greed. The other day a pauper, and now all the domain of his powerful relative seemed to be separated from him only by one life, and that life not only precarious but doomed.

He left his post directly, appointed a substitute, who was to communicate with him on important occasions, and he was at Smirnovo to receive Anna Petrovna. She came, worn out with fatigue and the struggles of her maternal heart, and next day she was seriously ill. Physicians sent for—advised darkened room—relief from business and anxieties—and poisoned her a little with mild narcotics.

Vladimir now read all her letters, and replied to all except two. These were from Alexis and Daria, entreating pardon with a filial anxiety and a loving tenderness that would have melted the mother at once. But this domestic fiend suppressed them, and the young pair got no reply whatever.

This marred in some degree their short-lived happiness. Still, they hoped all from time, and recovering by degrees the cruel rebuff, they were so happy that every day they blessed each other, and wondered whether any other mortals had attained such bliss on this side heaven.

Alas! in the midst of their paradise Fate struck them down. Alarming symptoms attacked Alexis. Physicians were sent for, one after another, and all looked grave. Daria wrote wildly to his mother: 'He is dying. Come, if you love him better than I do. Come, and take him from me for ever. Only save him.' Hope rose and fell, then dwindled altogether. Daria watched him day and night, and eyed every doctor's face so piteously that they had not the heart to speak out; but their looks and tones were volumes. At last the greatest physician in the empire came and stood with his confrères over that sad bed. He felt the patient's heart, his head, his limbs. He said but one word:

'Moribundus!'

Then he retired without losing a moment more, where science was as vain as ignorance.

Vladimir did not let Anna Petrovna see Daria's letter, but he went to her and said, with agitation, real or feigned: 'I hear Alexis is ill. I must go to him. I love the boy. If he is seriously ill, let me tell him you forgive him. Do not run a risk of shortening his life.'

The poor mother trembled, wept, and assented, and the hypocrite became dearer to her than ever.

He started at once for Petersburg, and, travelling day and night, soon reached the pleasant villa from which Daria's letter was written.

Outside were pink sun-blinds, marble pillars festooned with creepers, and all the luxuries of civilised existence; inside, the dire realities of life—the husband a corpse, the wife raving, and both of them in their prime. That no cruel feature might be absent, an official stood there, like an iron pillar, demanding the immediate interment of him, who, according to nature, had just begun to live.

There was no more temptation to be cruel. Vladimir buried the husband, got two good professional nurses for the wife, wrote feeling letters to the bereaved mother, and invited Daria's father to come to her at once. He even deceived himself into believing he was very sorry for all the hearts that were broken by this blow, and that he stayed in the capital to keep guard over the house of mourning, whereas what he stayed for was to enjoy the pleasures of the capital, and get himself appointed by the state administrator to Alexis, who, like most that love well, had died intestate, and left his love to battle for the rights he could have secured her by a stroke of the pen in season.

Alexis had drawn the rents of Staropolsk, his patrimony, and there was money in the house; but Vladimir thought it wise to connive at that, and fasten on a larger booty. Though older in years, he was somehow heir-at-law to Alexis, and, being administrator, had only to help himself.

From such a mind it is a relief to turn to sacred sorrow. An old man conveyed home by easy stages a pale young woman in a full cap, worn to hide the loss, by grief and brain-fever, of her lovely golden hair. It was the broken-hearted Daria.

A mother bereaved of her only son sought comfort in religion, and awaited her own summons, with thanks to God that she had not many years to live alone in *this* cruel world. This was the brave Anna Petrovna.

CHAPTER IV.

In the second month of her widowhood her father told Daria she ought to demand her third.

'My third!' said she. 'I have lost *him*, and would you comfort me with his money?' And she burst into such passionate weeping that the old man promised faithfully not to renew the subject.

In the fourth month of her widowhood she came and stood by her father as he was smoking his cigarette, put a hand light as a feather on his shoulder, looked down upon the floor, and said, in a low but rather firm voice, 'Yes.'

'Yes, what?' asked the old man.

'You can ask for our thirds.'

'Our thirds? Why, I have no claim.'

'No, not you; but——'

'What! Daria, my little soul. You blush. Is it so! Never mind your old father. Yes; well, then, now you are a woman, and your thirds you shall have, the pair of ye, or I'm not a man.'

By this time it was well known that Vladimir inherited and administered the estate of Alexis Pavlovitch Staropolsky, deceased; so Kyril Solovieff wrote to him with Russian politeness, hoped he was not premature or troublesome, but the widow of Alexis would be grateful if he would let her have her third, or a portion on account.

Vladimir, who had not been in a public office for nothing, wrote a line acknowledging receipt, and saying the matter should meet with due consideration. .

And so it did. He did not like parting with a third, but he had vague fears of a public discussion. He felt inclined to write back that he could not recognise the marriage as a legal one, but would respect the sentiments of his deceased relative, and disburse to her the same sum as if the marriage had been legal.

But before he could quite make up his mind a report reached him which, vague as it was, alarmed him seriously. He instantly employed spies, and they soon let him know that Daria Solovieff asked for her thirds because she had another to provide for—the offspring of her beloved Alexis.

This was told him with such circumstance and detail as left no doubt possible; and so the weak woman, who the other day lay at his mercy, struck terror to the very bones of this Machiavel; and all the better. It is a comfort to find that in the scheme of nature the weak can now and then confound the strong and cruel.

War to the knife now! This serf spawn, if it lived, would inherit the lands of Staropolsk and Smirnovo. Vladimir must not by word or deed admit the marriage.

He wrote, and denied all legal claim, but offered 5,000 roubles out of respect for the memory of Alexis.

This was declined, and proceedings commenced. A lawyer got up the case for Daria, instructed by her father.

Vladimir prepared his own case, and spent money like water; got the deacon of Samara out of the way to a better place twelve hundred miles off; had famous counsel from St. Petersburg, etc.

The case was tried in the district court. The defence was, 'No marriage at all, or else illegal by minority.'

On the question of minority the defence was upset, the Solovieffs made a hit there : they brought witnesses out of the enemy's camp—the nurse of Alexis, who had noted the very hour of his birth, four o'clock in the morning of the 9th of May, 1846.

Now the witnesses swore he was married 9th of May, at 11 A.M.

Three witnesses who knew Alexis, and had seen him married, had been spirited away for the time by the gold of Plutitzin. Eighteen natives of the town gave secondary evidence—swore to the bride there present, and that the bridegroom was a young man with swarthy complexion and wonderful black eyes, who passed for Alexis Pavlovitch Staropolsky.

This evidence led up to the direct testimony of old Kyril Solovieff, that he had driven Alexis from Smirnovo to Samara, and given him at the altar his daughter there present.

The last witness was Daria herself. Her beauty and sorrow and angelic candour, coupled with her situation, which was now very manifest, and a touching justification of her proceedings both in defence of her good name and her other rights, won every heart, and indeed made every word she spoke seem gospel truth.

She deposed to her adoption by Anna Petrovna,

her courtship by Alexis, their separation, his fidelity, their sojourn in Samara, their marriage, their cohabitation, her refusal to take these proceedings until she found herself pregnant.

When she was taken, sobbing and half fainting out of the box, defence seemed impossible. Many persons present wept, and among them was a young lawyer who never forgot that trial, never for a moment misunderstood a single point of it. It was the faithful, forgiving Ivan Ulitch Koscko.

The defendant's counsel rose calmly and alleged fraud. He admitted the attachment between Alexis and the plaintiff, and argued that to possess this beautiful woman he had lent her his name upon conditions which she and her friends never violated till death had closed his lips.

The person she had legally married was some tool bought for the job, and to leave the country for ever, and make way for the real possessor but fictitious husband.

Then they put in the book of registry, and, with a certain calm contempt, left their case entirely with the judge.

People stared and wondered.

The judge examined the book, and read from it: 'May 9, 1866, married Kusmin Gavrilovitch Petroff and Daria Kirilovna Solovieff, strangers.'

A chill ran round the court.

The judge asked the defendant's counsel in whose handwriting this entry was.

'In the same as the rest, apparently.

'And who wrote the rest?'

'We do not know for certain.'

'Well *I* must know before I admit it against sworn witnesses.'

He retired to take some refreshment, and on his return they had witnesses to swear that the entry in question and the notices that preceded it, and thirty-five per cent. that followed it, were all in the hand-writing of the last deacon.

'Where is he?' asked the judge.

'He was promoted some time ago to a church on the confines of Siberia.'

Then the judge expressed dissatisfaction at his not being there, and thereupon each counsel blamed the other. The plaintiff's counsel believed he had been spirited away. The defendant's counsel said that was an unworthy suspicion; the law relied on the book, not on the writer; he in many cases must be absent, since in many he was dead. It was for the other party, who had the book against them, to call the writer if they dared, and being plaintiff, they could have postponed the case until they had found him.

In this argument the barrister from the capital gained an advantage over the local advocate, and the judge nodded assent.

This concluded the trial, and the judge delivered the verdict and his reasons in a very few words.

'This a strange case,' said he—'a mysterious case. There is a conflict of evidence, all open to objection. The direct evidence for the plaintiff is respectable but interested; the evidence for the defendant is a book, and cannot be cross-examined. But then that book is the special evidence appointed by law to decide these cases. It can only be impugned by evidence of forgery or addition, mutilation or adulteration of some kind or other. It is not so impugned in this case; therefore it binds me. The verdict is for the defendant, the marriage of the plaintiff to Alexis Pavlovitch Staropolsky being not proved according to law, and, indeed, rather disproved.'

Daria's father went home furious at the defeat and the loss of money. Daria shed some patient tears, but bore the disappointment and the wrong with fortitude.

As the defeated ones drove out of the town in their humble vehicle they were stopped by an old friend—Ivan Ulitch. The meeting made them both uneasy. They had dismissed him so curtly, and what had they gained? The farmer even expected an affront, or ironical sympathy. But Ivan was not of that sort. He was 'humble fidelity' in person. Affectionate, not passionate, he had obeyed his beautiful friend, and left her in prosperity, but in her adversity he returned to her directly.

'Daria, my soul,' said he, 'do not be discouraged by this defeat. It is a fraud of some sort. Give me time; I shall unravel it. I live here now, and shall soon be a clerk no more, but a lawyer to defend your rights.'

'Good Ivan — kind, faithful Ivan!' said Daria, through her tears. 'What, are you still my friend?'

'More than ever, dear soul, now I see you wronged. Do not lose heart. This defeat is nothing. Your lawyer was weak: the other side were strong and unscrupulous, and have fought with gold and fraud. That is self-evident, though the fraud itself is obscure. No matter; I will work like a mole for you and un-ravel the knavery.'

Daria interrupted him. 'No, Ivan Ulitch; that you esteem me still is a drop of comfort, welcome as water to the thirsty. But no more law for me!'

And so they parted.

Ivan, though he seemed to acquiesce, was not to be discouraged. For months and years he patiently groped beneath the surface of this case, yet never men-tioned the case itself. He watched for the return of smuggled away witnesses; he listened in cafés and cabarets; he courted the priest and the deacon; he was artful, silent, patient, penetrating. Love by de-grees made him as dangerous as greed had made Vladi-mir Alexéitch.

Meantime that victorious villain hurried away to his head-quarters, and told Anna Petrovna there had been no difficulty after all. The very register of the place had shown that the person Daria was really married to was a serf.

'I do not doubt it,' said Anna Petrovna; 'but I can-not rejoice with you. Would to God my son had married her, and not died with *that* crime on his soul!'

Vladimir shrugged his shoulders, and made no reply. As for Anna Petrovna she never recurred to the subject; and indeed she hated the very name of Daria Solovieff. She was obliged to hear it now and then, but she never uttered it of her own accord.

Daria became the mother of a beautiful boy, and

the joys of maternity reconciled her to life.   Youth and health and maternal joy fought against grief, and in time gave her back all her beauty, with a pensive tenderness that elevated it.   Her position was painful, but the country people stood by her.   The women instinctively sided with her, and laid all the blame on the pride of the nobles.

She called her boy Alexis, and he was as dark as she was fair.   She had him well educated from his very infancy, and let everybody know that they must treat him like a noble, but herself like a peasant.   She never went near Smirnovo, nor did Anna Petrovna ever come her way.   Yet they often thought of each other, and each wondered how she could have so mistaken the other's character.   Their friends did not fail to keep the mutual repulsion alive, the impassable gulf open.

Ivan visited the cottage from time to time, and was always welcome.   One year after the birth of Alexis he offered marriage to Daria.   She thanked him for his fidelity, but calmly declined.   This restricted him to one topic; and, to do him justice, the enduring fellow did not cool in it one bit merely because Daria would not marry him.   He remained just as full of the law case and Plutitzin's knavery, to whose influence he had pretty well traced the false entry in the register, and the disappearance of the deacon, lost in that boundless empire, and separated from clerical functions, otherwise Ivan would have discovered him by his agents.

But Ivan's only eager listener was the old peasant. Daria had lost faith in human tribunals, and had no personal desire for wealth.   With her the heart predominated over the pocket.   Her great grief now was her alienation from the mother of Alexis, her old bene-factress. She often said that if any one would only confine her in one prison with Anna Petrovna, she would regain her confidence and her love. But her old patroness was physically inaccessible to her—at the capital nine months in the year, and shut up the rest; dragons at every door, under the chief dragon Vladimir, who seldom went near his office, but just cannily bribed everybody who objected to his frequent absences.

So rolled the years away, till one day Ivan Ulitch, now a keen lawyer in good practice, came to the cottage, 'bearded like the pard,' and somewhat changed in manner—more authoritative.

'The time is come,' said he; 'the plum is ripe.'

Daria rose quietly and was about to retire, but Ivan requested her to stay.

She said it was not necessary; her father would tell her; besides, Alexis was calling for her.

'Then let him come to you,' said Ivan, firmly. 'It is for him I have been working as well as for you. I think I have a right to look at him.'

'Oh yes,' said Daria, colouring up, and brought the boy in, and with her native politeness said to him, 'Alosha, this is a good friend to you and me; shake hands with him.'

Alexis shook hands directly.

'And now sit quiet, my dove.'

Her dove sat quiet, and opened two glorious eyes on Ivan Ulitch.

'Daria Kirilovna,' said Ivan, 'if you submit to that knave Plutitzin, you let him rob this boy out of his right. The moment your marriage is established, he is

the owner of Staropolsk and the heir of Anna Petrovna.
Now, do you love the son of Alexis Pavlovitch—great
Heaven! how like he is to his father!—do you love
him like a child or like a woman?'

The poor thing held out her arms to Alexis with an
inarticulate cry, the sacred music of a mother's heart.
Alexis ran to her. She was all over him in a moment,
and nestled his head in her bosom, and rocked a little
with him. Do I love my heart and soul? Do I love
my pigeon of pigeons?'

'I love *you*, mammy,' suggested Alexis.

'Ay, my heart of hearts; but not as your mammy
loves you. How could you?'

The men said nothing, but their eyes were moist,
and Ivan felt ashamed he had said anything that could
be construed into a doubt. He began to stammer
excuses.

'Nay, nay,' said Daria. 'I know what you meant,
and I deserve it. The love of my precious has been all
I needed. I ought to look forward to the days when he
will be a man, and perhaps ask why I neglected his
interests, and his good name as well as mine. My
faithful friend, if you are to be our lawyer, I will try
once more—for my Alexis. I will face that dreadful
court again for my Alexis.'

'Victory!' cried Ivan Ulitch, starting up and
waving his cap.

Alexis approved this behaviour highly. It was so
new in that staid house. 'Victory!' he cried, and
caught up his pork pie to wave it, but was cut short,
and nearly smothered with kisses.

'Here is a change of wind,' said the old man, drily;

'but excuse me, son Ivan, it is not victory yet. These young women they hang back and pull against you, and then all in a moment start off full gallop, and neat-leather reins won't hold them. But I must have my word too. The last trial cost me all my savings in one day. Will this cost as much?'

'The double!'

'And am I to pay it?'

'You will not pay one solkov. I shall pay it, and this boy's inheritance will repay it with interest.'

'Good! On these terms law is a luxury.'

'Not to me, if my best friend is to risk his money for us,' said Daria.

'That is my business,' retorted Ivan Ulitch, curtly.

Daria apologised with feigned humility, but made an appeal. 'Now, father——'

'Why, girl,' said he, 'the longer we live, the more we learn. He is not the calf he was when he first got tethered to your petticoats. He is a ripe lawyer now, by all accounts, and as sharp as a vixen with seven cubs. For all that, Mr. Lawyer, I should like to know whether that register book will come against us.'

'Of course it will; it is the pillar of the defence.'

'Then it will beat us again.'

'I think not.'

'Then how——'

Ivan interrupted. 'Kyril Kyrilovitch, you said right: "the longer we live, the more we learn." Well, I have lived long enough to learn that in ticklish cases it is best to tell nobody what cards we mean to play. The very birds of the air carry our words to the other side. I will say no more than this : I have spies in the very home of Anna Petrovna. At present she knows neither me nor Plutitzin. She shall know us both, and it is not *my* witnesses that the enemy's gold shall put out of the way during the trial. It is I who will bottle the wine, and keep it in cellar for use. All I require of you is not to breathe to a soul that we even intend to appeal against that judgment. If you breathe a syllable, you will cut your own throats and mine.'

Before he left he recurred to this, and once more exacted a solemn promise of secrecy. This done, he cut his visit short and went home.

It would be out of place and unnecessary to follow Ivan Ulitch Koscko in all his acts. Suffice it to say that he now began to gather certain fruits he had been years maturing. But one of the things he did was, to the best of my belief, new in the history of mankind. In the first place, it was a piece of knavery done by an honest man. That is unusual, but far from unique. But then it was done for no personal gain, and mainly out of love of justice, and justice had little chance of success without the help of this injustice. To this singular situation add the act itself and its unique details, and I think you will come to my opinion that, old as the world is, this precise thing was never done upon its surface before that day.

Well, then, Ivan Ulitch and the new deacon were bosom friends, and that friendship had been planted years ago, and sunned and watered and grown and ripened for this one day's work.

The deacon went a day's journey, leaving Ivan some ecclesiastical deeds to decipher and comment on in

his house.   Ivan breakfasted with him, and after his
·departure showed the deacon's house-keeper the work
he had before him, and said, ' Now, Tatnia, mind, I am
not here.   I can't do such work as this if I am interrupted.   Do not come near me till three o'clock, nor
let any one else.'

Tatiana, with whom he was a special favourite,
promised faithfully, and proved a very dragon.

Ivan took out of his lawyer's bag a cork-screw,
various phials containing inks and chemicals, paper,
numberless pens, and other things not worth enumerat-
ing, and out of his pockets magnifiers set in spectacles,
and things like surgeons' instruments.

He went to a little book-shelf, took out a book, and
found a key; with this key he opened an old oak chest,
clamped with iron, and found a book with vellum
leaves and a parchment cover brownish with age.   It
was the register.   This book was made near a century
ago by a priest who was an enthusiast.   Common as
skins are in Russia, this use of vellum was very rare.

He read several pages.   He put on magnifiers, and
examined the fatal entry; then, without removing his
magnifiers, he proceeded with his surgical instruments
to efface the name of Kusmin Gavrilovitch Petroff.   In
this work he proceeded with singular gentleness and
slowness.   He was full two hours effacing that one
name.   Then he heated an iron the size of a walnut,
and, after trying it on other parts of the book, ironed
down his work so that it was no longer visible to the
·naked eye, but only to a strong magnifier.

Then, with various inks and various pens, he set to
work to imitate on paper the hand-writing of the late

deacon and the words Kusmin Gavrilovitch Petroff, for which he had previously searched when he read the other pages, and found an example readily, for it was a common name.

When he had mastered the imitation, he took a hand-magnifier and wrote Kusmin Gavrilovitch Petroff over the place of the old signature. Then he put the book in the sun and let his work dry. It dried a trifle paler than the rest of the book, but with a crow's quill he added the requisite colour here and there.

The work was hardly finished when a heavy knock at the door made him start and tremble.

CHAPTER V.

'What is it?' said he.

'Five o'clock,' replied the voice of Tatiana.

And he thought it was about one.

He begged for half an hour more, and began to tie up the old papers with fingers that trembled now for the first time.

He put away the register, locked the chest, put the key in its hiding-place, unbolted the door, and asked Tatiana for a glass of brandy.

She brought it him directly, and said he needed it.

'No matter,' said he; 'the work is done.' He drank Tatiana's health, and went away gaily.

Tatiana went into the room, and found the pile of old papers all neatly done up and tied. 'Musty old things!' said she. ''Tis a shame a comely young man like that must bury his nose in such old-world muck.

Smells like the grave; no wonder he got pale over them, the nasty trash.'

Soon after this Ivan appeared at the cottage with affidavits to be signed by Daria, Kyril, and others, and in due course moved for a new trial upon numberless depositions alleging fraud, suppression of evidence, inefficient inquiry, recent discoveries, non-existence of an imaginary husband palmed upon the court, etc.

The notice of motion was served on Anna Petrovna and Vladimir Alexéitch. Anna Petrovna declined to move hand or foot. Vladimir opposed by powerful counsel, but the court could not burke an inquiry supported by such a mass of affidavits.

Vladimir, however, was very successful in another branch of policy. Even as Fabius wore out Annibal, he baffled the plaintiff, 'ad cunctando restituit rem.'

First, Anna Petrovna, whom he had the effrontery to call his leading witness, though he knew 'oxen and twain ropes would not drag her' into court.

Then at the end of three months he was ill himself.

Then, just as the trial was coming on, he could not find the late deacon. He had suddenly disappeared from Russia, and was said to be in Constantinople.

And so he sickened the adversaries' hearts, and they began to fear the new trial would not come on in their lifetime, if at all.

It was actually delayed eighteen months by these acts. But Ivan was not idle. He got the local press to insert timid hints of a most important trial unreasonably delayed. He even got a hint conveyed to the president that the right of postponement was being extended to a defeat of justice, and at last a sturdy judge said, 'No. At the last trial you relied mainly on an evidence that is easy of access. It is a sufficient defence, and you disclose no other. The cause ought to be tried during the lifetime of all the parties interested.'

Then he appointed a day.

The trial came on, with great expectation, in the leading court of Petersburg.

This time there were three judges.

To avoid weariness, I shall confine myself to such features of this trial as were new.

At the first trial Daria was dressed like a lady, and was interesting by her pale beauty and manifest pregnancy.

At this trial she was more beautiful, but dressed like a superior peasant, and her lovely boy like a noble, in rich silk tunic, boots, and cap with feather. So with a woman's subtlety did she convey that she came there for her son's rights, not her own.

The court was full of ladies, and they all found means to telegraph their sympathy, and keep up her fainting heart as she sat there, with her boy's hand in hers.

As to the evidence, the depositions of the old witnesses were taken down by the local court, and merely read at Petersburg. To these were now added certain facts, also proved on the spot, one being the adoption by Anna Petrovna of their client. They proved by many female witnesses her virtue from her youth, and that she was not the woman to live paramour with any man.

They were more particular as to the banns, and proved by oral testimony of several persons that not Kusmin Petroff, but Alexis Staropolsky, was cried in church with Daria Solovieff.

They then tried to prove a negative, that nobody had seen Petroff, but one of the judges stopped them. Said he, 'It does not lie on you to produce Petroff. The other side will do that.'

'We doubt it,' said the advocate.

'Then all the better for you,' said the judge.

From Daria herself they elicited that no man called Petroff had ever written or spoken to her either before or after her marriage, and that ten minutes after the wedding she and Alexis had met Vladimir Alexéitch, the real defendant, just outside the town, and her husband and he had exchanged looks of defiance.

They proved by another witness the arrival of Vladimir in the town about half an hour after the wedding, and that he was seen to go into the church at once and come out with the deacon.

Vladimir, there present, began to perspire at every pore.

When the defendant's turn came, his counsel told the court all this had been put forward at the last trial, and had been met triumphantly by an obvious solution, viz., that the late Alexis Staropolsky had loved a beautiful woman who had never deviated from the paths of virtue before, and was only persuaded under cover of a marriage ceremony. At that point, however, the young noble had protected himself against a mésalliance, and substituted a convenient husband, who was to disappear, and did disappear ; but the good, simple deacon had recorded all he saw or divined—the real marriage.

'A real marriage without banns,' suggested one of the judges.

'So it appears,' said counsel, indifferently. 'I am not here to bind the plaintiff to Petroff, but to detach her from Staropolsky. The register is here. The plaintiff married Petroff or *nobody*. The proof is technical, and is the proof the law demands. This court does not sit to make the law, nor to break the law, but to find the law.'

'That is so,' said the president. 'Let me see the book.'

The book was handed up. The judges examined it, and all looked grave.

Counsel proceeded to prove the handwriting, as before, by secondary evidence.

One of the judges objected. 'This writing is opposed to such a weight of oral testimony that we shall expect to see the writer of it.'

Counsel informed the court that they had hunted Russia for him, but could not find him. 'For years after this business he lived near Viatka, but now we have lost sight of him. Had the plaintiff appealed in a reasonable time, we should have had the benefit of his personal evidence.'

'There is something in that,' said the judge. Another remarked that entries in the same handwriting preceded and followed the entry in question. A third judge found another Petroff exactly like the writing of the fatal Petroff, and so, after a snarl or two, they excused the absence of the old deacon

Vladimir's counsel whispered him, 'You are lucky; the case is won.'

The judges retired to take some refreshment, and agree upon their judgment.

They left the register behind them. Ivan got it from the clerk and examined it carefully. The other side looked on sneeringly.

Ivan moved his finger over the entry, and whispered, 'It feels rough here.'

'Indeed,' said his counsel. 'Yes, I think it does. Don't say anything; get me a magnifier.'

Ivan went out and soon found a magnifier, having brought three with him into court for this little comedy. Counsel applied it.

'The vellum appears to be scraped in places,' said he. 'Now let me see. We will flatter the president.' Just then the judges entered, and this foxy counsel said, respectfully, 'We have found something rather curious in this entry, but my eyes are not so good as your excellency's. Would you object to examine it with a magnifier?'

The judge nodded assent. The book and magnifier were handed up to him. He examined them carefully, and said that he thought some name had been erased and another written over it.

At that there was an excited murmur.

'But,' said he, 'we must take evidence, for this is a serious matter. You must call experts. And *you*, please call experts on your side, for they seldom agree.'

The trial was postponed an hour, and the court seemed invaded with bees.

Ivan got experts, and sat quaking and wondering

how much experts really knew. ' *We* suspect erasure,' said he, to guide them.

In the box those two saw. erasure of some word previous to the writing of Petroff, but they could not say what word it was.   Did not think it was Petroff.

The other two saw erasures, or else scraping, but thought it was rather the light scraping of vellum that is sometimes done to get rid of the grease, etc., and make a better signature; but agreed with the others that the words were written over the scraping.

One of the plaintiff's experts was recalled, and asked his opinion of that evidence.

Said he, 'I was surprised at it, because in preparing parchment for writing nobody scrapes in the form of the coming signature; one scrapes a straight strip.'

Here the judge interposed his good sense. 'Look through the book,' said he, 'and tell me in how many places the vellum has been scraped before writing.' ·

He looked, and could not find one but this entry.

They battled over it to and fro, and at last one of the experts swore that Daria's name and Petroff's were not written with exactly the same ink; more gum in the latter.

After a long battle of experts the judges compared notes and the president delivered judgment:

'This is the case of Substance *v.* Shadow.   Here is a weight of evidence to prove that the plaintiff is a virtuous woman, adopted for her superior qualities by the mother of the deceased, and that mother, described before the trial as a leading witness, does not appear to contradict her on oath.   The plaintiff and Alexis Staropolsky are traced to Samara, seen there as lovers by many; their banns are called, and they are accompanied to church by living witnesses. They go from the church door and meet the defendant, who dares not enter the witness-box and deny this. They cohabit, and a son is born, but the husband dies. This calamity is taken advantage of to defeat the right with shadows. The first shadow is Kusmin Gavrilovitch Petroff; he is never seen to enter the church door or leave it. If he was present at the ceremony, he came in at the window, departed out of the window, and vanished into space. But more probably he is a *nom de plume*. A certain deacon erased some other name, and then wrote over the vacancy this *nom de plume*, and then made himself a shadow. We need not go into conjectures as to what name was originally written in that registry. That might be necessary under other circumstances, but here there is a chain of evidence of living witnesses to prove the marriage of Daria Kirilovna Solovieff and Alexis Pavlovitch Staropolsky. It is encountered by no man and no *thing*, but a mutilated book recording a *nom de plume* upon an erasure. The judgment must be for the plaintiff. The marriage was legal, and her son is legitimate. Their material rights will no doubt be protected in another court upon due application.'

The people rose, the ladies waved their handkerchiefs to Daria and her beautiful boy, and he actually kissed his hand to them with the instinct of his race.

Out of court there was a joyful meeting, and Daria actually took Ivan by the shoulders and kissed him on both cheeks. But she was away again so quick that the enraptured but modest lover never kissed her in return, he was so taken by surprise. However, he remembered the gentle onslaught with rapture. He sent her home with certain instructions. He remained to do her business. The case was reported, and he sent six copies of journals to the house of Anna Petrovna. One of the two copies sent to herself was in a light parcel surrounded by lace, for he felt sure Vladimir had taken measures to intercept information of any kind.

He then moved the Orphan Court to attach the separate estate of Alexis, deceased, give the widow her third, and put the rest in trust for Alexis, junior.

The other party, however, asked a brief delay to argue this, and meantime gave notice of appeal to the Senate on the question of marriage and legitimacy.

Vladimir wrote to Anna Petrovna, bidding her be under no anxiety as to the final result. They should accuse the other side of tampering with the register.

However, when this letter reached her, Anna Petrovna was another woman. The journals directed to her house were intercepted, but the parcel of lace reached her, and inside it was the report, and this line: 'Sent in this form because important communications to you have been constantly intercepted since you put yourself in the power of your son's worst enemy.'

'Can this be so?' said Madame Staropolsky. 'No, it is a calumny. I will not read this paper.' She tossed it from her.

On second thoughts she would read it, out of curiosity, just to see by what arts these people had deceived the judges.

She read the report word for word; read it with carefully-nursed prejudice fighting against native justice and good sense, and a sort of chill came over her. She had resigned her intelligence to Vladimir for seven years. Now she began to resume it.

'Oh, foolish woman,' she said, 'to go on year after year hearing but one side in such a case as this! Virtuous! Yes, she was—and he impetuous and wilful. How often have these two things led to a *mésalliance*!'

She went over all the points of the judgment, and could not gainsay them.

She sat all day and brooded over the past, and digested the matter, and was sore perplexed. Next day, while she was brooding, the old nurse of the family, whom Vladimir had been unable to corrupt, put into her hands a note.

'From whom?' she asked.

'From one who loves you, my heart's soul.

'Ah! What, has she bewitched *thee*?' She opened the note with compressed lips, but hands that trembled a little.

'ANNA PETROVNA,—How can we deceive you? You have eyes and ears, and more wisdom than the judges; pray, pray let us come to your feet for judgment. I will abandon all my rights if you look us in the face and bid me. 'DARIA.'

'The witch!' said Madame Petrovna, trembling a little. 'She thinks I cannot resist her voice. And can I? Ay, nurse, she will abandon her rights, but not her son's.'

'Can you blame her, my heart?'

'No,' said the lady, with a blunt honesty all her own.

Then she sat down and wrote, with her most austere face, 'Come, if you have the courage to meet the mother of Alexis.'

She sent the nurse off with this in a fast troika; and when the nurse was gone she regretted it. Daria was a woman now, and a mother defending her child. What chance would the truth have if she resisted it with that voice of hers and all a mother's art?

Then again she thought, 'No, I have my eyes as well as my ears, and I am a mother too. She cannot deceive me.'

Some hours passed, and the carriage did not return.

Then she said, 'I thought not. It was bravado. She is afraid to come.'

Then she began to be sorry Daria was afraid to come.

Meantime Daria was dressing the boy in a suit she had bought in St. Petersburg expressly for this long meditated, longed for, and dreaded interview. The suit was the very richest purple silk—cap, tunic, and trousers tucked into Wellington boots; in the cap a short peacock's feather. This was all the motherly art she practised. She prepared no tale nor bewitching accents, and she trembled at what she was going to do.

Anna Petrovna, finding she did not come, rang and inquired whether the nurse had come back.

'No.'

'Has the carriage returned?'

'No.'

Another hour of doubt, and wheels were heard.

Anna Petrovna seated herself in state, and steeled herself.

The door opened softly, and two figures came toward her down the vast apartment.

It was the young Alexis and his mother. I put him first because his mother did so. She kept him a little before her to bear the brunt; with a white hand on his shoulder she advanced him, and half followed, like a bending lily, with sweet obsequious Oriental grace.

As they advanced, Anna Petrovna rose rather haughtily at first; but no sooner were they near her than she uttered a cry so loud, so passionate, though devoid of terror, that it pierced and thrilled all hearts without alarming them.

'My boy, my child, come back from the dead— where—how? Am I mad—am I dreaming? No, it is my child, my beautiful child. He is seven years old— the painter has just left. Jesu! this is Thy doing. Thou hast had pity on another bereaved mother.'

Her age left her. She was down on her knees before the boy in a moment, and held him tight, and put back his hair, and gazed into his eyes, and devoured him with kisses. 'Lawyers, witnesses, judges, mortal men, this is beyond your power. Nature speaks. God gives me back my darling from the dead. Bless *you* for giving me back my own—my own, own, own. To my arms, my children!' Then all three were locked in one embrace, and the tears fell like rain. Blessed, balmy dew of loving hearts too long estranged!

CHAPTER VI.

THERE are scenes that cannot be prolonged on paper. It would chill them. I shall only say that, long after the first wild emotion had subsided, Anna Petrovna and her new-found daughter could not part even for a moment, but must sit with clasped hands looking at their child, to whom liberty was conceded in virtue of his sex, and he roamed the apartments inquisitive, followed by four eyes.

Another carriage was sent to the cottage for clothes. Daria and her boy were kept for ever ; and, to close the salient incidents of the day, Anna Petrovna hurried off a letter to Vladimir, peremptorily forbidding him to appeal against the decision, and promising him, on that condition, a liberal allowance during his life-time out of the personal estate of the writer, for she had saved a large sum on the estate.

Two days later came Ivan Ulitch, who had been at the cottage and learned the reconciliation. The object of his visit was to secure his beloved Daria from molestation from Vladimir Alexéitch, who, he felt sure, would return very soon. He brought with him a hang-dog looking fellow, who had been a servant in the great house, and expelled. Ivan sought an interview. Daria's influence secured it to him directly. He came into the room with this fellow crouching behind him.

Anna Petrovna, with her quick eye, recognised both Ivan and the man directly.

'I am pleased,' said she, ' to receive a faithful friend

of my dear daughter, and sorry to see him in bad company.'

'Madame,' said Ivan, 'do not regard him as anything but a minister of justice. A greater villain than he ever was intercepted two letters that even a fiend might have spared. This poor knave found them afterward in Vladimir's pocket, read them, and copied their contents, and placed his copies in the envelopes. Pray God for fortitude, dear lady, to read these letters, and know your enemies, since now you know your friends.'

As he spoke he held out two letters. Anna Petrovna took them slowly. She opened one of them with a piteous cry. It was from Alexis, announcing his marriage, but protesting love and duty, and asking pardon in tender and most respectful terms. 'Our lives,' said he, 'shall be given to reconcile you to my happiness.'

While she read, her face was so awful and so pitiful that by tacit consent they all retired from the room, and left her to see how she had been abused. When they came back they found her on her knees. She had been weeping bitterly to think that her son had died unforgiven because she had been deceived by a reptile.

As she suffered deeply, so she acted earnestly.

She called all her servants, and gave them a stern order.

She dismissed the steward on the spot for complicity with Vladimir, and she offered Ivan the place, with rooms in the house. He embraced the offer at once, to be near Daria.

Daria and she were rocking together, and Daria's sweet voice was comforting her with a long prospect of love and peace, when grinding wheels and barking curs announced the return of Vladimir.

Ivan left the room hastily, saying, 'Leave him to me.'

For the first time in the memory of man, the great door of that house did not open to a visitor. Vladimir had to knock. The hall re-echoed with the heavy hammer.

Then the door opened slowly, and displayed a phalanx of servants planted there grimly, not to receive but to obstruct.

They forbade him, by order of Anna Petrovna, to enter, and were as insolent as they had been obsequious.

He threatened violence. They prepared to resort to it. When he saw that, the Asiatic re-appeared in him. 'May I ask for a reason?' said he, very civilly.

Ivan stepped forward. 'Sir,' said he, 'a dishonest servant took two letters you intercepted. They were written at Petersburg after the marriage. He substituted copies, and the bereaved mother is weeping over the originals.'

'Ah!' said Vladimir, and was silent. He literally fled. His face was never seen again in that part of Russia. Yet he had the hardihood to claim the promise of a pension, and that high-minded woman, who could not break a promise, flung it him yearly through her steward, Ivan Ulitch.

Balmy peace and love descended now on the house, and abode there. Alexis and Ivan grew older, but Anna Petrovna younger. Her daughter's voice and her daughter's love were ever-flowing fountains of gentle joy; still, like Naomi of old, her bliss was in her boy. His father and he seemed blended in her heart, and that heart grew green again.

Ivan is calmly happy in the present, and in the certainty that Daria will never marry any man but him, and in the hope that one day Anna Petrovna will let him marry her. At present he is afraid to ask her for the mother of Alexis. But Alexis is paving the way by calling him 'my father.' It rests with Anna Petrovna; for, if she says the word, Daria will marry Ivan merely to please a good friend, and afterward be surprised to find how happy he can make her.

He has never revealed, and never will, that masterstroke of fraud with which he baffled fraud, and perpetuated right by wrong.

He is right not to boast of it, and I hope I may not be doing ill to record it. The expression so many French writers delight in, 'a pious fraud,' is the most Satanic phrase I know.

I did not invent the manœuvre which is the point of this tale, and I pray Heaven no man may imitate it.

RUS.

[My dear lamented brother, William Barrington Reade, was first
a sailor, then a soldier, then a county squire, and had from
his youth an eye for character and live facts worth noting
by sea or land. . He furnished me from his experiences
several tid-bits that figure in my printed works; for instance,
in 'Hard Cash,' the character and fate of Maxley, and the
manœuvres of the square-rigged vessel attacked by the
schooner: also the mad yachtsman, and his imitation of
piracy, in 'The Jilt,' etc. So now I offer the public his
little study of a real character in rural life. Indeed, such
quiet things may serve to relieve the general character of my
work; for, pen in hand, I am fond of hot passions and pictorial incidents, and, like the historians, care too little for the
'middle of humanity.']

GEORGE MOORE, a shoemaker, with a shock head of
black hair, a new wife, half a hundred of leather, and
two sovereigns, came over from Ewelme to Ipsden, and
applied to my father for a cottage on Scott's Common.
It was a very large cottage; the kitchen between
twenty and thirty feet long; old style—smoked rafters,
diamond panes, etc.

A shed, pigsty, and two paddocks went with the
tenement. Rent of the lot, 11*l.* Moore became the
tenant, made boots and shoes incessantly for years, and
sold them at Henley, Reading, or Wallingford market.

He would carry in a sackful on his back, stand behind them in the market-place, and if he got rid of them, would often buy a pig or a cow, or even a pony, with such excellent judgment that he always made a profit; and when he bought at a fair he often sold his purchase on the road, for the nimble shilling tempted him. One of his declared axioms was, 'Quick come and safe keep.'

In 1849 my brother inherited the Ipsden estates, and a year or two afterward occupied an old house of his near Scott's Common, and so he became Mr. Moore's neighbour. He soon found out to his delight that this shoemaker was a character, his leading traits ostentatious parsimony, humorous avarice, and jolly dissatisfaction; his phraseology a curious mixture of rural dialect and metropolitan acumen.

As many of his sayings sounded like proverbs, my brother once, to gratify him doubly, said : 'Mr. Moore, neighbours should be neighbourly,' and set him to measure his growing family for shoes. He might as well have given the order to Procrustes : Moore made shoes for *shops*; he expected feet to fit his shoes; and, after all, live leather is more yielding than dead.

The bill was settled one half-penny short. From that day, although Moore's conversations with my brother rambled over various topics, they always ended one way—'Beg pardon, sir, but there was a half-penny to come last account.'

Then the humorist would fumble for this half-penny, but never find it. He used it as a little seton.

Moore once related to him his visit to a road-side hotel in the old coaching days.

'I came in mortal hungry, Squire, and there was a table spread. Don't know as ever I saw so much vittles all at one time. Found out afterward it was for the passengers' dinner. Sets me down just before the beautifulest ham—a picture—takes the knife and fork, and sets there with my fistes' (pronounced mediævally 'fisteys') 'on the table, and the knife and fork in 'em. "Landlerd," says I to a chap in a parson's tie, "be you the landlerd?" No; he was the waiter. "Then," says I, "you tell the landlerd I wants to speak to 'un very particular;" so presently the landlerd comes, as round as a bar'l mostly. "Landlerd," says I, with my fistes on the table, and the knife p'inting uppards, "I must know what the reckoning ool be afer I sticks my ferk into 't."'

Somebody with whom he traded wanted one shilling and tenpence more than his due in a considerable transaction. Moore made the parish ring.

However, he appears in this case to have thought he owed mankind in general, and Scott's Common in particular, an explanation, so he gave it to the game-keeper, Will Johnstone—Johnstone retailed it at the 'Black Horse,' and round it came to my humorist *via* the gardener.

'Ye may say one shilling and tenpence is a very little sum. Here's Moore running all over the parish after one ten. But it's a beginning. A text is a little thing; but parson can make half an hour's sermon on't.'

Rustic Oxfordshire has never within the memory of

man accepted that peevish rule of the grammarians,
'Two negatives make an affirmative.' We have a
grammatical creed worth two of that. We hold that
less than two negatives might be taken for an affirmative, or at least for an assent.

A Cambridge man, whom his college, St. John's,
transplanted into my county as an incumbent, declared
to me once that he heard a native of my county address a band of workmen thus: 'Ha'n't never a one of
you chaps seen nothing of no hat ?'

Moore accumulated negatives as if they were half-
pence. A neighbour to whom he had now and then
lent a spade, or a frying-pan, or a faggot, offended him,
and they slanged each other heartily over the palings.
Moore wound up the controversy thus: 'Don't you
never come to my house for nothing no more, for ye
won't get it.'

The population of Scott's Common is sparse, but
the dialogue being both long and loud, seven girls had
collected, from four to thirteen years old. With this
assembly Moore shared his triumph. 'There, you
gals, I have sewed up *his* stocking,' said George
Moore.

Scott's Farm was a small holding surrounded by
woods, flat enough when you got up to it, but on very
high ground. Not a drop of well-water for miles. The
men drank no liquid but beer; the women tea and
tadpoles.

None of the larger tenants would be bothered with
'Scott's.' But small farmers are poor farmers and
unsuccessful. One or two failed on it, and it was
vacant. The homestead was a picture to look at, and

in the farm-yard a natural cart-shed, perhaps without its fellow, an old oak-tree twenty-seven feet in girth, and of enormous age. The top was gone entirely, so was the inside. Nothing stood but a large hollow stem with three or four vertical chasms, one so broad that a cart could pass into the wooden funnel—yet that shell put out the greenest oak-leaves in all the conntry side. An artist could have lived at Scott's Farm and made money. But the acres attached to the delightful residence made it a bad bargain to farmers; for the acres and the low rent tempted the tenants to farm.

Now you must understand that for a long time past Ireland has been telling England a falsehood, and England swallowing it for a self-evident truth, and building rotten legislation on it, viz., that the rent is the principal expense of a farm.

It is not one-fifth the expense of a well-tilled farm; and of an ill-cultivated farm not one-tenth, for it is the last thing paid.

Scott's Farm was one out of a hundred examples I have seen. The rent of seventy-five acres, plus a charming house and homestead, was fifty pounds. Yet one bad farmer after another broke on it, and grumbled at the rent, though it could not have been the rent that hurt him, for he never paid it.

Well, Mr. Moore called on my brother, and offered to rent Scott's Farm.

My brother stared with amazement, then said, drily, 'Did you ever do me an injury?'

'Not as I know on, Squire; nor don't mean to.'

'Then why should I do you one? Scott's! Why, they all break on it.'

'Oh,' said Moore, 'folk as ha'n't got no head-piece, nor no money neither, are bound to break on a farm. 'Tain't to say George Moore is agoing to break.'

My brother replied, 'Oh, I know you are a good judge of live-stock, and I dare say you have picked up a notion of farming; but you see it requires capital.'

'Well, Squire,' said the shoemaker, 'I'm not a thousand-pound man, but I'm a nine-hundred-pound man. I'll show you some on't;' and he actually pulled out of his breeches pocket seven hundred pounds in bank notes, and presented them as his references. In short, he rented Scott's Farm.

But my brother could never bear anybody who *amused* him to come to grief, and so for a time he was in anxiety lest Moore should lose the money he had acquired by his industry, and kept by his economy. However, the new tenant stocked the farm, which his predecessors had not done, and let fall remarks indicating prosperity, as that a farmer had no business to go to his barn-door for rent, and that *he* could make a living anywhere. Besides, the rising ricks spoke for themselves.

I believe he had been tenant nine months when, one day, my brother, seeing him smoking a pipe over his farm-yard gate, dismounted expressly to talk to him.

Mr. Moore's first sentence betrayed that he was no longer a shoemaker.

'Look 'ee here, Squire, a farmering man wants to have four eyes and three hands; two for work; one is always wanted in his pocket—rent, tithe, labour, taxes, rates. Why, the parish tapped me three times last month. My wife got behind in her washing through wasting of her time counting out the money I had .to pay away. As to my men—I be counted sharp, but I must be split in two to be sharp enough for they.'

'I was afraid you would find the rent heavy,' said my brother, innocently.

'The rent?' cried Mr. Moore; 'I don't vally it that!' and he snapped his fingers at it. 'But how about the labour—men and horses and women; and the three crops of weeds on one field, through me coming after tipplers and fools as left the land foul for Moore to clean after they. And then——' He paused, and, jerking his thumb over his shoulder, added: ' THE BLACK SLUG THAT EATS UP THE TENTH OF THE LAND.'

My brother did not understand the simile one bit till he followed the direction of Mr. Moore's thumb, and beheld a beneficed clergyman crossing the common like a lamb, all unconscious of the injurious metaphor shot after him by oppressed agriculture.

Having suppressed a grin with some difficulty, my brother said, gravely, 'I'll tell ye what it is, Moore; if you went to church a little oftener, you would find out that the clergy are worth their money to those who go by their advice in this world, and so learn not to forget the next. Come, now; our parson has no tithes, and only a very small stipend, yet I never see you at church. Surely you might go once on a Sunday.'

Now I must premise that Mr. A——, justly dissatisfied with the morals of that parish, preached sermons which were in fact philippics.

'Why, Squire,' said Moore, 'I have tried 'un. But

I do take after my horses; I can't stand all whip and no carn.'

Undaunted by the comparison, his landlord gravely reminded him that there were prayers as well as a sermon, and prayers full of charity, and fitted to all conditions of life.

'Well, Squire,' said the farmer, half apologetically, 'I'll tell you the truth; I never was a hog at prayers.'

It was a pity he could not add he never was greedy of this world's goods.

One day my brother heard his voice rather loud in the yard, and found him bargaining with a lad in a smock-frock—a stranger.

At sight of the Squire the injured farmer appealed to him. 'Look at 'un,' said he, 'a-standing there.' The lad remained impassive as the gate-post under the scrutiny thus dramatically invited. 'A wants ten shilling a week, and three pound Michaelmas.' Then, turning from my brother to the lad, 'Now, what did you have at your last place—without a lie?'

'Six shillings, and a pound at Michaelmas,' said the young fellow, calmly.

'And you thinks to rise me ten shillings! Now, tell 'ee what it is, young man, you hire yourself to keep the mildew out o' my wheat and the rot out o' my sheep, or else draa no wages out o' me. You make me safe as my horses shan't go broken-winded, nor blind, nor lame, while you be driving on 'em, nor my cows shan't slip their calves, nor my sows shan't lay over their litters and smother 'em. I maunt have no fly in my turmots under you, my barley and wuts must come to the rick nice and dry and bright, and then I'll pay you half-a-sovereign a week.'   With sudden friendliness— 'Where did 'ee come from ?'

'Cholsey village.'

'However did 'ee find your way all up here?

The lad said it was only six miles; he had found his way easy enough.

'Then you'll find it easier back.   Good-morning.'

And off he went.   The lad put his hands in his breeches-pockets and strolled away unmoved in another direction ; and my brother retired swiftly to take down every syllable of this inimitable dialogue.   It afterward appeared that his was the only genuine exit; the other two were examples of what the French dramatists call *fausse sortie.*   For the very next day this Cholsey lad was at work for Mr. Moore.

'Halloo!' said my brother. 'Why, you parted never to meet again—far as the poles asunder.   Ha! ha!'

'Oh, that is how we *begins!*' explained Moore, with a grin.   'Bought him at my own price.   But' (with sudden gloom) 'a *wool* have two pound Michaelmas, the risolute to-a-d.'

Moore had a cur his wife implored him to hang out of her way.   'Well,' said he, 'anything for a quiet life. You find the card; I'll find the labour.'

Ere a cord was found Moore caught sight of the good, easy Squire ; he came out and told him Toby had been poaching on his own account, and had better be tied up except when wanted.   Offered him for three half-crowns, praised him up to the skies.

Squire Easy submitted to the infliction, and Toby was sent to the kennel.

Next week, Moore had made a bad bargain. 'I let 'ee have Toby too cheap; I hear of all sides as he's the best rabbiter you ha' got, a regular hexpeditious good dog.'

He gave his landlord a piece of advice, which, to tell the truth, that gentleman needed sorely; for he was never known to make one good bargain in all his life. Said Mr. Moore: 'Don't you never listen to a chap as won't say aforehand how much he'll give or take to a farthing, or a halfpenny at the *very* outside. When that there humbug says to you, "Oh, we shan't quarrel," says you, "I'll take care of that, for down you puts it to a farthing." When he says, "Oh, I'll not hurt you," says you, "Oh yes, ye will, if I give you a chance; put it down to a farthing, or I'm off."'

He let his parlour and a bedroom to a lodger for fifteen shillings a week, a sum unheard of in those parts.

This transpired in a few months, and my brother congratulated him.

Here is his reply, *ad verbum*:

'Why, Squire, it doesn't all stick to me. There's my missus she is took off her work to attend to he. Then there's a gre-at hearty gal I'm fossed to hire. There goes eighteenpence a week and her vittels. I tried to get a sickly one as wouldn't eat my head off, but there warn't a sickly one as 'ud come. Feared of a little work! Now' (with sudden severity), 'do I get half-a-guinea out of he?' Then with a shout: 'No!' Then with the sudden calmness of unalterable conviction: 'Not by sixpence.'

This seems a tough man, not to be easily moved, a wary man, not to be outwitted; yet misfortune befell him, and rankled for years.

My brother left Oxfordshire and settled in a milder climate. During his long sojourn there, a vague report reached him that bad money had been passed on Moore, and he had made the district ring.

When after seven years my brother returned to his native woods, he looked in at Scott's Farm, and there was Moore, the only familiar face about which did not seem a day older. After other friendly inquiries my brother said:

'But how about the bad money that was passed on you? Tell me all about it.'

'That I wool,' said Moore, delighted to find a good listener to a grievance which to him was ever new, though the circumstance was five years old. 'I was at dung-cart most of that day, and then I washed, and tried to get a minute to milk the cow; but bless your heart, they never will let me milk her afore sunset. It's Moore here, and Moore there, from half a dozen of 'em; and Mr. Moore here, and Mr. Moore there, from the one or two as have learned manners, which very few of 'em have in these parts; and between 'em they allus contrive to keep me from my own cow till dusk. Well, sir, I had got leave to milk her, hurry-scurry as usual, and night coming on when a man I had sold a fat hog to came into the yard to pay. 'Wait a minute,' says I. But no, he was like the rest, couldn't let me milk her in peace; wanted to settle and drive the baacon home. So I took my head out o' the cow, and I went to him without so much as letting my smock down,

and he gave me the money, 6*l.* 17*s.*   I took the gold
in one hand so, and the silver in t'other so, and I went
across the yard to the house, and I asked the missus to
get a light, and then I told the money before her, six
sovereigns and seventeen shillings, and left her to
scratch him a receipt, while I went back to my cow,
and I thought to milk her in peace at last.   But before
I had drained her as should be, out comes my missus,
and screams fit to wake the dead: " George ! George !"
" I be coming," says I ; so I up with the milk-pail and
goes to her.   "Whose cat's dead now ?" says I, "for
mercy's sake."

' " Come in, come in," says she.   " George, whoever
is that man?   He have paid us a bad shilling ; look at
that."   Well, we tried that there shilling on the table
first, and then on the hearth : 'twas bad ; couldn't be
wus.   " Run after him," says she ; "run this moment."
" Lard," says I, "they be half way to Wallingford by
this time.   Here, give me a scrap of paper.   I'll carry
it about in my fob; he goes to all the markets ; he will
change it, you may be sure."

' Well, the very next Friday as ever was I met him
at Wallingford market, pulls out the paper, shows him
the shilling, tells him it warn't good.   He looks at it
and agreed with me.   " Then change it, if you please,"
says I.   " What for ?" says he.   " I don't want no bad
shillings no more nor you do."   " But," says I, " price of
hog was six seventeen, and you only paid six sixteen in
money."   "Yes, I did," says he.   "I gave you six
seventeen."   " No, ye didn't."   " Yes, I did."   " No, ye
didn't; you gave me six sixteen and *this*.   Now, my
man." says I, " act honest and pay me t'other shilling."

No, he wouldn't. There was a crowd by this time, so I said, " Look here, gentlemen, I sold this man a hog, and he gave me this in part pay, which it ain't a *real* shilling, and mine was a genuine hog ; " so they all said it warn't a shilling at all. When the man heard that he was for slipping off, but I stepped after him with half the market at my heels. " Will you pay me my shilling ? " " I don't owe you no shilling," says he. " You do," says I ; " and pay me my shilling you shall." " I won't." " You shall ; I'll pison your life else."

'Next time of asking, as the saying is, was Reading market. Catches him cheapening a calf. Takes out shilling. " Now," says I, " here's your bad shilling as you gave me for my hog—which it is a warning to honest folk with calves to sell," says I. " Be you going to change it ? " " No, I bain't." " You bain't ? " says I. " You shall, then," says I. " Time will show," says he, and bid me good-day, ironical. I let him get a little away, and then I stepped after him. " Hy, stop that gentleman," I hallooed. " He have given me a bad shilling." You might hear me all over the market. Then he threatened defanation or summat ; I didn't keer ; I bawled him out o' Reading market that there afternoon.

'Met him at Henley next ; commenced operations —took out the shilling. He crossed over directly, I after 'un, and held out the shilling. " 'Tain't no use," says I. " You shan't do no business in this here county till you have changed this here shilling. Come, my man, 'tis only a shilling ; what is all this here to-do about a shilling ? " says I ; " act honest and give me

my shilling, and take this here *keepsake* back." "I
won't," says he. "You won't?" says I; "then I'll
hunt you out of every market in England. I'll hunt
ye into the wilderness and the hocean wave."

'He got very sick of me in a year or two's market-
ing, I can tell you; for I never missed a market *now*,
because of the shilling. He had to give up trade
and go home whenever he saw my shilling and me
a coming.'

'And so you tired him out?'

'That I did.'

'And got your shilling?'

'That I did not. He found a way to cheat me,
after all' (with a sudden yell of reprobation). 'He
went and died—and here's the shilling.'

BORN TO GOOD-LUCK.

I.

PATRICK O'RAFFERTY was a small farmer in the County Leinster. He and his fatl er before him had been yearly tenants to Squire Ormsby for fifty years on very easy terms.

Patrick, more uneasy than his sire, now and then pestered this Squire for a lease. Then the Squire used to say, 'Well, if you make a point of it, I will have the land valued, and a lease drawn accordingly.' But this iniquitous proposal always shut O'Rafferty's mouth for a time. He was called in the village Paddy Luck; and certainly he had the luck to get into a good many fights and other scrapes, and to get out of them wonderfully. It was he who set the name rolling; his neighbours did but accept it.

He professed certain powers akin to divination, and they were not generally ridiculed, for he was right one time in five, and that was enough, for credulity always forgets the usual and remembers the eccentric.

This worthy had a cow to sell, and drove her in to the nearest fair. He put twelve pounds on her and was laughed at. She was dry and she was ugly. 'Twelve pounds! Go along wid ye.' 'Never mind *her*,' was

Pat's reply. 'I'm Paddy Luck, and it's meself that will sell the baste for twelve pounds, and divil a ha'penny less.' This was his proclamation all the morning. In the afternoon he condescended to ten pounds, just to oblige the community. At sunset he managed to get eight pounds, and a bystander told him he was a lucky fellow.

'That is no news, thin,' said he. It was dark, and he was tired; his home was twelve Irish miles off; he resolved to sleep in the town. In the meantime he went to a tavern and regaled his purchaser, drank, danced, daffed, showed his money, got drunk, and was robbed by one of the light-fingered gentry who prowl about a fair.

The consequence was that the next time he ordered liquor on a liberal scale—for he was one who treated semicircularly in his cups—he could not find a shilling to pay, and the landlord put him out into the street. He cooled himself at a neighbouring pump, and went in search of gratuitous lodgings. The hard-hearted town did not provide these, so he walked out of it into sweeter air. He was not sick nor sorry. Quite the reverse. He congratulated himself on his good luck. 'Sure, now,' said he, 'if I had sold her for twelve pounds, it's four pounds I'd be losing by that same bargain.'

Some little distance outside the town he found a deserted hovel; there was no door, window, nor floor; but the roof was free from holes in one or two places, and there was a dry corner and a heap of straw in it. Paddy thanked his stars for providing him with so complete and gratuitous a shelter, and immediately burrowed into the straw, and was about to drop asleep when the glimmer of a lantern shot in through the doorway, and voices muttered outside.

Patrick nestled deeper in the straw; he was a tres-passer, and it seemed too late and yet too early for the virtues, charity included, to be afoot.

Two men came in with a sack, a spade, and a lantern; one of them lifted the lantern up and took a cursory glance round the premises. Patrick, whom the spade had set a-shivering, held his breath. Then the man put the lantern down, and his companion went to work and dug, not a grave, as panting Pat expected, but a big round hole.

This done, they emptied the sack; out rolled and tinkled silver salvers of all sizes, coffee-pots, teapots, forks, spoons, brooches, necklaces, rings—a mine of wealth, that glowed and glittered in the light of the lantern.

Patrick began to perspire as well as tremble. The men filled in the hole, stamped the earth firmly down, and then lighted their pipes and held a consultation. The question was how to dispose of these valuables. After some differences of opinion, they agreed that one Barney was the fence they would invite to the spot, and if he would not give one hundred pounds for the spoil, they would take it to Dublin. It transpired that Barney lived at some distance, but not too far to come to-morrow evening and inspect the booty. Then, if he would spring to their price, they would go home with him and receive the coin.

'My luck!' thought Patrick. 'What need had they to light their pipes and chatter like two old women about such a trifle, without searching the straw first, the omadhauns!' The thieves retired, and lucky Pat went quietly to sleep.

He awoke in broad daylight, and strolled back into the town. He walked jauntily, for, if he had no money, he possessed a secret. He was too Irish and too sly to go to the police-office at once; his little game was to try and find out who had been robbed, and what reward they would give.

Meantime, he had to breakfast off a stale roll given him by a baker out of charity. About noon he passed through a principal street, and lo! in a silversmith's shop was a notice, written very large:

'THIRTY GUINEAS REWARD!

'Whereas these premises were broken into last night, and the following valuable property abstracted:'

Then followed an inventory a foot long.

'The above reward will be paid to any person who will give such information as may lead to the conviction of the thieves and the recovery of the stolen goods, or any considerable part thereof.'

Patrick walked in and asked to see the proprietor. A little fussy man in a great state of agitation responded to that query.

'Are you in arnest now, sorr?' asked Pat.

'In earnest! Of course I am.'

'What if a dacent poor boy like me was to find you the silver and thieves and all?'

'I'd give you the thirty guineas, and my blessing into the bargain.'

'Maybe ye wouldn't like to give me my dinner an' all, by raison I'm just famishing with hunger?'

This proposal raised suspicion, and the proprietor asked his name.

'Patrick O'Rafferty. I'm tenant to Squire Ormsby.'

'I know *him*. Well, Patrick, I suppose you can give me some information. I'll risk the dinner, anyway.'

'Ah, well, sorr,' said Patrick, 'they say "fling a sprat to catch a whale." A rumpsteak and a quart of ale is a favourite repast of mine; when I have had 'em I'll arn 'em, by the holy poker!'

'Step into my back parlour, Mr. Rafferty,' said the silversmith.

He then sent for the rump-steak very loud, and for a policeman in a whisper.

The steak came first, and was most welcome. When he had eaten it, the modest O'Rafferty asked for a pipe and pot.

While he smoked and sipped calmly the disguised policeman arrived, and was asked to examine him through a little window.

'Does he look like crime?' whispered the silversmith.

'No,' said the policeman. 'Calf-like innocence and impudence galore.'

The jeweller asked O'Rafferty to step out. 'Now, sir,' said he, 'you have had your dinner, and I don't grudge it you; but if this is a jest, let it end here, for I am in sore trouble, and it would be a heartless thing to play on me.'

'Och, hear to him!' cried Patrick, with a whine as doleful as sudden. 'Did iver an O'Rafferty make a jist of an honest man's trouble, or ate a male off his losses? But what is a hungry man worth? I could not see how to do your work while I was famished; but now my belly is full, and my head fuller, glory be to God!'

'I don't know how it is,' said the jeweller, aside to the detective, 'he tells me nothing, and yet somehow he gives me confidence. But, Mr. O'Rafferty, do consider—time flies, and I'm no nearer my stolen goods. What is the first step we are to take?'

'The first step was to fill my belly; the next step is to find me—och, murther, it is a rarity!'

'Never mind,' said the disguised officer. 'Find you what?'

'A policeman—that isn't a fool.'

II.

This was a stinger, and so sudden, his hearers looked rather sheepish at him. It was the policeman who answered.

'If you will come to the station, I will undertake to find you that.'

Patrick assented, and on the way they made friends; his companion revealed himself, and forgave the stinger, and Patrick, pleased with his good-temper, let him into the plan he had matured while smoking his pipe and appearing to lose time. All Patrick stipulated was that he himself should be the person in command; and as he alone knew where the booty was, and was manifestly as crafty as a badger, this was cheerfully acceded to. So, an hour before dusk, four fellows that looked like countrymen drove a cart full of straw up to the hovel, and made a big heap by adding it to what was there already.

Then two drove the cart back to the edge of the town, and put the horse up, and rejoined their companions in ambush, all but one, and he hid in a dry ditch opposite. They were all armed, and the outside watcher had a novel weapon—a powerful blue light in the shape of a fat squib.

It is a dreary business waiting at night for criminals who may never come at all, or, if they do, may be desperate, and fight like madmen, or wild cats.

Eight o'clock came—nine—ten—eleven—twelve: the watchers were chilled and stiff, and Patrick sleepy.

One of the policemen whispered to him, 'They won't come to-night. Are you sure they have not been and taken up the swag?'

'Not sure; but I think not.' The policeman growled, and muttered something about a mare's-nest.

'Hush!' said another.

'What?' in an agitated whisper.

'Wheels!'

Silence.

They all remained as still as death. The faint wheels, that would have been inaudible by day, rattled nearer and nearer. It was late for a *bona fide* traveller to be on the road. Would the wheels pass the hovel?

They came up fast; then they stopped suddenly. To the watchers everything was audible, and every sound magnified. When the drag stopped it was like a railway train pulling up. Men leaped out, and seemed to shake the ground. When three figures bustled into the hovel it sounded like a rush of men. Then came a thrilling question : Would the thieves examine the premises before they looked for the booty? The chances were they would.

Well, they did not. They were in great anxiety, too, but it took the form of hurry. They dug furiously, displayed the booty to Barney all in a hurry, and demanded their price.

' Now, then, one hundred pounds, or take your last look at 'em.'

' One hundred pounds ! ' whined Barney. ' Can't be done.'

' Very well ; there's no time to bargain.'

' I'll give eighty pounds. But I shall lose money by 'em.'

' Blarney ! They are worth a thousand. Here, Jem, put 'em up ; we can do better in Dublin.'

Barney whined and remonstrated, but ended by consenting to give the price.

The words were hardly out of his mouth, when the hovel gleamed with a lurid fire, so vivid and penetrating that every crevice of it and the very cobwebs came out distinct.

The thieves yelled with dismay, and one ran away from the light, slap into the danger, and was dazzled again with opening bulls' eyes, and captured like a lamb. The other rushed blindfold at the entrance, but his temple encountered a cold pistol, and a policeman immovable as a statue. He recoiled, and was in that moment of hesitation pinned from behind and hand-cuffed—click ! As for Barney, from whom no fight was expected, he was allowed to clamber up the walls like a mouse in a trap, then tumble down, until the four-wheel they had come in was brought up by Paddy O'Rafferty. Then the thieves were bundled in, and sat each of them between two honest men, and the fence was attached by the wrist to a policeman, who walked him to the same destination; but, like friend Virgil's bull, *multa reluctantem*, hanging back in vain, and in vain bribing the silent, impenetrable Bobby.

Pat slept at the station, and next morning the jeweller gave his thirty guineas with a good heart, but omitted the blessing. Patrick whined dismally at this very serious omission, and the worthy little fellow gave it him with glistening eyes, 'For,' said he, 'I'll own now the loss would have ruined me. I find by my books they cost me thirteen hundred pounds.' So then he blessed him solemnly, and Pat went home rejoicing. 'I'll have more luck than ever now,' said he. 'I'll have all sorts of luck now—good, bad, and indifferent.'

When he got home he told the story inaccurately, and like a monomaniac; that is to say, he suppressed all the fortitude and sagacity he had shown. These were qualities he possessed, so he thought nothing of them.

Luck and divination were what he prided himself on. His version ran thus: he had the luck not to sell his cow till nightfall, the still better luck to be robbed of his money, and compelled to sleep in the neighbour-hood. Then, thanks to his superlative luck, the Queen's jeweller had been robbed of silver salvers the size of the harvest-moon, two gallon teapots, pearls like hazel nuts, and diamonds as big as broad beans; and seeing no other way to recover them, and hearing that the wise man of Gannachee was in the town, had given him a good dinner and his pipe, and begged him to use all his powers as a seer; of all which the upshot was that he had put the police on the right track, and recovered the booty, and caged the thieves, and marched home with the reward.

In telling this romance, he was careful to take out the thirty sovereigns, and jingle them, and this musical appeal to the senses so overpowered the understandings of his neighbours that they swallowed the wondrous tale like spring water.

After this few were bold enough to resist his pretensions to luck and divination. He was often consulted, especially about missing property, and as he now and then guessed right, and sometimes had taken the precaution to hide the property himself, which materially increased his chances of finding it, he passed for a seer.

One fine day Squire Ormsby learned to his dismay that his pantry had been broken into and a mass of valuable plate taken. Mr. Ormsby was much distressed, not only on account of the value, but the length of time certain pieces had been in his family. He distrusted the police and publicity in these cases, and his wife prevailed on him to send for Patrick O'Rafferty.

That worthy came, and heard the story. He looked at the lady and gentleman, and his self-deception began to ooze out of him. To humbug his humble neighbours was not difficult nor dangerous, but to deceive and then undeceive and disappoint his landlord was quite another matter.

He put on humility, and said this was a matter beyond him entirely. Then the Squire was angry, and said, bitterly: 'No doubt he would rather oblige his neighbours, or a shopkeeper who was a stranger to him, than the man whose land had fed him and his for fifty years.' He was proceeding in the same strain when poor Pat, with that dismal whine the merry soul was subject to occasionally, implored him not to murder him entirely with hard words; he would do his best.

'No man can do more,' said Mr. Ormsby. 'Now, how will you proceed? Can we render you any assistance?'

Patrick said, humbly, and in a downcast way, he would like to see the place where the thieves got in.

He was taken to the pantry window, and examined it inside and out, and all the servants peeped at him.

'What next?' asked the Squire.

Then Patrick inwardly resolved to get a good dinner out of this business, however humiliating the end of it might be. 'Sorr,' said he, 'ye'll have to give me a room all to myself, and a rump-steak and onions; and after that, your servants must bring me three pipes and three pints of home-brewed ale. Brewers' ale hasn't the same spiritual effect on a seer's mind.'

The order was given, and set the kitchen on fire with curiosity. Some disbelieved his powers, but more believed them, and cited the jeweller's business and other examples.

When the first pipe and pint were to go to him a discussion took place between the magnates of the kitchen who should take it up. At last the butler and the housekeeper insisted on the footman taking it. Accordingly he did so.

Meantime, Patrick sat in state digesting the good food.   He began to feel a physical complacency, and to defy the future ; he only regretted that he had confined his demand to one dinner and three pots.   To him in this frame of mind entered the footman with pipe and pint of ale as clear as Madeira.

Says Patrick, looking at the pipe, 'This is the first of 'em.'

The footman put the things down rather hurriedly and vanished.

'Humph,' said Pat to himself, '*you* don't seem to care for my company.'

He sipped and smoked, and his mind worked.

The footman went to the butler with a scared face, and said, 'I won't go near him again; he said I was one.'

'Nonsense!' said the butler: 'I'll take up the next.'

He did so.   Patrick gazed in his face, took the pipe, and said, *sotto voce* :

'This is the second;' then, very regretfully, 'Only one more to come.'

The butler went away much discomposed, and told the housekeeper.

'I can't believe it,' said she.   'Anyway, I'll know the worst.'

So in due course she took up the third pipe and pint, and wore propitiatory smiles.

'This is the làst of 'em,' said Patrick, solemnly, and looked at the glass.

The housekeeper went down all in a flutter. 'We are found out, we are ruined,' said she. 'There is nothing to be done now but— Yes, there is; we must buy him, or put the comether on him before he sees the master.'

Patrick was half dozing over his last pipe when he heard a rustle and a commotion, and lo! three culprits on their knees to him. With that instinctive sagacity which was his one real gift—so he underrated it—he said, with a twinkling eye:

'Och, thin, you've come to make a clane brist of it, the three Chrischin vartues and haythen graces that ye are. Ye may save yourselves the throuble. Sure I know all about it.' .

'We see you do. Y'are wiser than Solomon,' said the housekeeper. 'But sure ye wouldn't abuse your wisdom to ruin three poor bodies like us?'

'Poor!' cried Patrick. 'Is it poor ye call yourselves? Ye ate and drink like fighting cocks; y'are clothed in silk and plush and broadcloth, and your wages is all pocket-money and pin-money. Yet ye must rob the man that feeds and clothes ye.'

'It is true! it is true!' cried the butler.

'He spakes like a priest,' said the woman.

'Oh, alanna! don't be hard on us; it is all the devil's doings; he timpted us. Oh! oh! oh!'

'Whisht, now, and spake sinse,' said Patrick, roughly. 'Is it melted?'

'It is not?'

'Can you lay your hands on it?'

'We can, every stiver of it. We intended to put it back.'

'*That's* a lie,' said Patrick, firmly, but not in the least reproachfully. 'Now look at me, the whole clan of ye, male and faymale. Which would you rather do—help me find the gimcracks, every article of 'em, or be lagged and scragged and stretched on a gibbet and such like iligant divarsions?'

They snatched eagerly at the plank of safety held out to them, and from that minute acted under Mr. O'Rafferty's orders.

'Fetch me another pint,' was his first behest.

'Ay, a dozen, if ye'll do us the honour to drink it.'

'To the divil wid your blarney! Now tell the master I'm at his sarvice.'

'Oh, murder! what will become of us? Would you tell him after all?'

'Ye omadhauns! can't ye listen at the dure and hear what I tell him?'

With this understanding Squire Ormsby was ushered in, all expectation.

'Yer honour,' said Patrick, 'I think the power is laving me. I am only able to see the half of it. Now, if you plaze, would you like to catch the thieves and lose the silver, or to find the silver and not find the thieves?'

'Why, the silver, to be sure.'

'Then you and my lady must go to Mass to-morrow morning, and when you come back we will look for the silver, and maybe, if we find it, your honour will give me that little bit of a lease.'

'One thing at a time, Pat; you haven't found the silver yet.'

At nine o'clock next morning, Mr. and Mrs. Ormsby returned from Mass, and found O'Rafferty waiting for them at their door. He had a long walking stick with a shining knob, and informed them, very solemnly, that the priest had sprinkled it for him with holy water.

Thus armed, he commenced the search. He penetrated into out-houses, and applied his stick to chimneys and faggots and cold ovens, and all possible places. No luck.

Then he proceeded to the stable-yard, and searched every corner: then into the shrubbery; then into the tool-house. No luck. Then on to the lawn. By this time there were about thirty at his heels.

Disgusted at this fruitless search, Patrick apostrophised his stick: 'Bad cess to you, y'are only good to burn. Ye kape turning away from every place; but ye don't turn to anything whatever. Stop a bit! Oh, holy Moses! what is this?'

As he spoke, the stick seemed to rise and point like a gun. Patrick marched in the direction indicated, and after a while seemed to be forced by the stick into a run. He began to shout excitedly, and they all ran after him. He ran full tilt against a dismounted water-barrel, and the end of the stick struck it with such impetus that it knocked the barrel over, then flew out of Patrick's hand to the right, who himself made a spring the other way, and stood glaring with all the rest at the glittering objects that strewed the lawn, neither more nor less than the missing plate.

Shouts and screams of delight. Everybody shaking hands with Patrick, who, being a consummate actor, seemed dazzled and mystified, as one who had succeeded far beyond his expectations.

To make a long story short, they all settled it in their minds that the thieves had been alarmed, and hidden the plate for a time, intending to return and fetch it away.

Mr. Ormsby took the seer into his study, and gave him a piece of paper stating that for a great service rendered to him by Patrick O'Rafferty, he had, in the name of him and his, promised him undisturbed possession of the farm so long as he or his should farm it themselves, and pay the present rent.

Pat's modesty vanished at the Squire's gate; he bragged up and down the village, and henceforth nobody disputed his seership in those parts.

But one day the Sassenach came down with his cold incredulity.

A neighbour's estate, mortgaged up to the eyes, was sold under the hammer, and Sir Henry Steele bought it, and laid some of it down in grass. He was a breeder of stock. He marked out a park wall, and did not include a certain little orchard and a triangular plot. The seer observed, and applied for them. Sir Henry, who did his own business, received the application, noted it down, and asked him for a reference. He gave Squire Ormsby.

'I will make inquiries,' said Sir Henry. 'Good morning.'

He knew Ormsby in London, and when he became his neighbour the Irish gentleman was all hospitality. One day Sir Henry told him of O'Rafferty's application, and asked about him.

'Oh,' said Ormsby, 'that is our seer.'

'Your what?'

'Our wise man, our diviner of secrets; and some wonderful things he has done.'

He then related the loss of his plate, and its supernatural recovery.

The Sassenach listened with a cold, incredulous eye and a sardonic grin.

Then the Irishman got hot, and accumulated examples.

Then the Sassenach, with the obstinacy of his race, said he would put these pretensions to the test. He had picked out of the various narratives that this seer was very fond of a good dinner, and pretended it tended to enlighten his mind; so he laid his trap accordingly.

At his request Patrick was informed that next Tuesday, at one o'clock, if he chose to submit to a fair test of his divining powers, the parcel of land he had asked for should be let him on easy terms.

Patrick assented jauntily. But in his secret soul he felt uneasy at having to encounter this Sassenach gentleman. Sir Henry was the fortunate possessor of what Pat was pleased to call 'a nasty, glittering eye,' and over that eye Pat doubted his ability to draw the wool as he had done over Celtic orbs.

However, he came up to the scratch like a man. After all, he had nothing to lose this time, and he vowed to submit to no test that was not preceded by a good dinner. He was ushered into Sir Henry Steele's study, and there he found that gentleman and Mr.

Ormsby.   One comfort, there was a cloth laid, and
certain silver dishes on the hobs and in the fender.

‘Well, Mr. O’Rafferty,’ said his host, ‘I believe you
like a good dinner?’

‘Thrue for you, sorr,’ said Pat.

‘Well, then, we can combine business with pleasure;
you shall have a good dinner.’

‘Long life to your honour!’

‘I cooked it for you myself.’

‘God bless your honour for your condescinsion.’

‘You are to eat the dinner first, and then just tell
me what the meat is, and the parcel of land is yours
on easy terms.’

Patrick’s confidence rose.   ‘Sure, thin, it is a fair
bargain,’ said he.

The dishes were uncovered.   There were vegetables
cooked most deliciously; the meat was a *chef-d’œuvre*;
a sort of rich ragout done to a turn, and so fragrant
that the very odour made the mouth water.

Patrick seated himself, helped himself, and took a
mouthful; that mouthful had a double effect.   He
realised in one and the same moment that this was a
more heavenly compound than he had ever expected to
taste upon earth, and that he could not and never
should divine what bird or beast he was eating.   He
looked for the bones; there were none.   He yielded
himself to desperate enjoyment.   When he had nearly
cleaned the plate he said that even the best-cooked
meat was not the worse for a quart of good ale to wash
it down.

Sir Henry Steele rang a bell and ordered a quart of
ale.

Patrick enjoyed this, too, and did not hurry; he felt it was his last dinner in that house, as well as his first.

The gentlemen watched him and gave him time. But at last Ormsby said: 'Well, Patrick?'

Now, Patrick, while he sipped, had been asking himself what line he had better take; and he had come to a conclusion creditable to that sagacity and knowledge of human nature he really possessed, and underrated accordingly. He would compliment the gentlemen on their superior wisdom, and own he could not throw dust in such eyes as theirs; then he would beg them not to make his humble neighbours as wise as they were, but let him still pass for a wise man in the parish, while *they* laughed in their superior sleeves. To carry out this he impregnated his brazen features with a world of comic humility.

'And,' said he, in cajoling accents, 'ah, your honours, the old fox made many a turn, but the dogs were too many for him at last.'

What more of self-depreciation and cajolery he would have added is not known, for Sir Henry Steele broke in loudly, 'Good heavens! Well, he *is* an extraordinary man. It *was* an old dog-fox I cooked for him.'

'Didn't I tell you?' cried Ormsby, delighted at the success of his countryman.

'Well, sir,' said Sir Henry, whose emotions seldom lasted long, 'a bargain's a bargain. I let you the orchard and field for—let me see—you must bring me a stoat, a weasel, and a polecat every year. I mean to get up the game.'

Mr. O'Rafferty first stared stupidly, then winked cunningly, then blandly absorbed laudation and land; then retired invoking solemn blessings; then, being outside, executed a fandango, and went home on wings; from that hour the village could not hold him. His speech was of accumulating farms at peppercorn rents, till a slice of the county should be his. To hear him, he could see through a deal board, and luck was his monopoly. He began to be envied, and was on the way to be hated, when, confiding in his star, he married Norah Blake, a beautiful girl, but a most notorious vixen.

Then the unlucky ones forgave him a great deal: for sure, wouldn't Norah revenge them? Alas! the traitress fell in love with her husband after marriage, and let him mould her into a sort of angelic duck.

This was the climax. So Paddy Luck is now numbered among the lasting institutions of ould Ireland (if any).

May he live till the skirts of his coat knock his brains out, and him dancing an Irish fling to 'the wind that shakes the barley!'

'THERE'S MANY A SLIP 'TWIXT THE CUP AND THE LIP.'

CHAPTER I.

MR. SAMUEL SUTTON, wool-stapler, had a large business in Frome, inherited from his father, and enlarged by himself; also a nest-egg of 150,000*l.* invested at four per cent. in solid securities. He lived clear out of the town in a large house built by himself, and called Merino Lodge, with lawn, gardens, conservatories, stables, all of them models. He loved business, and spent his day in the office; he loved his wife, and enjoyed his evenings at home. But this life of calm content was broken up in one month; his wife sickened and died, leaving him utterly desolate and wretched. No child to reflect her beloved features, and no live thing to cherish but her favourite dog, an orphan girl she had taken into the house eight years before, and the immortal memory of a watchful and unselfish affection.

Under this stunning blow messages of consolation poured in upon him, many of them delicately and admirably worded, all written with a certain sympathy, but with dry eyes. His very servants spoke with bated breath and sorrowful looks before him, but he heard the squawks of the women and the guffaws of the men out in the yard. Only one creature beside himself suffered. It was his wife's *protégée*, Rebecca Barnes. For many a day this girl, like himself, never smiled, and often burst into tears all in a moment over her work. This was not lost on the mourner; hitherto he had hardly noticed this humble figure; but now he looked at her with interest, and told her, once for all, he would be a friend to her, as his beloved wife had been.

The young woman, thus distinguished, was attractive: she was tall and straight, but not bony, nor nipped in at the waist. She had the face of an English rural beauty: light brown hair, a very white skin, dark grey eyes, and a complexion not divided into red and white, but with a light brick-dusty colour, very sweet and healthy, diffused all over two oval cheeks; a large but shapely mouth and beautiful teeth made her winning; a little cocked-up nose spoiled her for a beauty; and she might be summed up as comely in person.

Educated by a lady with great good-sense, she could read aloud fluently and with propriety, could write like a clerk, cook well, make pickles and preserves, sweep, dust, cut and sew dresses, iron and get up lace and linen; but could not play the piano nor dance a polka.

Mrs. Sutton always intended her to be housekeeper; and the widower now told her to try and qualify herself in time; she was too young at present.

Months rolled on, but Samuel Sutton's loneliness did not abate. He had only one relation who interested him; Joe Newton, son of a deceased sister, a bold Eton boy he had often tipped. Joe was now at Oxford, and Mr. Sutton invited him for the long vacation, and prepared to like him.

While he is on the road, let us attempt his character —at that period: a goodish scholar, excellent athlete ; rowed six in the college boat, and was promised a place in the University Eleven for fair defence, hard hitting, and exceptional throwing.

He used to back himself against both the universities to fling the hammer and construe Demosthenes ; the College tutor heard and remonstrated. 'It was not the thing at Oxford to brag ; why, Stilwell made a hundred and fifteen against Surrey the other day, but he only said he had been very *lucky*. That is the form at present,' said the excellent tutor, stroke of the university boat in his day. Joe explained largely. Of course he knew there were two men who could beat him at throwing the hammer, one Oxford, one Cambridge, and a lot who could eclipse him at construing Greek orators. 'But you see, sir,' said he, slily, 'the fellows that can construe Demosthenes can't fling the hammer ; and the happy pair that can take the shine out of me at the hammer can't construe Demosthenes. I can do both after a fashion.'

'Oh,' said the tutor, 'that alters the case. So it was only an enigma ; sounded like a brag.'

Add to the virtues indicated above pugilism, wrestling, good spirits, six feet, broad shoulders, abundance of physical, and a want of moral, courage, and behold Joe Newton, aged twenty-one.

He came to Merino Lodge, and filled the place with sudden vitality. He rowed everybody on the lake ; armed both sexes with fishing-rods ; mowed and rolled a paddock into a cricket ground, organised matches between county clubs; drew on his uncle for copious luncheons, chaffed, talked, and enlivened all the family and neighbourhood, and gazed at Rebecca Barnes till he troubled her peace, and set her heart in a flutter.

One fine summer evening there was a harvest-home supper, and the rustics drank the farmer's cider without stint. Returning from this banquet, a colossal carter met Rebecca Barnes and proceeded to some very rough courtship. She gave him the slip and ran and screamed a little. It was near the cricket-ground that Joe was rolling for a match to come off. He heard the signals of distress, and vaulted over the gate in front of Rebecca, just as the carter caught her, and she screamed violently.

'Come, drop that, my man,' said Joe, good-humouredly enough.

'Who be you?' inquired the rustic, disdainfully, and challenged him to fight.

'No, don't, sir, pray don't,' cried Rebecca. 'He is bigger than you, and he thrashes them all.'

Joseph hesitated out of good nature. The bully called him a coward, and took off his coat. Joseph said, apologetically:

'He wants a lesson. I won't detain you a minute. Now, then, sir, let us get it over.' And without taking off his coat, put himself in his favourite attitude. The carter made a rush, got it right and left as if from Heaven, and stood staring with two black eyes; came on again more cautiously, but, while endeavouring a tremendous rounder that would probably have finished the business his way, received a dazzler with the left followed by a heavy right-hander on the throat that felled him like a tree.

Joe then gave his arm to Rebecca, who was trembling all over. She took it with both hands, and an inclination to droop her head on his shoulder, which made the walk home slow, amusing, and delightful to Joe.

After that evening, Rebecca, who was already on the verge of danger, began to be divinely happy and unreasonably depressed by turns. She was always peeping at Joe, and coming near him, and avoiding him; and then he took to spooning upon her, and she was coy, but fluttered with wild hopes, and thrilled with innocent joys.

At last energetic Joe spooned on her so openly that Mr. Sutton observed.

He made short work with both culprits.

'Rebecca,' said he, 'be good enough to keep that young fool at a distance. Joe, let that girl alone. She is only a servant, after all, and I will not have her head turned.'

Rebecca blushed and cried and tried to obey.

Joe affected compliance, got impatient, and one day watched for Rebecca, caught her away from home, declared his love for her, and urged her to run away with him.

The instinct of virtue supplied the place of experience, and she rejected him with indignation, and after that kept out of his way in earnest.

However, before he left he owned his fault, begged her pardon, and asked her to wait for him till he got his family living, and was independent of everybody.

This was another matter, and female love soon

forgives mild audacity.   Reckless Joe overcame her reasonable misgivings, and fed her passion by letters for three whole years, and she refused young Farmer Mortlock, an excellent match in every way.

By-and-by Joe's letters cooled and became rare. He even declined his uncle's invitations on pretence of reading with a tutor in Wales.

Then Rebecca paled and pined, and divined that she was abandoned.   Soon cruel suspense gave way to certainty.   Joe was ordained priest, took the family living, and married Melusina Florence Tiverton, a young lady of fashion, high connections, and eight thousand pounds, which, before the marriage, was settled on her and her children.

Mr. Sutton announced this to his friends with satisfaction, and he even told it to Rebecca Barnes, whom .he happened to find at a passage window sewing buttons on his shirts.   He was fond of Joe, and thought his good marriage ought to please everybody, and so he was in a good humour, and told Rebecca all about it, and that he had promised the happy pair a thousand pounds to start with.

Rebecca turned cold as a stone, and kept on sewing, but slower and slower every stitch.

'Well, you might wish them joy,' said Mr. Sutton.

'I wish—them—every—happiness,' said Rebecca, slowly and faintly, and went on sewing mechanically.

Mr. Sutton looked at her inquiringly, but had already said more to her than was his custom at that period of her service, so he went about his business.

She sewed on still, feeling very cold, and soon the

patient tears began to trickle, and then she put her work aside, and laid her brow against the corner of the shutter that the tears might run their course without spoiling her master's collars and cuffs.

Not long after this the housekeeper left, and Mr. Sutton sent for Rebecca 'You are young,' he said, half hesitating, ' but you are steady and faithful.' Then he turned his back on her and looked at his wife's portrait. 'Yes, Jane,' said he, 'we can but try her.' Then, without turning from the picture, ' Rebecca, take the housekeeper's keys and let us see how you can govern my house.'

'I will try, sir,' said she ; then curtsied and left the room, with the tear in her eye at him consulting the picture of her they both loved.

Rebecca Barnes had made many observations upon servants and their ways, and entered on office with some fixed ideas of economy and management.

She did not hurry matters, but by degrees waste was quietly put down, the servants were compelled, contrary to their nature, to return everything to its place ; the weekly bills decreased, and yet the donations to worthy people increased.

She had held the keys, and nearly doubled their number, about eight months, when Mr. Sutton gave her an order. ' Barnes,' said he, ' Joe and his wife are coming to see me next Wednesday at five o'clock. Get everything ready for them at once—give them the best bedroom—and make them comfortable.'

'Yes, sir,' said she, and went about it directly.

She summoned maids, saw fires lit, beds and

blankets put down to them, not sheets only; took linen out of her lavender cupboard, ordered flowers, and secured the comfort of the visitors, though heats and chills pervaded her own body by turns at the thought of receiving Joe Newton and the woman he had preferred to herself. 'She is beautiful, no doubt,' thought Rebecca. 'I wonder whether she knows? Oh, no; surely he would never tell her. He would be ashamed.' The mere doubt, though, made her red and then pale.

The pair arrived with their own maid; a house-maid under orders showed them to their rooms; Rebecca Barnes kept out of their way at first, and steeled herself by degrees to the inevitable encounter.

She took her opportunity next day, and approached Mrs. Newton first with a civil inquiry if she could do anything for her.

'You are the—the—' drawled the lady.

'The housekeeper, madam.'

'The housekeeper? You are very young for that.'

'Not so young as I look, perhaps; and I have been sixteen years in the house.' She then renewed her question.

'Not at present,' was the reply. 'I will send for you if I require anything.'

The words were colourless in themselves, but there was a hard, unfriendly, and superior tone in them rather out of place in a house where she was a guest, and a new one, and kindly civility just being shown her.

Downstairs the lady did not charm. She desired to please, but had not the tact. Her voice was high-pitched, and she could not listen. Her husband, however, was in ecstasy over her, and rather wearied his uncle with descanting on her perfections.

Things went on well enough until she got a little more familiar with Uncle Samuel; and then, looking on him as virtually a bachelor, she must needs advise him from the heights of her matronly experience. She told him his housekeeper was too young for the place.

'She *is* young,' said he, 'but she has experience, and my dear wife taught her.'

Instead of listening to that, and saying, 'Ah, that alters the case,' as most men or women would, this tactless young lady went on to say that she was too young and good-looking to be about a widower. It would set people talking, and so she strongly advised him to change her for some staid, respectable person.

'Mind your own business, my dear,' replied the wool-stapler, with such contemptuous resolution that she held her tongue directly, and contented herself just then with hating Rebecca Barnes for this repulse; but when she got hold of Joe, she scolded him well for the affront; she never saw she had drawn it on herself. It was not in her nature to see a fault in herself under any circumstances whatever.

Joe, physical hero, moral coward, dared not say a word, but took his unjust punishment meekly.

However, after dinner, owning to himself that this infallible creature had made a blunder, he set himself to remove any ill impression. He descanted on her virtues, above all, her generosity and her zeal for her friends' interests, etc.

Uncle Sutton got sick of his marital mendacity, and said, 'Now, Joe, don't you be an uxorious ass.

She is your wife, and she is well enough; but she is no paragon.'   And so he shut *him* up.

They stayed a fortnight, and then went home. As Melusina had intruded her opinion on Rebecca, Mr. Sutton, who came more into contact with the latter now she was housekeeper, had the sly curiosity to ask her, in a half-careless way, what she thought of Joe's wife.

'Well, sir,' said Rebecca, wiser and more on her guard than Melusina, 'he might have done better, I think, and he might have done worse.'

'Voice too shrill for me,' said the master. 'But I suppose he took her for her good looks.'

'Good looks, sir! What, with a beak for a nose and a slit for a mouth?'

Mr. Sutton laughed. 'How you women do admire one another. Stop; now I think of it, this is ungrateful of you, for she told me you were too good-looking.'

'Too good-looking!' said Rebecca.   'What did she mean by that? Ah! she wanted you to part with me.'

'Stuff and nonsense,' said he; but he coloured a little at the abominable shrewdness of females in reading one another at half a word.

Rebecca was too discreet to press the matter; she pretended to accept the disavowal, but she did not. Joe's wife to come into the house on her first visit, and instantly endeavour to turn out the poor girl that had been there from a child!

'And he could look on and let her,' said she; 'he that thought it little to defend me against that giant. Men are so strange, and hard to understand.'

Next year Joe came by himself, and charmed everybody. Rebecca at last kept out of his way, for she found the old affection reviving, and was frightened.

Two years more, and the pair came on a visit at one day's notice. But all was ready for them in that well-ordered house.

The motive of this hasty visit soon transpired. They had spent more than double their income since they married, owed two thousand pounds, and had an execution in the house.

Uncle Sutton was displeased. 'Debt is dishonest,' said he. 'We can all cut our coat according to our cloth.' But he ended by saying, 'Well, make out a list of all the debts. Try if you can tell the truth now, both of you, and put them all down.'

By this time Rebecca had become his accountant in private matters, and her fidelity and discretion had gradually earned his confidence. He actually consulted her on the situation—not that she could have influenced him against his own judgment. No man was more thoroughly master than Sam Sutton. But he was a solitary man, and it is hard to be always silent.

'Bad business, Rebecca. Now I wonder what you would do in my place?'

'Do, sir? Why, pay Master Joe's debts directly. You will never miss it. But when I *had* paid them, I'd tell her not to come begging here again with a fortune on her back.'

'Come, come,' said Sutton, 'she is dressed plainer than any lady in Frome. I will say that for her.'

'La, sir! where are your eyes? What! with those furs and that old point lace? Three hundred guineas

never bought them.   There are no such furs in Frome.
I've seen their fellows in London.   They are Russian
sables, the finest to be had for money.   And look at
her fingers, crippled with diamonds and rubies.   There's
four or five hundred more, and that is how Master Joe's
money goes.   I pity him; he couldn't have done worse
if he had married—a servant.'

Mr. Sutton looked very grave.   However, he sold
out and drew the cheque.   But, unfortunately, instead
of lecturing the wife, he took the husband to task.   He
said he was sorry to see Mrs. Joseph so extravagant in
dress.

'My dear uncle,' replied he, 'why, she is anything
but that; she is most self-denying.   I am the only one
to blame, believe me.'

'Now, you uxorious humbug,' cried Uncle Samuel,
'can't you see she has got three hundred guineas on
her back in lace and sable furs, and as much more on
her fingers?   Where are your eyes?'

Joe looked sheepish.   'I am no judge of these
things, uncle; but I feel sure you are mistaken.'

'No, I am not mistaken.   Everybody knows the
value of sables and diamonds.'

Joe retailed this conversation very timidly to his
wife, not to make her less extravagant, but more
cautious under Uncle Sutton's eye.   He took care to
draw that distinction for the sake of peace.

His finesse was wasted.   'It's the woman,' said she,
as quick as lightning.

'What woman?'

'The woman Barnes.   She has told him—to make
mischief.'

'No, no; the old fox has got eyes of his own.'

'Not for sables. It is the woman.'

'Well, dear, I don't think so; but if it is, then I wouldn't give her the chance again.'

'Me take off my sables because a woman is envious of them? *What do you think I bought them for?* I'll wear them all the more—ten times more.'

'Hush! hush!' implored the weak husband, for the peacock voice, raised in defiance, was audible through doors at a considerable distance.

All this mortified Mrs. Joe's vanity, and that was her stronger passion. She came no more to Merino Lodge.

But she sent her husband once a year with orders to bring home some money, and get rid of the woman Barnes.

He was to tell Mr. Sutton that Barnes was a mercenary woman, and kept his wife away. But Joe's subservience relaxed when he got to Merino Lodge and his pea-hen could not watch him. He made himself agreeable to everybody.

One fine day he discovered that Rebecca was consulted in matters of domestic account, and that he owed the cheque he always took home in some degree to her good word as well as to his uncle's affection. Upon that he forgot he was to undermine her, and began to spoon a little on her; but this was received with a sort of shudder that brought him to his senses.

So the years rolled on, confirming the virtues and the faults of all these characters, for nothing stands still.

Joe Newton was forty-one, and looked forty-five;

Rebecca Barnes thirty-eight, and looked twenty-five. Mrs. Newton was forty, and looked fifty; and Uncle Sutton, though fifty-seven, looked five-and-forty, thanks to sober living, good-humour, and a fine constitution.

Joe's inheritance seemed distant, and he was always in debt, though often relieved.

But who can foretell? The stout wool-stapler was seized with a mysterious malady, frequent sickness, constant depression. He struggled manfully, went to his office ill, came back no better, but at last had to stay at home.

By-and-by he took to his bed.

Rebecca wrote to Joe Newton. He came and found his uncle eternally sick, and turning yellow.

Joe spoke hopefully, said it was only jaundice, but went away and told a different tale at home.

There he and his wife, demoralised by debt, discussed the approaching death of a great benefactor in hypocritical terms, through which eager expectation pierced.

'You are sure he has not made a fresh will? That woman has his ear.'

'Make your mind easy, dear. He told me all about it himself not six months ago. He leaves us and our children all his money, except five thousand pounds to Rebecca Barnes.'

'Five thousand pounds to a servant?'

'And only two hundred thousand pounds to us!' said Joe, hazarding a little humour.

'Tied up, I'll be bound.'

'Well, dear!' said Joe, 'even if it should be, our children will benefit, and we shall have enough.'

'Five thousand pounds to that woman! And not tied up, of course.'

Joe could have told her from his uncle's own lips why he was to have a life-interest only in that large fortune. 'Your wife is vain, selfish, and extravagant, and you are her slave. She shall not waste my money as she has yours. It is all secured to you and your children.'

But Joe preferred peace to admonition, and kept his uncle's treasons to himself.

Mr. Sutton was tenderly nursed night and day by Rebecca Barnes and a young orphan girl she had brought into the house, as she herself had been brought thirty years ago. He was attended by Dr. Stevenson, an old friend.

But neither physic nor nursing could stop the fatal sickness that prostrated the strong man.

At last Dr. Stevenson and a physician he had summoned from London told Rebecca to prepare for the worst. He must die of inanition, and that shortly.

Rebecca sent a mounted messenger to Joe: 'Come at once, or you will not see him alive.'

Joe sent back word he would come by the first train.

But before he went his wife gave him instructions: 'Now mind, if he knows you, and can speak, do nothing. But if he is insensible, you must begin to think of your interests; you are executor; you told me so.'

'One of them.'

'And the one on the spot. There are quantities of

plate and valuables in the house. You must fix seals, and ask Barnes for her keys.'

'Will not that be premature?'

'No, stupid; it will be just in time.'

'Hum! she has been a faithful servant. I am afraid it would wound her feelings.'

'The feelings of a menial! Besides, there are two ways of doing these things. Of course you will flatter her, and say you only want to relieve her of responsibility. But mind you secure her keys, or I'll never forgive you.'

'Very well,' said Joe. 'I suppose you are right; *you always are.*'

He reached the Lodge, and Rebecca met him with a despairing cry, 'Oh, Mr. Joseph!' and led the way to the sick room.

They found Mr. Sutton yellow and yet cadaverous, gasping and almost rattling for breath.

'He is dying,' said Joe, awestruck. 'He will not live an hour.'

Presently the patient gasped desperately and tried to raise himself.

'Lift him!' cried Rebecca, and seized a basin, while Joe's strong arm raised him.

Instantly there burst from the patient a copious discharge of black blood, or what looked like it.

Joe turned pale, and cried, 'Oh, it is the substance of the liver,' and he felt faint at the sight.

Rebecca stood firm. She gave the basin quickly to the girl, and filled Joe a glassful of neat brandy. He tossed it off, and it revived him.

They laid the patient back gently, and Rebecca felt his pulse.   It was scarcely perceptible.

'He is going,' she said.   Then, looking round in despair, she seized a table-spoon, filled it with brandy, slightly diluted, and opening his mouth, placed the spoon at the root of the tongue, and so got the contents down his throat.

As he retained it, she repeated the dose three times.

The patient lay motionless, no longer gasping, but just faintly breathing, as men do before life's little candle flickers out.

They sat down on each side of him in silence.   He had been a good friend to both.

By-and-by Joe's dinner was announced.   He asked Rebecca to come down and eat a morsel with him.

Rebecca was hospitable, but could not leave the moribund even for a moment.   'No,' said she; 'I saw *her* die, and I must see *him* die.'

Joe assured her he would not die till night, and said he could not eat alone.

Accustomed to oblige, Rebecca consented, though unwillingly.   She summoned an elderly woman that was in the house, and bade her watch him with the young girl, and send down to her the moment there was any change.

Then she went reluctantly, and sat down opposite Joseph Newton, pale and woe-begone.   He had recovered himself, and ate a tolerable dinner.   She tried, out of complaisance, but could only get a morsel or two down.

After a hasty meal, and two glasses of port, the Rev. Joseph Newton opened his commission.   He began

as dirccted.   He dilated upon her long and faithful
service, and then told her he knew she was not forgotten,
or he would have felt bound to take care of her.

While he delivered these sugar-plums he did not
look her in the face, and so he did not observe that her
eye was fixed on him and never moved.

Having thus prepared the way, he proceeded in a
briefer style to say that he was his uncle's executor, and
a great responsibility was now about to fall on him;
unfortunately, he could not stay here all night to discharge those sad duties, so perhaps it would be as well
to intrust him with her keys before he left.

Then Rebecca, who had hitherto been keenly
observant and silent, said, very quietly, ' Give you my
keys, sir ?   What! do you mistrust me ? '

' Of course not; my only object is to relieve you of
so great a responsibility, where there are so many
servants and so many valuables about.'

' Valuables about!   That is not my way, sir. There
is nothing loose in this house more than I can keep my
eye on.'

' An excellent system,' said Joe, warmly. ' I promise to follow it.   But, to do so, I must have an
executor's power.   Come, Rebecca, I must return by
the five o'clock train ; please oblige me with your keys;
the places that have none you and I will seal up
together.'

Rebecca Barnes rose from the table so straight she
seemed six feet high, and the eyes that had watched
him like a cat from the first syllable he had uttered
flashed lightning at him.

' You have spoken a woman's mind ; take a woman's

answer. What! you couldn't wait till the breath was out of that poor dear body before you must lay your greedy hands upon his goods.'

Joe rose in his turn. 'Rebecca, you forget yourself.'

'No, I remember too well. Twenty years ago you did your best to ruin me; and, when you couldn't, you trifled with my affections, held me in hand for years, and flung me away without one grain of pity—you broke my heart, and made me a servant for life. Now you insult the faithful servant, you that were false to the faithful lover. Trust you with my keys, you false-hearted— No, sir.' And she folded her arms superbly. 'Go back to your wife and tell her if she wants to *rob* him she must *kill* him first, and me too; for while he lives I am mistress of this house, and she and you are—NOBODY.'

Then she turned her back on him as only a tall, disdainful woman can, and flew wildly upstairs to her dying master.

CHAPTER II.

AFTER all, once in twenty years is not often to vent one's outraged feelings, and those who smother their fiery wrongs too long owe nature an explosion.

But Rebecca Barnes, though wild with passion, was by nature anything but a virago. So, even as she flew up the stairs, the rain followed the thunder, and it was in a wild distress, not fury, she darted into her master's room, hurried the other women out of it, and flung herself on her knees by his side. 'Oh, master, master!'

she cried;' 'is it come to this?   They wish you dead!
They want your plate; they want your china; they
want your money; they don't want you.   For all the
good you have done only one poor woman will shed a
tear for you.'   Then she began to mumble his hand and
wet it with her honest tears.

'Now I understand my dream,' said a calm, faint
voice that seemed to come from the other world.

Rebecca sprang to her feet with a scream, and eyed
him keenly.

'You are better.'

'I am.   There was something growing inside me.
I always said so.   It has broken.   I feel lighter now.'

Rebecca flung herself on her knees again.

'Oh, master! then don't give in. Try, try, try, and
you'll get well.   If you won't get well to please poor
me, do pray get well to spite those heartless creatures.
They couldn't wait.   They demanded my keys, they
were so hot to take possession.'

'Joe and his wife?'

'Put her first; he is her slave.   He has no heart or
conscience when she gives the order.   But let's, you
and I, baffle them.   Let us get well.'

'I mean to,' said he slowly, 'so where's the sense of
your sobbing and crying like that?'

'Dear heart, what can I do?   The fear of losing
you—the affront—my anger—my hope—my joy—of
course I must cry.   Oh! oh! oh!   La! how you smell
of brandy!'

'Ay, brandy has been my best friend.   I drank about
a pint while you were downstairs.'

'Oh, goodness gracious me! a pint of brandy!'

'Tell ye it saved me.   I'm sleepy.'

He went off to sleep.   Rebecca covered him up warm and fanned him gently.   He slept some hours, and on awaking asked for brandy and yolk of egg.   He took this at intervals.

Dr. Stevenson came, examined and felt him all over, and found him full of vital warmth, looked at what had come from him, and said, 'Better an empty house than a bad tenant.'   In a word, pronounced him out of danger.

During his convalescence, Mr. Sutton talked more to Rebecca than he had ever done, and told her that at one time he never expected to live, 'For,' said he, solemnly, 'I was as near my dear wife as I am to you. I could not see her, unfortunately, but she spoke to me.'

'Oh, sir, tell me ; you'll tell *me*.   I loved her ; I had reason.'

'Yes, I will tell *you*,' said he.   'She said, "Not now, Samuel.   There was only one woman shed a tear for me, and only one will shed a tear for you."'   He reflected a little.   'Now I think of it, that was bidding me to live this time.   Yes, Jenny, my love, I'll live and teach some folk a lesson—they have taught *me* one.'

He ordered Rebecca to write and ask his lawyer to come to him at once with two witnesses.

Rebecca had cooled by this time, and began to be a little alarmed at the turn things were taking ; so she said she had been a good deal put out about the keys, and he must not take to heart every word an angry woman said.

'Mind your own business,' was his reply. 'Write as I bade you.'

The lawyer came with his witnesses. Rebecca retired.

When she re-appeared she seemed so uneasy that he said to her, 'You needn't look as if you had robbed a church. I have not disinherited Joe.'

'I am right down glad of that.'

'But I have cut him down a bit, and I've changed my executor. Now please remember—the next time I die—*you* are my sole executor; and your keys never leave you.'

She cast a beaming look of affection and gratitude on him. He had applied the right salve to her wound. She belonged to a sex that does not always weigh things in our balances. She was not very greedy of money, but to take her keys from her was to dishonour her in her office.

It was soon public that Mr. Sutton had made a new will—contents unknown. Lawyers do not reveal such secrets spontaneously.

'We are disinherited,' cried Joe's wife; 'and by that woman Barnes. I always warned you how it would end; but you never would get rid of her. We have you to thank for it, the children and I.'

Joe resisted for once. 'No,' said he, 'it is all your doing. She would have let you alone if you had let her alone. But you were in such a hurry to insult her you could not wait till it was safe.'

What, ho! Mutiny! Rebellion! And by the head of the house, paragon of submission hitherto! Mrs. Joe went into a fury, and threatened to leave

him and take the children—a menace I would have
welcomed with rapture : but it ended in his apologising
for his gleam of reason.

When Mr. Sutton had kept them on tenterhooks for
a month and more, and was in better health than ever
he had been, he instructed his lawyers to answer the
questions of coarse or interested curiosity, and it soon
became public that he had made an equal division, half
to his nephew's family, with life interest to Joseph himself, and half to Rebecca Barnes and her heirs for ever,
the said Rebecca being his wife's *protégée*, and his
faithful housekeeper and nurse.

Joe liked this much better than being disinherited.
'Come, Melly,' said he, 'blood is thicker than water.
I am content. A hundred thousand pounds is not
starvation.'

Mrs. Joe, however, did not seem to think so; at
least, she complained rather louder than before. 'To
share our inheritance with a menial,' said she, and
repeated this in more places than one. She even
inoculated Dr. Stevenson with this gentle phrase, and
prevailed on him to offer friendly advice to his late
patient, and gave him hints what to say. Mrs. Joe was
his best client, being full of imaginary disorders, so he
adopted her course; called on Mr. Sutton, was heartily
welcomed, promised him thirty years more, and then
took the liberty of an old friend to advise him. Joe
had a young family. The division was not equal, and
would it not be a pity to leave disproportionate wealth
to a menial ?

'A menial ?' inquired Sutton, affecting innocent
ignorance of his meaning.

'Well, it is a harsh term, but it is what people are saying just now, and would say louder over your tombstone; and, after all, whoever you pay wages to is a menial, and if large fortunes are left to them, especially females, why, somehow, it always makes scandal, and throws discredit on an honoured name. I hope you will not be angry with me for speaking freely—we are old friends.'

Mr. Sutton seemed to ponder. 'I am afraid you are right. It is too much money to leave to a *menial*.' Then, suddenly—'Seen Joe and his wife lately?'

'I saw them only yesterday,' said the doctor, off his guard. 'May I venture to tell them you will reconsider the matter?'

'Not from me. But you can tell who you like that, on second thoughts, I ought not to make a *menial* my executor.'

'You are right. And I suppose you will not leave such a very large fortune——'

'To a *menial?* No.'

The doctor went away pleased at his influence. Mr. Sutton rang the bell, and bade a servant send Rebecca to him.

When she came he handed her a draft for one hundred pounds, and told her she must get a wedding-dress ready made, and waste no time, for she was to be married right off by special licence.

'Me!' said she, staring, and then blushing. 'Never.'

'Next Monday at half-past ten,' said he, calmly.

'No, sir,' said she, resolutely. 'I'll never leave my master. I always respected you, and now—I have

nursed you. I—Don't ask me to leave you—for I won't.
Forgive me. I cannot. How could I? The idea!'

'Who asks you, goose? It is me you have got to
marry.'

'You, sir?' She blushed like a girl, she laughed,
she looked at him to see if he were in earnest; then
she said, 'Well, I never!'

'Come, Becky,' said he, 'you are a woman now;
don't waste time like a girl.'

'I *am* a woman,' said she, 'and too much your
friend to do this foolishness. Where's the use? I
shall never leave you, whether or no. And finely the
folk would talk if you were to marry your servant.
See how they always do on such occasion. No, sir; if
you will be ruled by me for.*once*' (she had been guiding
him for years), 'you will let well alone. As a servant
you have got a very good bargain in Becky Barnes; but
I should be a bad bargain as a wife.'

'Don't you—teach me—my business—Becky Barnes,'
said the master, severely. 'I have been making bar-
gains all my life, and never a bad one. "Try 'em before
you buy 'em" is a safe rule, and terribly neglected in
marriages. I have had you under my eye twenty years
in health and sickness. You are a good housekeeper, a
tender nurse, a faithful friend, and you are going to be
a good wife. Come, you'll have to obey me at last, so
don't waste words, and don't waste time.'

By this time Rebecca's face was red and her eye
moist at such unwonted praise from a man who never
exaggerated or flattered.

She looked at him softly, and said, with a pretty air
of mock defiance:

'I'll tell everybody you *made* me.'

'Say what you like, my dear, and do what I bid you.' So then he drew her to him and kissed her; put the draft into her hand, and despatched her to make her purchases.

Her pride was gratified. The nursing had brought their hearts nearer to each other, and she said to herself:

'After all, what does it matter to *me*? And if *he* is unhappy, why, it will be my fault. He shall not be unhappy?'

She made her own wedding dress for fear of unpunctual milliners.

Sunday night she had one cry over the illusions of her youth. It was but a short one. She asked herself if those two men stood before her now which she should take.

'Why, the man, and not the cur.'

They were married privately on Monday at half-past ten.

At eleven came by appointment the lawyer and two witnesses. Mrs. Samuel Sutton was sent upstairs to put on her travelling dress. Meantime, Mr. Sutton and the lawyer did business.

'Mr. Dawson, my second will was open to objection. I left too much to a menial.'

'Well, sir,' said the lawyer, 'it was not for me to advise.'

'But you agree with me.'

'Perfectly.'

'Well, then, cancel will two.'

'Both wills are cancelled by your marriage, sir.'

'Ah! I forgot.   Well, draw me a will on the lines of my first.   Only, no rigmarole this time.   I'm in a hurry.   You can charge me for a volume, but put it all in the ace of spades, that's a good soul.'

The lawyer consented, and handed Mr. Sutton testament number one to peruse, and reminded him that in that testament the whole property was left to the Rev. Joseph Newton and his children—all but five thousand pounds to Rebecca Barnes.

'My menial?'

'Yes.   But five thousand pounds was not excessive.'

'Not at all, if you knew the two parties.   Well, sir, I don't think we can improve on the *form* of that will. Just reverse the provisions, that is all.'

The lawyer stared.

'Leave the five thousand pounds to my nephew to play ducks and drakes with, and all my real and personal estate to my wife, Rebecca Sutton, and her heirs for ever.'

The lawyer stared, bowed, and set to work.   Mr. Sutton left him to prepare for his journey, but in a few minutes came back and hurried him.

'Come, polish that off,' said he.   'We have only half an hour to get to the station.'

'I could engross it, and send it up to you for signature,' suggested the solicitor.

'What, me go by rail intestate?   No, thank you.'

The will was drawn and attested, and as he signed it Sutton said to the lawyer, 'You see I have not left my fortune to a menial;' then bitterly, 'nor yet to mercenaries.'

The wedded pair dashed up to London.   Each

looked lovingly at the other on the road, and Sutton said to himself, 'I have done this marriage in a vulgar way. She was entitled to more sentiment; and—by Jove! *now I look at her*—she is a duck.'

He was right; every woman likes to be courted; and this one deserved it. Well, he first courted her after marriage instead of before; courted her as if she were a complete novelty; presents, nosegays, attentions of every kind; always by her side, and finding her some pleasure or another; and always good-humoured, kind, and courteous in a plain, manly way.

She came back beaming with happiness, and he wore a conquering air that made folks smile.

Sneers flew about at home and abroad, and Mr. Sutton was now and then discomposed.

Rebecca's watchful eye saw it. She never said a word about it, but she ruminated.

One day the study door was ajar, and she heard Mr. Sutton's voice louder than usual. A tradesman was there and had said something blunt; she gathered as much from Mr. Sutton's answer. 'Why, here's a to-do because a plain man of business has married his house-keeper that was brought up by his wife; and her father was just what I am, only not so lucky. One would think a duke had gone and married his kitchen wench. Well, yes, I took a peach out of my own garden instead of a prickly pear out of a swell hot-house; and all the better for me, and all the worse for Joe Newton.'

Rebecca heard this in passing, turned round and put the tips of the fingers of both hands to her lips and blew the speaker a kiss through the door with an ardour, an abandon, and a grace that would have adorned a lady of distinction.

Next morning she went to work in her way. 'My dear,' said she, gaily, 'I wonder whether you would give me a treat?'

'Well, Becky, I am not fond of denying you.'

'No, indeed, you over-indulge me. But the truth is, I have a great desire to see foreign countries, if it is agreeable to you, dear.'

'Agreeable to me! Why, I have been going to do it these thirty years.'

'Oh, I am so glad! Then will you arrange a tour for us—a nice long one?'

Mr. Sutton fell into this without seeing all that lay behind. It was a fair specimen of Rebecca's handiwork. By this means the house was shut up, the satirical servants discharged without a wrangle, and his friends and neighbours taught the value of Samuel Sutton by his absence.

The couple travelled Europe wisely ; never bound themselves to leave a place half enjoyed, nor stay in it exhausted. They were eighteen months away, but spent the last six in a lovely villa near the Bois de Boulogne.

They came home with a thumping boy and a Norman nurse, and both parents looked younger than when they went.

The news spread like wildfire.

'They bought that child abroad,' said Mrs. Joe.

Alas ! for that romantic theory, Rebecca nursed him herself and gloated over him, as mothers will, and fourteen months later produced a lovely girl.

The parents were happy in their children and themselves; both found in their own hearts unsuspected treasures of tenderness.

The wool-stapler was dictatorial in his own house; his wife docile whenever he laid down the law; but, if he directed, she suggested, and he generally went her way, sometimes without knowing it. Under her gentle influence he arranged a large, business-like system of personal charity, and this increased so as to find them both occupation, and withdraw him by degrees from active trade without subjecting him to *ennui*.

He became a sleeping partner in the wool trade and an active partner in a large scheme of education, and judicious loans and relief, much of which emanated by degrees from an enlarged housekeeper feeling her way, and possessed of administrative ability.

When they drove out together they often sat hand in hand as well as side by side, and one plain friend who saw their ways declared they were a young couple, and he would prove it.

'Ay, prove that, you dog,' said Samuel Sutton, laughing.

'Well, I will. "A man is as old as he feels, and a woman's as old as she looks."'

The proverb was admitted and the application thereof.

After a long struggle between poverty and pride, the Rev. Joseph Newton wrote to his uncle a piteous tale of his young family, and begged relief.

He received an answer by return of post:

'My dear Joe,—This sort of thing is in your aunt's department. You had better write to her.'

Then there was fury in the house of Newton. Reproaches—defiance. 'Apply to that woman—never!'

A few more months and County Court summonses, and Joe was reproached as a bad father, who could not sacrifice his pride to his children's welfare.

So then Joe sent the hat to his aunt. He got a word of comfort and one hundred pounds by return of post. He was melted with gratitude, and said so openly.

Mrs. Joe snubbed him, and said it was a mere drop out of the ocean the woman had robbed them of.

Not a year passed without a contribution of this kind, sometimes unasked, sometimes solicited. Aunt Rebecca drew the cheques, Uncle Samuel connived with a shrug; it was money thrown into a bottomless pit, and he knew it.

Only once did Aunt Rebecca send advice to her dilapidated nephew: 'You have enough if you could but be master in your own house.'

Which was wasted most, the advice or the money, is a problem to be solved by him who shall have squared the circle.

Years have rolled on, but they are all alive, these little studies; to call them characters might seem presumptuous.

When last seen, Mr. Sutton was eighty, and looked sixty; Joe sixty-two, and looked seventy; Rebecca sixty, and looked forty—thanks to goodness, a nature affectionate, not passionate, and her light brick-dust colour; Mrs. Joseph Newton sixty-one, and looked eighty.

'Scornful dogs eat dirty puddings.' She still

speaks disdainfully of 'that woman,' and takes that woman's money, and awaits the decease of Uncle Samuel, and he looks the very man to outlive her.

The title of this story is a fine one, and there are many examples of its truth in history besides the above tale, the leading incident of which is true to the letter. That title, though it reads idiomatic, is but a happy translation. The original is Greek, and comes down to us with an example. To the best of my recollection, the ancient legend runs that a Greek philosopher was discoursing to his pupil on the inability of man to fore-see the future—ay, even the event of the next minute. The pupil may have, perhaps, granted the uncertainty of the distant future, but he scouted the notion that men could not make sure of immediate and con-secutive events. By way of illustration, he proceeded to fill a goblet.

'I predict,' said he, sneeringly, 'that after filling this goblet, the next event will be I shall drink the wine.

Accordingly he filled the goblet. At that moment his servant ran in. 'Master, master! a wild boar is in our vineyard!'

The master caught up his javelin directly, and ran out to find the boar and kill him.

He had the luck to find the boar, and attacked him with such spirit that Sir Boar killed him, and the goblet remained filled.

From that incident arose in Greece the saying,

Πολλα μεταξυ πελει κυλικος και χειλεος ακρου.

This has been Englished thus:

> There's many a slip
> 'Twixt tho cup and tho lip.

And to my mind the superiority of the English language is shown here, for an original writer has always a certain advantage over a translator; yet the English couplet expresses in eleven syllables all that the Greek hexameter says in sixteen; and our couplet, close as it is, can be reduced to seven syllables without weakening or obscuring the sense—

> Many a slip
> 'Twixt cup and lip

THE TWO LEARS.

GEOFFREY of Monmouth tells the old British legend of King Leir. Holinshed repeats it, and from him Shakspeare took it, and made the dry bones live. In that great master's hands the tale broadened and deepened. It became more tragical than the original record.

This is the outline of Shakspeare's story:

King Lear, being old, and disposed to enjoy ease and dignity without the cares of state, resolved to divide his kingdom among his three daughters. Their names were Goneril, Duchess of Albany, Regan, Duchess of Cornwall, and Cordelia, unmarried, but courted by the King of France and the Duke of Burgundy, then a powerful monarch, though nominally vassal to the French King.

When it came to the division, the old King was weak enough to tell his daughters he should give the larger share to the one who loved him best, and should prove her love by words.

This was to invite cheap protestations, and accordingly two of the ladies, Goneril and Regan, vied in lip-love. Goneril said she loved him more than words could utter, yet she found words to paint filial love in tolerably glowing terms; for she went so far as to say that she loved him dearer than eyesight, space, or liberty, and no less than honour, beauty, health, and life itself; with more to the same tune.

Regan could not soar above this; so she had the address to say that her sister had spoken her very mind, only she, Regan, went a little farther, and detested all other joys but that of filial love.

The royal parent believed all this, and then turned to his favourite, his youngest, and asked her what she could say to draw from him a larger dowry than her sisters had just earned—with their tongues.

> *Cordelia.* Nothing, my lord.
> *Lear.* Nothing?
> *Cordelia.* Nothing.
> *Lear.* Nothing can come of nothing: speak again.

Cordelia was a little frightened at her father's anger; but she would only say that she loved her father as a daughter should; she obeyed him, loved him, honoured him, and thought it no merit, but a thing of course. She also declined frankly to believe that her sisters, who were wives, had no love for their husbands, only for their father; nor could she promise to reserve all her love for her father, and give none to the man she might wed.

The fact is, she being a woman, her sisters were such transparent humbugs to her that it made her rather blunt in her honesty, and she did not gild the pill.

> *Lear.* So young, and so untender?
> *Cordelia.* So young, my lord, and true.
> *Lear.* Let it be so; thy truth then be thy dower.

He then went into a violent passion, and disowned

her as his daughter, and ordered her from his presence, while he settled with his favoured daughters what retinue he was to have as a retired King, and where he was to live.

Afterward he sent for Cordelia and the princes her suitors; he told them to her face he had disinherited her, and he used terms of invective so ambiguous that Cordelia, who had borne all the rest in silence, now interfered, and appealed to his justice to tell those gentlemen she had lost his favour not by any unchaste or dishonourable act, but for want of a greedy eye and a flattering tongue.

Lear evaded this remonstrance, and upbraided her again in general terms; but Cordelia's appeal was not lost upon her suitors. Burgundy, indeed, only offered to take her with the dowry originally proposed, and on the King refusing this, he declined her hand. But thereupon this pitiable scene was redeemed by a trait of nobility. France, who had come there for a rich dowry as well as a bride, was now fired with nobler sentiments, and welcomed a pearl of womanhood, without land or money:

> Fairest Cordelia, thou art most rich, being poor;
> Most choice, forsaken; and most loved, despised !
> Thy dowerless daughter, King, thrown to my chance,
> Is Queen of us, of ours, and our fair France:
> Not all the dukes of wat'rish Burgundy
> Shall buy this unprized, precious maid of me.

Even this noble burst did not enlighten or soften the impetuous old King, whose vanity had been publicly wounded. He actually took the arm of Burgundy, the paltry duke who had admitted he wooed the lady only for her substance, and he bade the only daughter who really loved him begone,

> Without his love, his grace, his benison.

France was as glad to have her as he to part with her, and so she disappeared for a time from the scene.

Now the terms of Lear's retirement, which I alluded to above, were these: he was to retain the title of a King, and a retinue of a hundred knights, to be kept at the expense of his regal daughters, and he and that retinue were to reside a month at a time with each princess in turn.

He began his new life in the palace of his daughter Goneril.

He and his knights soon became burdensome to that lady, and she made the most of every little offence. She resolved to shift him on to her sister, and gave insidious instructions to her major-domo:

> Put on what weary negligence you please,
> You and your fellows; I'd have it come to question.
> If he dislike it, let him to my sister,
> Whose mind and mine, I know, in that are one—
> Not to be overruled. Idle old man,
> That still would manage those authorities
> That he hath given away.

These perfidious instructions bore fruit immediately. Goneril's head-servant was insolent to Lear; the impetuous King beat him, and was soon afterward confronted by his daughter, who, to his amazement, took him to task in cold and lofty terms for his disorderly conduct and that of his train. With regard to the latter, she told him plainly he must discharge one-half of them, or she should do it for him.

This cool insolence, coming so soon after the violent protestations, put Lear in a fury.

> Darkness and devils !
> Saddle my horses; call my train together.
> Degenerate bastard, I'll not trouble thee !
> Yet have I left a daughter.
>
> *Goneril.* You strike my people, and your disordered rabble
> Make servants of their betters.

These two speeches alone may serve to show which was likely to prevail in this unnatural combat—the hot-headed, warm-hearted King, or his cold-blooded, iron daughter. Lear's rage broke into curses, but ended in tears that were like drops of blood from his wounded heart, and at last he turned away from that ungrateful serpent, and journeyed to the court of Regan.

But a letter from Goneril reached that palace before the ex-King, and he actually found some difficulty in obtaining an audience of his own daughter.

At last she and her husband met him, but outside the house.

At sight of her his swelling breast overflowed, and he told her her sister was ungrateful, and had struck him to the heart. 'Oh, Regan !' he sobbed.

Regan calmly begged him to be patient, and said he had misunderstood her sister : it was for his own good she had restrained the riots of his followers. She reminded him he was old, insinuated he was in his dotage, and needed the control of wiser people; and to conclude, she coolly advised him to return to her sister, and beg her pardon.

P

'What!' cried he; 'when she has abated me of half my train, looked black upon me, and struck her serpent fangs into my heart?' He then, in his rage, called down all manner of curses on his eldest daughter.

Says Regan, 'Why, you will be cursing me next.'

In the midst of this who should arrive but Goneril and her attendants, on a visit to Regan.

Regan received her instantly with a cordiality she had not shown to her father and benefactor.

Lear was amazed at that, after what he had said, and exclaimed, 'Oh, Regan, will you take her by the hand?'

It was Goneril who replied to this, and with the most galling and contemptuous insolence:

> Why not by the hand, sir?　How have I offended?
> All's not offence that indiscretion finds
> And dotage terms so.

At this the poor old King prayed to Heaven for patience.

Regan paid no attention to that, but coldly stuck to her point. She advised him to comply with Goneril's terms, strike off half his knights, and conclude his month. After that he could come to her. At present his visit would not be convenient.

Lear refused, hotly.

'As you please,' said Goneril, coldly.

Regan persisted, and said that, in fact, fifty followers were too many in another person's house. How could so many people, under two commands, hold amity?

Then Goneril put in her word. Why could he not be attended on by *their* servants?

'To be sure,' said Regan. 'Then, if they were disrespectful, we could control them. At all events,' said she, 'when you come to me, bring no more than twenty-five.'

He asked her if that was her last word. She said it was. Then the poor old King said Goneril was better than she was. Yes, he would go back with Goneril, and dismiss half his retinue.

One would have thought these clever, heartless women had bandied the poor old man to and fro enough. But Goneril had no mercy; this was her reply, when he consented to her own proposition :

Goneril.   Hear me, my lord:
What need you five-and-twenty, ten, or five,
To follow in a house where twice so many
Have a command to tend you ?
    Regan.   What need *one*?

So they trumped each other's cards, and coldly drove him wild.

He raged and stormed at them unheeded. He wept with agony unheeded. He left them both, and went forth into the stormy night a houseless King, a banished father.

Crushed vanity is hard to bear. Wounded affection is hard to bear. Under the double agony the poor old King lost his reason, and wandered about the kingdom like a beggar.

Meantime his despised curses began to work, for his wicked daughters prepared their own chastisement by their own crimes; and here the poet has well shown that the hearts cold to divine affection could be hot with illicit love as well as spurred by greed.

But now it was reported in France how the old King had been abused, and Queen Cordelia, indignant, invaded the kingdom with a French army. Her emissaries found the poor King in a miserable condition, living in rags, and sleeping in out-houses and stables. She had him laid, all unconscious, on a fair bed in her own tent, with music softly playing, and her own physician waiting on him. She herself nursed him with deep anxiety for his waking.

All was changed. She who in his hour of pride and prosperity had said she loved him only as every daughter ought to love her father, now overflowed with passionate tenderness. She took his gray head to her filial bosom, and bemoaned him. 'Was this a face,' said she, 'to be opposed to the warring winds? On such a night too! Why, I would have given shelter to my enemy's dog, though he had bitten me. And wast thou fain, poor father, to hovel thee with swine on musty straw?'

While she was thus lamenting over him the sore-tried King awoke; but not his memory. He thought he had been dead and told them they did wrong to take him out of the grave where he rested from his sufferings. The happy change in his condition brought him no joy at first; it did but confuse and puzzle him. He looked at Cordelia, and saw she was a Queen, and tried to kneel to her. But she would not let him, and kneeled to him instead, and begged him to hold his hand over her and give her a parent's blessing. Seeing so great a lady at his feet craving his blessing let some light into his distracted mind, and drew from the once fiery old man sweet piteous words that have made many an eye wet,

> Pray do not mock me:
> I am a very foolish fond old man,
> Fourscore and upward; and, to deal plainly,
> I fear I am not in my perfect mind.
> Methinks I should know you, and know this man;
> Yet I am doubtful—for I am mainly ignorant
> What place this is—and all the skill I have
> Remembers not these garments; nor I know not
> Where I did lodge last night. Do not laugh at me;
> For, as I am a man, I think this lady
> To be my child Cordelia.
>
> *Cordelia.*   And so I am, I am.

Then the poor soul, seeing her weep, bade her not cry, and offered to drink poison if she chose; for he said she had far more reason to hate him than her sisters had.

But she soon convinced him of her love, and from that time they never parted.

At this very time Goneril and Regan died by poison and suicide, and so paid the forfeit of their crimes.

But all this was on the eve of a battle between the French and English forces, and in that battle, deplorable to relate, Cordelia was slain, and Lear mustered strength to kill her assassin, and then the last chord of his sore-tried heart gave way, and he died by the side of his loved daughter, who had professed so little, yet had done so much and died for him.

This is the heart of Shakespeare's story. There is an inferior hand visible in parts of it; it is clogged with useless characters and superfluous atrocities, and the death of Cordelia is revolting, and a sacrifice of the narrative to stage policy. But all that pertains directly to King Lear is exquisite, and so masterly that the tale

has extinguished the legend.   Historically incorrect, it
is true in art, all but the sacrifice of Cordelia, which,
coupled with the other deaths, turns the theatre into a
shambles, and, above all, disturbs the true motive of
the tale.   When the reader finds the sore-tried old man
lying on a soft couch tended by Queen Cordelia, and
when at last he knows her, and they mingle their tears
and their love, the reader sees this is the lightening
before death, and the mad King has recovered his wits
to be just to his one child, and then to fall asleep after
life's fitful fever.   Against such a tale, so told, no
previous legend can fight.   Under such a spell you can
neither conceive nor believe that Lear recovered his
kingdom and caroused again at the head of his knights,
and toasted his one child.   Youth may recover any
wound; but old age and royal vanity crushed and
trampled on, and paternal love struck to the heart by
the serpent's tooth of filial ingratitude, what should
they do but rage and die ?

Yet there is a legend, almost as old as Lear, of a
father whom his children treated as Goneril and Regan
treated Lear ; but he suffered and survived, and his
heart turned bitter instead of breaking.

Of this prose Lear the story is all over Europe, and,
like most old stories, told vilely.   To that, however,
there happens to be one exception, and the readers of
this collection shall have the benefit of it.

In a certain part of Ireland, a long time ago, lived
a wealthy old farmer whose name was Brian Taafe.
His three sons, Guillaum, Shamus, and Garret, worked
on the farm.   The old man had a great affection for

them all; and finding himself grow unfit for work, he resolved to hand his farm over to them and sit quiet by the fireside. But as that was not a thing to be done lightly, he thought he would just put them to their trial. He would take the measure of their intelligence, and then of their affection.

Proceeding in this order, he gave them each a hundred pounds, and quietly watched to see what they did with it.

Well, Guillaum and Shamus put their hundred pounds out to interest, every penny; but when the old man questioned Garret where his hundred pounds was, the young man said, 'I spent it, father.'

'Spent it!' said the old man, aghast. 'Is it the whole hundred pounds?'

'Sure I thought you told us we might lay it out as we plaised.'

'Is that a raison ye'd waste the whole of it in a year, ye prodigal?' cried the old man; and he trembled at the idea of his substance falling into such hands.

Some months after this he applied the second test.

He convened his sons, and addressed them solemnly. 'I'm an old man, my children; my hair is white on my head, and it's time I was giving over trade and making my sowl.' The two elder overflowed with sympathy. He then gave the dairy-farm and the hill to Shamus, and the meadows to Guillaum. Thereupon these two vied with each other in expressions of love and gratitude. But Garret said never a word; and this, coupled with his behaviour about the hundred pounds, so maddened the old man that he gave Garret's portion, namely, the home and the home-farm, to his elder brothers to hold in common. Garret he disinherited on the spot, and in due form. That is to say, he did not overlook him nor pass him by; but even as spiteful testators used to leave the disinherited one a shilling, that he might not be able to say he had been inadvertently omitted and it was all a mistake, old Brian Taafe solemnly presented young Garret Taafe with a hazel staff and a small bag. Poor Garret knew very well what that meant. He shouldered the bag and went forth into the wide world with a sad heart but a silent tongue. His dog, Lurcher, was for following him, but he drove him back with a stone.

On the strength of the new arrangement, Guillaum and Shamus married directly, and brought their wives home, for it was a large house, and room for all.

But the old farmer was not contented to be quite a cipher, and he kept finding fault with this and that. The young men became more and more impatient of his interference, and their wives fanned the flame with female pertinacity—so that the house was divided, and a very home of discord.

This went on getting worse and worse, till at last, one winter afternoon, Shamus defied his father openly before all the rest, and said, 'I'd like to know what would plaise ye? Maybe ye'd like to turn us all out as ye did Garret?'

The old farmer replied, with sudden dignity, 'If I did, I'd take no more than I gave.'

'What good was your giving it?' said Guillaum; 'we get no comfort of it while you are in the house.'

'Do you talk that way to me too?' said the father, deeply grieved. 'If it was poor Garret I had, he wouldn't use me so.'

'Much thanks the poor boy ever got from you,' said one of the women, with venomous tongue; then the other woman, finding she could count on male support, suggested to her father-in-law to take his stick and pack and follow his beloved Garret. 'Sure he'd find him begging about the counthry.'

At the women's tongues the wounded parent turned to bay.

'I don't wonder at anything I hear *ye* say. Ye never yet heard of anything good that a woman would have a hand in—only mischief always. If ye ask who made such a road, or built a bridge, or wrote a great histhory, or did a great action, you'll never hear it's a woman done it; but if there is a jewel with swords and guns, or two boys cracking each other's crowns with shillalahs, or a didly secret let out, or a character ruined, or a man brought to the gallows, or mischief made between a father and his own flesh and blood, then I'll engage you'll hear a woman had some call to it. We needn't have recoorse to histhory to know your doin's, 'tis undher our eyes; for 'twas the likes o' ye two burnt Throy, and made the King o' Leinsther rebel against Brian Boru.'

These shafts of eloquence struck home; the women set up a screaming, and pulled their caps off their heads, which in that part was equivalent to gentlefolks drawing their swords.

'Oh, murther! murther! was it for this I married you, Guillaum Taafe?'

'Och, Shamus, will ye sit an' hear me compared to the likes? Would I rebel against Brian Boru, Shamus, a'ra gal?'

'Don't heed him, avourneen,' said Shamus: 'he is an ould man.'

But she would not be pacified. 'Oh vo! vo! If ever I thought the likes 'ud be said of me, that I'd rebel against Brian Boru!'

As for the other, she prepared to leave the house. 'Guillaum,' said she, 'I'll never stay a day undher your roof with them as would say I'd burn Throy. Does he forget he ever had a mother himself? Ah! 'tis a bad apple, that is what it is, that despises the tree it sprung from.'

All this heated Shamus, so that he told the women sternly to sit down, for the offender should go; and upon that, to show they were of one mind, Guillaum deliberately opened the door. Lurcher ran out, and the wind and the rain rushed in. It was a stormy night.

Then the old man took fright, and humbled himself:

'Ah, Shamus, Guillaum, achree, let ye have it as ye will; I'm sorry for what I said, a'ra gal! Don't turn me out on the high-road in my ould days, Guillaum, and I'll engage I'll niver open my mouth against one o' ye the longest day I live. Ah, Shamus, it isn't long I have to stay wid ye, anyway. Yer own hair will be as white as mine yet, plaise God; and ye'll be thanking him ye showed respect to mine this night.'

But they were all young and of one mind, and they turned him out and barred the door.

He crept away, shivering in the wind and rain, till he got on the lee side of a stone wall, and there he stopped and asked himself whether he could live through the night.

Presently something cold and smooth poked against his hand; it was a large dog that had followed him unobserved till he stopped. By a white mark on his breast he saw it was Lurcher, Garret's dog.

'Ah,' said the poor old wanderer, 'you are not so wise a dog as I thought, to follow me!' When he spoke to the dog, the dog fondled him. Then he burst out sobbing and crying. 'Ah, Lurcher! Garret was not wise either; but he would niver have turned me to the door this bitter night, nor even thee.' And so he moaned and lamented. But Lurcher pulled his coat, and by his movements conveyed to him that he should not stay there all night; so then he crept on and knocked at more than one door, but did not obtain admittance, it was so tempestuous. At last he lay down exhausted on some straw in the corner of an out-house; but Lurcher lay close to him, and it is probable the warmth of the dog saved his life that night.

Next day the wind and rain abated; but this aged man had other ills to fight against besides winter and rough weather. The sense of his sons' ingratitude and his own folly drove him almost mad. Sometimes he would curse, and thirst for vengeance, sometimes he would shed tears that seemed to scald his withered cheeks. He got into another county and begged from door to door. As for Lurcher, he did not beg; he used to disappear, often for an hour at a time, but always returned, and often with a rabbit or even a hare in his mouth. Sometimes the friends exchanged them for a gallon of meal, sometimes they roasted them in the woods. Lurcher was a civilised dog, and did not like them raw.

Wandering hither and thither, Brian Taafe came at last within a few miles of his own house ; but he soon had cause to wish himself farther off it ; for here he met his first downright rebuff, and, cruel to say, he owed it to his hard-hearted sons. One recognised him as the father of that rogue, Guillaum Taafe, who had cheated him in the sale of a horse, and another as the father of that thief Shamus, who had sold him a diseased cow that died the week after. So, for the first time since he was driven out of his home, he passed the night supperless, for houses did not lie close together in that part.

Cold, hungry, houseless, and distracted with grief at what he had been and now was, nature gave way at last, and, unable to outlast the weary, bitter night, he lost his senses just before dawn, and lay motionless on the hard road.

The chances were he must die ; but just at death's door his luck turned.

Lurcher put his feet over him and his chin upon his breast to guard him, as he had often guarded Garret's coat, and that kept a little warmth in his heart ; and at the very dawn of day the door of a farmhouse opened, and the master came out upon his business, and saw something unusual lying in the road a good way off. So he went toward it, and found Brian Taafe in that condition. This farmer was very well-to-do, but he had known trouble, and it had made him charitable. He

soon hallooed to his men, and had the old man taken
in; he called his wife too, and bade her observe that it
was a reverend face, though he was all in tatters. They
laid him between hot blankets, and, when he came to a
bit, gave him warm drink, and at last a good meal.
He recovered his spirits, and thanked them with a
certain dignity.

When he was quite comfortable, and not before,
they asked him his name.

'Ah, don't ask me that!' said he, piteously. 'It's
a bad name I have, and it used to be a good one, too.
Don't ask me, or maybe you'll put me out, as the others
did, for the fault of my two sons. It is hard to be
turned from my own door, let alone from other honest
men's doors, through the vilyins,' said he.

So the farmer was kindly, and said, 'Never mind
your name, fill your belly.'

But by-and-by the man went out into the yard, and
then the wife could not restrain her curiosity. 'Why,
good man,' said she, 'sure you are too decent a man to
be ashamed of your name.'

'I'm too decent not to be ashamed of it,' said Brian.
'But you are right; an honest man should tell his name
though they druv him out of heaven for it. I am Brian
Taafe—that was.'

'Not Brian Taafe, the strong farmer at Corrans?'

'Ay, madam; I'm all that's left of him.'

'Have you a son called Garret?'

'I had, then.'

The woman spoke no more to him, but ran screaming to the door: 'Here, Tom! Tom! come here!'
cried she; 'Tom! Tom!' As Lurcher, a very sympa-

thetic dog, flew to the door and yelled and barked fiercely in support of this invocation, the hullabaloo soon brought the farmer running in.

'Oh Tom, asthore,' cried she, ' it's Mister Taafe, the father of Garret Taafe himself!'

'Oh, Lord!' cried the farmer, in equal agitation, and stared at him. 'My blessing on the da you ever set foot within these doors!' Then he ran to the door and hallooed: 'Hy, Murphy! Ellen! come here, ye divils!'

Lurcher supported the call with great energy. In ran a fine little boy and girl. 'Look at this man with all the eyes in your body!' said he; 'this is Misther Taafe, father of Garret Taafe, that saved us all from ruin and destruction entirely.' He then turned to Mr. Taafe, and told him, a little more calmly, 'that years ago every ha'porth they had was going to be carted for the rent, but Garret Taafe came by, put his hand in his pocket, took out thirty pounds, and cleared them in a moment. It was a way he had; we were not the only ones he saved that way, so long as he had it to give.'

The old man did not hear these last words; his eyes were opened, the iron entered his soul, and he over-flowed with grief and penitence.

'Och, murther! murther!' he cried. 'My poor boy! what had I to do at all to go and turn you adrift, as I done, for no raison in life!' Then, with a piteous apologetic wail, 'I tuck the wrong for the right; that's the way the world is blinded. Och, Garret, Garret, what will I do with the thoughts of it? An' those two vilyins that I gave it all to, and they turned me out in

my ould days, as I done you. No matther!' and he
fell into a sobbing and a trembling that nearly killed
him for the second time.

But the two friends of his son Garret nursed him
through that, and comforted him; so he recovered.
But, as he did live, he outlived those tender feelings
whose mortal wounds had so nearly killed him. When
he recovered this last blow he brooded and brooded,
but never shed another tear.

One day, seeing him pretty well restored, as he
thought, the good farmer came to him with a fat bag
of gold. 'Sir,' said he, 'soon after your son helped us,
luck set in our way. Mary she had a legacy; we had
a wonderful crop of flax, and with that plant 'tis kill or
cure; and then I found lead in the hill, and they pay
me a dale o' money for leave to mine there. I'm almost
ashamed to take it. I tell you all this to show you I
can afford to pay you back that thirty pounds, and if
you please I'll count it out.'

'No!' said Mr. Taafe, 'I'll not take Garret's
money; but if you will do me a favour, lend me the
whole bag for a week, for at the sight of it I see a way
to—— Whisper.'

Then, with bated breath and in strict confidence, he
hinted to the farmer a scheme of vengeance. The
farmer was not even to tell it to his wife; 'for,' said
old Brian, 'the very birds carry these things about; and
sure it is knowing divils I have to do with, especially
the women.'

Next day the farmer lent him a good suit and drove
him to a quiet corner scarce a hundred yards from his
old abode. The old farmer got down and left him.

Lurcher walked at his master's heels. It was noon, and the sun shining bright.

The wife of Shamus Taafe came out to hang up her man's shirt to dry, when, lo! scarce thirty yards from her, she saw an old man seated, counting out gold on a broad stone at his feet. At first she thought it must be one of the good people—or fairies—or else she must be dreaming; but no! cocking her head on one side, she saw for certain the profile of Brian Taafe, and he was counting a mass of gold. She ran in and screamed her news rather than spoke it.

'Nonsense, woman!' said Shamus, roughly: 'it is not in nature.'

'Then go and see for yourself, man!' said she.

Shamus was not the only one to take this advice. They all stole out on tiptoe, and made a sort of semicircle of curiosity. It was no dream; there were piles and piles of gold glowing in the sun, and old Brian with a horse-pistol across his knees, and even Lurcher seemed to have his eyes steadily fixed on the glittering booty.

When they had thoroughly drunk in this most unexpected scene, they began to talk in agitated whispers; but even in talking they never looked at each other—their eyes were glued on the gold.

Said Guillaum: 'Ye did very wrong, Shamus, to turn out the old father as you done; see now what we all lost by it. That's a part of the money he laid by; and we'll never see a penny of it.'

The wives whispered that was a foolish thing to say: 'Leave it to us,' said they, 'and we'll have it all one day.'

This being agreed to, the women stole toward the

old man, one on each side. Lurcher rose and snarled, and old Brian hurried his gold into his ample pockets, and stood on the defensive.

'Oh, father! and is it you come back? Oh, the Lord be praised! Oh, the weary day since you left us, and all our good-luck wid ye!'

Brian received this and similar speeches with fury and reproaches. Then they humbled themselves and wept, cursed their ill-governed tongues, and bewailed the men's folly in listening to them. They flattered him and cajoled him, and ordered their husbands to come forward and ask the old man's pardon, and not let him ever leave them again. The supple sons were all penitence and affection directly. Brian at last consented to stay, but stipulated for a certain chamber with a key to it. 'For,' said he, 'I have got my strong box to take care of as well as myself.'

They pricked up their ears directly at mention of the strong-box, and asked where it was.

'Oh, it is not far, but I can't carry it. Give me two boys to fetch it.'

'Oh, Guillaum and Shamus would carry it or anything to oblige a long-lost father!'

So they went with him to the farmer's cart and brought in the box, which was pretty large, and, above all, very full and heavy.

He was once more king of his own house, and flattered and petted as he had never been since he gave away his estate. To be sure, he fed this by mysterious hints that he had other lands besides those in that part of the country, and that, indeed, the full extent of his possessions would never be known until his will was read; which will was safely locked away in his strong-box—*with other things.*

And so he passed a pleasant time, embittered only by regrets, and very poignant they were, that he could hear nothing of his son Garret. Lurcher also was taken great care of, and became old and lazy.

But shocks that do not kill undermine. Before he reached threescore and ten Brian Taafe's night-work and troubles told upon him, and he drew near his end. He was quite conscious of it, and announced his own departure, but not in a regretful way. He had become quite a philosopher; and indeed there was a sort of chuckle about the old fellow in speaking of his own death, which his daughters-in-law secretly denounced as unchristian, and, what was worse, unchancy.

Whenever he did mention the expected event, he was sure to say, ' And mind, boys, my will is in that chest.'

' Don't spake of it, father,' was the reply.

When he was dying, he called for both his sons, and said, in a feeble voice, ' I was a strong farmer, and come of honest folk. Ye'll give me a good wakin', boys, an' a gran' funeral ? '

They promised this very heartily.

' And after the funeral ye'll all come here together and open the will, the children an' all—all but Garret. I've left him nothing, poor boy, for sure he's not in this world. I'll maybe see him where I'm goin'.'

So there was a grand wake, and the virtues of the deceased and his professional importance were duly howled by an old lady who excelled in this lugubrious art. Then the funeral was hurried on, because they were in a hurry to open the chest.

The funeral was joined in the churchyard by a stranger, who muffled his face, and shed the only tears that fell upon that grave. After the funeral he stayed behind all the rest and mourned, but he joined the family at the feast which followed ; and, behold ! it was Garret, come a day too late. He was welcomed with exuberant affection, not being down in the will; but they did not ask him to sleep there. They wanted to be alone, and read the will. He begged for. some reminiscence of his father, and they gave him Lurcher. So he put Lurcher into his gig, and drove away to that good farmer, sure of his welcome, and praying God he might find him alive. Perhaps his brothers would not have let him go so easily had they known he had made a large fortune in America, and was going to buy quite a slice of the county.

On the way he kept talking to Lurcher, and reminding him of certain sports they had enjoyed together, and feats of poaching they had performed- Poor old Lurcher kept pricking his ears all the time, and cudgelled his memory as to the tones of the voice that was addressing him. Garret reached the farm, and was received first with stares, then with cries of joy, and was dragged into the house, so to speak. After the first ardour of welcome, he told them he had arrived only just in time to bury his father. 'And this old dog,' said he, 'is all that's left me of him. He was mine first, but when I left he took to father. He was always a wise dog.'

'We know him,' said the wife; 'he has been here before.' And she was going to blurt it all out, but her man said, 'Another time,' and gave her a look as black .

as thunder, which wasn't his way at all, but he explained to her afterward. 'They are friends, those three, over the old man's grave. We should think twice before we stir ill blood betune 'em.' So when he stopped her she turned it off cleverly enough, and said the dear old dog must have his supper. Supper they gave him, and a new sheepskin to lie on by the great fire. So there he lay, and seemed to doze.

The best bed in the house was laid for Garret, and when he got up to go to it, didn't that wise old dog get up too with an effort, and move stiffly toward Garret, and lick his hand; then he lay down again all of a piece, as who should say, 'I'm very tired of it all.' 'He knows me now at last,' said Garret, joyfully. 'That is his way of saying good-night, I suppose. He was always a wonderful wise dog.'

In the morning they found Lurcher dead and stiff on the sheepskin! It was a long good-night he had bid so quietly to the friend of his youth.

Garret shed tears over him, and said, 'If I had only known what he meant, I'd have sat up with him. But I never could see far. He was a deal wiser for a dog than I shall ever be for a man.'

Meantime the family party assembled in the bed-room of the deceased. Every trace of feigned regret had left their faces, and all their eyes sparkled with joy and curiosity. They went to open the chest. It was locked. They hunted for the key; first quietly, then fussily. The women found it at last, sewed up in the bed; they cut it out and opened the chest.

The first thing they found was a lot of stones. They

glared at them, and the colour left their faces. What deviltry was this?

Presently they found writing on one stone, 'Look below.' Then there was a reaction, and a loud laugh. 'The old fox was afraid the money and parchments would fly away, so he kept them down.'

They plunged their hands in, and soon cleared out a barrowful of stones, till they came to a kind of paving-stone. They lifted this carefully out, and discovered a good new rope with a running noose, and—the will.

It was headed in large letters, finely engrossed:

THE LAST WILL AND TESTAMENT OF BRIAN TAAFE.

But the body of the instrument was in the scrawl of the testator:

I bequeath all the stones in this box to the hearts that could turn their father and benefactor out on the highway that stormy night.

I bequeath this rope for any father to hang himself with who is fool enough to give his property to his children before he dies.

This is a prosaic story compared with the Lear of Shakspeare, but it is well told by Gerald Griffin, who was a man of genius. Of course I claim little merit but that of setting the jewels. Were I to tell you that is an art, I suppose you would not believe it.

I have put the two stories together, not without a hope that the juxtaposition may set a few intelligent people thinking. It is very interesting, curious, and instructive to observe how differently the same events operate upon men who differ in character. And perhaps 'The Two Lears' may encourage that vein of observation: its field is boundless.

DOUBLES.

WE live in an age of bad English.   There is a perverse preference for weak foreign to strong British phrases, and a run upon abstract terms, roundabout phrases, polysyllables, and half-scientific jargon on simple matters, like velvet trimming on a cotton print.

Addison could be content to write : 'My being his nearest neighbour gave me some knowledge of his habits ; ' but our contemporaries must say, 'The fact of my being his nearest neighbour gave me,' etc.   Now observe : in the first place, it is not 'the fact' but 'the circumstance ; ' and in the next, both 'fact' and 'circumstance' are superfluous and barbarous.   Probably the school-boys who invented this circumlocution had been told by some village schoolmaster that a verb can only be governed by a noun substantive.   Pure illusion! it can be governed by a sentence with no nominative case in it, and the Addisonian form is good, elegant, classical English.   All the Roman authors are full of examples ; and, unless my memory fails me, the very first Latin line cited as good syntax in the old Eton grammar is :

Ingenuas didicisse fideliter artes
Emollit mores, nec sinit esse feros.

Try your nineteenth-century grammar on this—it is

a fair test: 'Factum discendi ingenuas artes emollit mores.' Why is this so glaringly ridiculous in Latin, yet current in English? Simply because bad English is so common, and bad Latin never was.

To die is landing on some distant shore.

This line of Garth's turned into nineteenth-century English would be, 'The fact of dying is identical with landing on some distant shore.'

If I could scourge that imbecile phrase, 'the fact of,' out of England, I should be no slight benefactor to our mother-tongue. I may return one day to the other vices of English I have indicated above. At present I will simply remark that what I call 'Doubles,' the writers of the new English call '*cases of mistaken identity.*' Phœbus! what a mouthful! This is a happy combination of the current vices.

1. Here is a term dragged out of philosophy to do vulgar work.

2. It is wedded to an adjective, which cannot co-exist with it. You may mistake a man for A, or you may identify him with A. But you cannot do both; for if you mistake, you do not identify, and if you identify, you do not mistake.

3. Here are ten syllables set to do the work of two. Now, in every other art and science economy of time and space is the great object; only the English of the day aims at *parvum in multo.* But, thank Heaven, good old 'Double' is not dead yet, though poisoned with exotics and smothered under polysyllables.

There are always many persons on the great globe who seem like other persons in feature when the two

are not confronted ; but, setting aside twins, it is rare
that out of the world's vast population any two cross
each other's path so like one another as to bear comparison. Where comparison is impossible, the chances
are that the word ' Double' is applied without reason.
Sham Doubles are prodigiously common. My note-
books are full of them. Take two examples out of
many. Two women examine a corpse carefully, and
each claims it as her husband. It is interred, and by-
and-by both husbands walk into their wives' houses
alive and—need I say—impenitent. A wife has a man
summoned for deserting her. Another woman identifies
him in the police-court as her truant husband. This
looks ugly, and the man is detained. Two more wives
come in and swear to him. A pleasing excitement per-
vades the district. Our lady novelists had kept to the
trite path of bigamy : but truth, more fertile, was
going to indulge us with a quadrigamy. Alas ! the
quadrigamist brought indisputable evidence that he
had been a public officer in India at the date of all the
four marriages, and had never known one of these four
injured females, with the infallible eyes cant assigns to
that sex.

Sometimes the sham Double passes current by be-
guiling the ears in a matter where the eyes, if left to
themselves, would not have been deceived. The most
remarkable cases on record of this are the false Martin
Guerre and the sham Tichborne. A short comparison
of these two cases may serve to clear the way to my
story.

Fifteenth century : Martin Guerre, a small peasant
proprietor in the south of France, and a newly married

man, left his wife and went soldiering, and never sent
her a line in eight years.   Then came a man, who, like
Martin, had a mole on his cheek-bone and similar
features, only he had a long beard and moustache.   He
said things to the wife and sister of Martin Guerre
which no stranger could have said, and, indeed, reminded the wife of some remark she had made to
him in the privacy of their wedding-night.   He took
his place as her husband, and she had children by him.
But her uncle had always doubted, and when the
children came to divert the inheritance from his own
offspring, he took action and accused the new-comer of
fraud.   It came to trial; there was a prodigious number of respectable witnesses on either side; but the
accused was about to carry it, when stump—stump—
stump—came an ominous wooden leg into the court,
and there stood the real Martin Guerre, crippled in the
wars!   The supposed likeness disappeared all but the
mole, and the truth was revealed.   The two Martins
had been soldiers, and drunk together in Flanders, and
Martin had told his knavish friend a number of little
things.   With these the impostor had come and be-
guiled the ears, and so prejudiced the eyes.   French
law was always severe.   They hanged him in front of
the real man's door.

Orton's case had the same feature.   His witnesses
saw by the ear.   He began by pumping a woman who
wanted to be deceived, and from her and one or two
more he obtained information with which he dealt
adroitly, and so made the long ears of weak people
prejudice their eyes.   As for his supposed likeness to
Tichborne, that went not on clean observation, but on

wild calculation. 'If Martin Guerre, whom you knew beardless, had grown a long beard, don't you think he would be like this?'

'Yes, I do; for there's his mole, and he knew things none but Martin Guerre could.'

'If Roger Tichborne, whom you knew as thin as a lath, had become as fat as a porpoise, don't you think he would be like this man?'

'Yes, I do; for his eyes twitch like Roger's, and he knows some things Roger knew.'

Eleven independent coincidences prove the claimant to be Arthur Orton; and three such coincidences have never failed to hang a man accused of murder. But that does not affect the question as to whether he was like Tichborne. There is, however, no reason whatever to believe that he was a bit like him. In the first place, it is not in the power of any man to divine how a very lean man would look were he to turn very fat in the face; and, in the next place, the fat was granted contrary to experience—for it is only a plump young man who gets fat at thirty; a lean man at twenty-one is never a porpoise till turned forty. To conclude, this is no case of Doubles, but the shallowest imposture recorded in all history; and the fools who took a fat living snob, with a will of iron, for a lean dead aristocrat, with a will of wax, have only to thank their long ears for it: no downright delusive appearance ever met their eyes.

A much nearer approach to a Double occurred almost under my eyes.

A certain laughter-loving dame, the delight of all who knew her, vanished suddenly from her father's house, where she was visiting. Maternal tenderness took the alarm, emissaries searched the town north, south, east, and west, and a young lady was found drowned, and immediately recognised as my sprightly friend. Her father came and recognised her too. In his anguish he asked leave to pray with her alone; and it was only in the act of prayer that his eye fell upon some small thing that caused a doubt; but examining her hair and forehead more narrowly, he found the drowned girl was not his child.

As for her, poor girl, she was young, and had dashed off to Brighton in very good company, and, like the rest of her prodigious sex, had grudged a shilling for a telegram, though she would have given all she had in the world rather than cause her parents so serious an alarm.

Even in this case calculation enters: the drowned girl, when alive, may not have looked so like my laughter-loving friend. Still, we must allow them Doubles, or very near it.

Having thus narrowed the subject, I will now give the reader the most curious case of Doubles my reading, though somewhat rich in such matters, furnishes:

The great Molière married Armande Bejart, a sprightly actress of his company. She was a fascinating coquette, and gave him many a sore heart. But the public profits by a poet's torments; wound him, he bleeds, not ephemeral blood, but immortal ichor— thoughts that breathe, and words that burn, and characters that are types more enduring than brass. The great master has given us, in a famous dialogue, the defects and charms of the woman he had the misfortune to love. This passage, in which a disinterested speaker runs her down and a lover defends her, is charming; and the interlocutors are really the great observer's judgment and his heart. The contest ends, as might be expected, in the victory of the heart.

Covielle, *alias* Molière's judgment: 'But you must own she is the most capricious creature upon earth.'

Cléonté, *alias* Molière's heart: 'Oui, elle est capricieuse, j'en demeure d'accord; mais tout sied bien aux belles; on souffre tout des belles.'—*Le Bourgeois Gentilhomme*, Act III., Scene IX.

But Armande Bejart entered more deeply into Molière's mind, and but for her the immortal Célimène —a character it will take the world two hundred years more to estimate at its full value—would never have seen the light. Célimène is a born coquette, but with a world of good sense and keen wit, and not a bad heart, but an untruthful—a pernicious woman, not a bad one. She has an estimable lover, and she esteems him; but she cannot do without two butterfly admirers, whom she fascinates and deceives. They detect her, and expose her insolently. She treats them with calm contempt. Only to the worthy man she has slighted she hangs her head with gentle and even pathetic penitence. She offers to marry him; but when he makes a condition that would render infidelity impossible, her courage fails, and she declines, yet not vulgarly. This true woman, with all her suppleness, ingenuity, and marvellous powers of fence, whether she has to parry the just remonstrances of her worthy lover, or soothe the vanity of her butterfly dupes, or pass a polished rapier through the body of a female friend who comes to her with hypocrisy and envenomed blandishments, is Armande Bejart. That is one reason why I give a niche in my collection to a strange adventure that befell her after the great heart she so played with had ceased to beat, and the great head that created Célimène had ceased to ache. The widow Molière, after her husband's death, carried on her gallantries with greater freedom, but in an independent spirit, for she remained on the stage, a public favourite; and her lovers, though not restricted as to number, must please her eye. She does not appear to have been accessible to mere ignoble interests. Monsieur Lescot, a person of some importance, President of the Parliament of Grenoble, saw her repeatedly on the stage, and was deeply smitten with her. He had heard it whispered that she was not quite a vestal, and he resolved to gratify his fancy if he could. In those days the stage at night was a promenade open to any gentleman of fashion; but President Lescot did not care to push in among the crowd of beaus and actors, so he consulted a lady who had been useful to many distressed gentlemen in similar cases. This Madame Ledoux had a very large acquaintance with persons of both sexes; and such was her benevolence, that she would take some pains, and even exert some ingenuity, to sweep obstacles out of the path of love, and bring agreeable people together. She undertook to sound Mademoiselle Molière, as the gay widow was called, and, if possible, to obtain Monsieur Lescot an interview.

After some days she told Lescot that the lady would go so far as to pay her a visit at a certain time, and he could take this opportunity of dropping in and paying his addresses.

He came, and found a young lady whose quiet appearance rather surprised him. La Molière on the stage was celebrated for the magnificence of her costumes; but here she was dressed with singular modesty. He had a delightful conversation with her, and one that rather surprised him. She was bitter against the theatre, its annoyances, and mortifications, and confessed she felt not altogether unwilling to make a respectable acquaintance who had nothing to do with it.

In the next interview Lescot was urgent and the lady coy; nevertheless, she held out hopes, provided he would submit to certain positive conditions. Lescot agreed, and expected that a settlement of some kind would be required.

Nothing of the sort. What she demanded, and upon his word of honour, was that he would never come after her to the theatre, nor, indeed, speak to her in public, but only at the house of their mutual friend, Madame Ledoux. The condition was curious, but not sordid. President Lescot accepted it, and very tender relations ensued. Lescot was in paradise, and Madame Ledoux took advantage of that to bleed him very freely; but his inamorata herself showed no such spirit. She threw out no hints of the kind, and the most valuable present she accepted from him was a gold necklace he bought for her on the Quai des Orfévres. She assured him, too, that the intrigues ascribed to her were utterly false, and that what most attracted her in him was his being in every way unlike her theatrical comrades—a man of position, and a friend apart, with whom she could forget the turmoil of her daily existence and the stale compliments of the coxcombs who throng the theatre.

At this time the works of Thomas Corneille, nephew of the great dramatist, had a vogue which has now entirely deserted them. His ' Circe ' was produced, and Mademoiselle Molière played the leading part, and astonished the town by the splendour and extravagance of her dresses. Lescot saw her from his box and admired her, and applauded her furiously, and with raptures of exultation, to think that this brilliant creature belonged to him in secret, and came to him dressed like a nun. But this new *éclat* set tongues talking, and Lescot listened and inquired. He learned on good authority that La Molière had two lovers— one a man of fortune, M. Du Boulay, and another an actor, called Guérin, whose affections she had stolen from an actress of the same company. *Item*—that Du Boulay had offered her marriage, but finding her incapable of fidelity, had retired, and at present she was on discreditable terms with the actor in question.

Lescot, who was now tenderly attached to his fascinating visitor, put her on her defence, addressed the bitterest reproaches to her, and lamented his own misfortune in having listened to her perfidious tongue, and bestowed a constant heart upon a double-faced coquette. She seemed surprised and alarmed; but recovering herself, used all her address to calm him. She shed many tears, and declared she loved no one but him, and had kept him out of the theatre for this very reason—that it was, and always had been, a temple of lies and odious calumnies.   Lescot was half appeased, but, his jealousy being excited, demanded more frequent interviews. She consented readily, made a solemn appointment for next day, and took good care not to come.

This breach of faith revived all Lescot's jealousy, and after waiting for her, and raging and storming for two hours, he could bear his jealous doubts and fears no longer, but broke his word and went straight to the theatre. As any gentleman could sit on the stage during the performance, President Lescot claimed that right, and sat down upon a stool during the performance of 'Circe.' In this situation, being only one of many gentlemen there, and under the public eye, he managed to restrain himself, though greatly agitated, and at first contented himself with watching to see her start at the sight of him. She did not seem to notice him, however; to be sure, she was warm in her part. At last it so happened that she walked past him with that grand reposeful slowness which is, and always was, one of a graceful actress's most majestic charms. He seized that opportunity. 'You are more beautiful than ever,' he said, quite audibly; 'and if I was not in love with you already, I should be now.'

Whether La Molière was warm in her part and did not hear, or was used to these asides, she paid no attention whatever.

That piqued the distinguished member of Parliament, and he sat sullen till the play ended. Then he was on the alert, and followed La Molière so sharply that he entered her dressing-room at her heels. Her maid requested him to leave. He stood firm, and requested the maid to retire, as he had something particular to say to Mademoiselle. Mademoiselle wanted to remove the glorious but heavy trappings of tragedy, so she said, rather sharply, 'Say it, then, sir. I do not think there can be any secrets between you and me.'

'Very well, madame,' said Lescot, bitterly: 'then what I have to say is that your conduct is unjustifiable.'

'What cause of displeasure have I given you?'

'You made an appointment with me; I keep it, you break it. I come here, disheartened and unhappy, to learn the reason, and you receive me like a criminal.'

'The man is mad!' said La Molière, and eyed him with a look of haughty disdain that would have crushed him had he been less sure right was on his side. As it was, though it staggered him, it provoked him more. He confronted her with equal hauteur, and cried out, 'You had better say you do not know me.'

Thus challenged, and being aware she knew a great many gentlemen, she looked at him hard and full, not to make a mistake, then she said, 'I don't even know your name!'

Lescot put his hand to his heart, and was wounded to the quick. 'What!' he cried, 'after all that has passed between us! Why, you must be the basest of God's creatures to use me so!'

'Ah!' cried La Molière. 'Jeannette, call some people to turn this man out of the place.'

'By all means,' cried the other. 'Call all Paris to hear me give this woman her true character before I leave the place.'

'He seized her wrist with his left hand, and with his right he tore the necklace off her neck, and dashed it to the ground'

'Ruffian, you shall smart for this insolence!' said La Molière, grinding her white teeth.

By this time two or three actors and a dozen actresses had come running and half dressed. The disputants being French, both spoke at once, and at the top of their voices; La Molière declaring this ruffian a perfect stranger to her, who had burst into her dressing-room, and outraged her with the grossest calumnies, the very meaning of which was an enigma to her, and Lescot relating all the particulars of his secret intrigue with her. Detail convinces, and La Molière had the mortification to see by the sniggering of the actresses, who knew her real character, that they believed the gentleman and not her.

'Why, look!' cried he, suddenly; 'the ungrateful creature has a necklace on I gave her. I bought it for her on the Quai des Orfévres.'

This was too much. La Molière, red as fury, and her eyes darting flame, sprung at him with her right hand lifted to give him such a box on the ear as she had never yet administered on the stage; but he had the address to seize her wrist with his left hand, and with his right he tore the necklace off her neck and dashed it to the ground.

Then La Molière called the guard; and as personal violence is always severely treated in France, the President of the Parliament of Grenoble cooled his heels in prison that night.

Next morning the President Lescot was released on bail, after a short hearing, in which he declared loudly that he had a perfect right to expose a courtesan, whose lover he was, and who had the effrontery to say publicly she did not know him. 'That right,' said he, 'I am prepared to maintain in any tribunal.'

He held the same language in society; and, on the whole, the world took his part in the matter.

Supposing the allegation to be false, La Molière had her proper remedy. She had only to proceed against Lescot for violence and slander.

She hesitated, and this confirmed the public opinion. It spread to the theatrical audiences, and the favourite actress began to be received with sneers and chuckles, or ominous silence.

She was alarmed, and went to an old actress called Châteauneuf, who had a long head, and had often advised her in matters of intrigue.

La Châteauneuf said the case was plain. She must take proceedings.

'Nay, but I dare not,' said La Molière. 'They will search into my whole life.'

The older fox laughed, but said, 'Never mind that, child. You are innocent for once; that is an accident you must put to profit, and so throw a doubt on your real indiscretions. Commence proceedings at once. You are ruined if you submit.'

The young fox listened to the old fox with the respect due to our seniors, and laid a criminal information against Lescot.

He stood firm as a rock, persisted in his statements, and brought a very ugly witness, the goldsmith from the Quai des Orfévres. This trader swore to La Molière's necklace as one he had sold, and to her as the lady who was with Lescot when he sold it.

This evidence was fatal to the accuser, both in the

court and with the public. But when Lescot went after Madame Ledoux, to complete his defence, she was not to be found. He let this out, and that he had relied on her. The accuser's agent then smelled a rat, and set the police on to find Ledoux.

Meantime La Molière was the butt of Paris.

But the police succeeded in finding Ledoux, and her examination put a new face on the matter. Ledoux confessed that Monsieur Lescot, being madly enamoured of Mademoiselle Molière, had asked her assistance; that she, not caring to meddle with an intrigue of that kind, had introduced to him a young lady who perfectly resembled Mademoiselle Molière. This young lady, she said, had for maiden name Marie Simonnet, but called herself the widow of a Monsieur Harvé de la Tourelle, a gentleman of Brittany.

On this hint the accuser searched for the young lady in question. They soon found traces of her, and that she was called by her friends 'La Tourelle.'

La Tourelle had disappeared. 'And never will appear, being a phantom,' said Lescot. 'Was ever so audacious a figment? as if one woman could have the face, the figure, the manners, the cough, and the necklace of another!'

Well, the officers of justice caught La Tourelle in the suburbs of Paris, and were astonished at the resemblance.

She was confronted with Mademoiselle Molière in the judge's room, in presence of Ledoux and the President Lescot.

The ladies faced each other like two young stags ready to butt each other. The injured Molière folded her arms grandly, and cocked her nose high, and would fain have looked the other down as a criminal. But the other jade saw she was the younger of the two, and wore a demure air of defiant complacency.

But, setting aside fleeting expression, they were literally one in stature, form, and feature. If each had looked into a mirror, she would have seen the hussey that now faced her.

Amazement painted itself on every face; most of all on Lescot's.

Ledoux persisted in her confession; and both she and La Tourelle were imprisoned, to await the trial.

Lescot now found himself in the wrong box; and it became very important to him that the trial should never come off. With this view he exerted all his influence to bail La Tourelle, meaning, no doubt, to forfeit his recognizances-and send her out of the country. But the judges would accept no bail, and the day of trial was fixed.

Then Lescot bribed the jailer; and he showed La Tourelle how to make her escape in a very ingenious way, that had never occurred to the lady whose genius, like that of many other ladies, was mainly confined to matters of love and intrigue.

Lescot sent her away into the depths of Dauphiné, and her absence suspended that trial.

But La Molière's blood was up, and she appealed personally to men in power, and used all her charms and all her arts.

The result was a new process, under which not one of those who had offended her escaped.

The President Lescot was condemned to stand at

La Molière.

La Tourelle.

The Doubles Confronted.

the bar, and read a paper in presence of La Molière and four witnesses, to be by her chosen:

'I, François Lescot, admit and declare that I, by recklessness and mistake, have used violence against Mademoiselle Molière, here present, and slandered her foully, but without malice of heart, having taken her for another person.'

He was also fined two hundred francs.

By the same judgment the women Ledoux and La Tourelle had to pay a fine of twenty francs each to the King, one hundred francs each to La Molière, and to be whipped, naked, before the gate of the Châtelet, and also before the house of Mademoiselle Molière.

Lescot made his *amende honorable*, and paid his fine. Ledoux paid her fine, and was whipped before the Châtelet and before La Molière's windows; but La Tourelle was more fortunate. Nature has her freaks; she profited by one of them. Lescot, who had now compared in many ways the hussey he adored with the jade who had personated her, was as much enamoured as ever, if not more; but, by Jupiter! it was not the actress but her double he was now in love with. He joined her in Dauphiné, and rewarded her with a life-long attachment, which she is believed to have shared.

La Molière, as her foxy adviser had prophesied, was wonderfully re-established in character. Men said, 'And, no doubt, she was always calumniated.' The judgment of the Châtelet operated as a certificate of her good morals.

The goldsmith's evidence is accounted for thus. There were no jewels to the necklace. A number of gold necklaces had been made on one pattern. The goldsmith swore to La Molière's because he saw the lady, as he thought.

While the affair was yet warm the tragi-comedy of Thomas Corneille, called 'L'Inconnu,' was produced. La Molière was the countess, and in the play a gipsy looked at her hand, and spoke these lines:

> Cette ligne, qui croisse avec celle de vie,
> Marque pour volre gloire un moment très fatal;
> Sur des traits ressemblants on en parlera mal,
>   Et vous aurez une copie.
>   N'en prenez pas trop de chagrin:
>   Si votre gaillarde figurè
> Contre vous, quelque temps, cause un fâcheux murmure,
>   Un *tour de ville* y mettra fin,
>   Et vous rirez de l'aventure.

The public, always quick to fit fiction to reality, seized on these verses at once and applied them to the recent event, and showed their sympathy with the actress by storms of applause.

The favourite, her popularity embellished by a *coup de maître,* now married her actor—and continued her gallantries.

But Célimène, at bottom, lacked neither judgment nor heart. Hence I am able to conclude with a good and touching trait. On the anniversary of Molière's death, which befell in winter, she always collected the poor round his grave, and there bestowed charity on them, and lighted great fires to warm them as they ate the food she bestowed without stint upon them at that great master's tomb.

Poor Célimène. Adieu!

THE KNIGHT'S SECRET.

THOMAS ERPINGHAM was knighted by Henry the Fourth for good and valiant service.

This Sir Thomas Erpingham, Knight of the Garter, afterward fought by the side of Henry the Fifth in his French wars, and was made Warden of the Cinque Ports, but retired to Norwich, his native place. He married a beautiful, pious lady, and after a turbulent career and the horrors of war, desired to end his days in charity. Being wealthy, and of one mind, he and Lady Erpingham built a goodly church in the city, and also erected and endowed a religious house for twelve monks and a prior, close to the knight's house and parted only by a high wall.

But though the retired soldier wished to be at peace with all men, two of his friars were of another mind. Friar John and Friar Richard hated each other, and could by no means be reconciled; neither had ever a good word for t'other; and at last Friar John gave Friar Richard a fair excuse for his invectives. Lady Erpingham came ever to matins in the convent, and Friar John would always await her coming, and attend her through the cloister, with ducks and cringes and open adulation; whereat she smiled, being in truth a most innocent lady, affable to all, and slow to think ill of any man.

But Richard denounced John as a licentious monk, and some watched and whispered; others rebuked Richard; for it was against the monastic rule to put an ill construction where the matter might be innocent.

But Richard stood his ground; and, unfortunately, Richard was right. Misunderstanding the lady's courtesy and charity, Brother John thought his fawning advances were encouraged; and this bred in him such impudence that one day he sent her a fulsome love-letter, and had the hardihood to beg for a private interview.

The lady, when she opened this letter, could hardly believe her senses; and at last, as gentlewomen will be both unsuspicious and suspicious in the wrong place, she made up her mind that the poor, good, ridiculous. friar could never have been so wicked as to write this; nay, but it was her husband's doing, and a trial of her virtue: he was older than herself, and great love is oft tainted with jealousy.

This brought tears into her eyes, to think she should be doubted; but soon anger dried them, and she took occasion to put the letter suddenly into Sir Thomas's hand, and fixed her eyes on him so keenly that, if there had been a flaw in his conjugal armour, no doubt those eyes had pierced it.

The knight read the letter, and turned black and white with rage; his eyes sparkled with fury, and he looked so fearful that the lady was very sorry she had shown him the letter, and begged him not to take a madman's folly to heart.

'Not take it to heart,' said he. 'What! these beggarly shavelings that I have housed and fed, and so lessened my estate and thine—they shall corrupt thee, and rob me of my one earthly treasure? Sit thou down and write.'

'Write, Thomas! what?—to whom?'

'Do as I bid thee, dame,' said he, sternly, 'and no more words.'

Those were days when husbands commanded and wives obeyed; so she sat down trembling, and took the pen.

Then he made her write a letter back to the friar, and say she compassionated his love, and her husband was to ride toward London that night, and her servant, on whom she could depend, should admit him to her by a side-door of the house.

Friar John, at the appointed time, took care to be in the town, for he knew the lay brother who kept the gate of the priory would not let him out so late. He came to the side-door, and was admitted by a servant of the knight, a reckless old soldier, who cared for neither man nor devil, as the saying is, but only for his master. This man took him into a room and left him, then went for the knight: he was not far off. Now the unlucky monk, being come to the conquest of a beautiful lady, as he vainly thought, had fine linen on, and perfumed like a civet. The knight smelled these perfumes, and rushed in upon him with his man, like dogs upon the odoriferous fox, and, in a fury, without giving him time to call for help or to say one prayer, strangled him and left him dead!

But death breeds calm; the knight's rage abated

that moment, and he saw he had done a foul and remorseless deed.   He would have given half his estate to bring the offender back to life.   Half his estate? His whole estate, ay, and his life, were now gone from him: they were forfeited to the law.   So did he pass from rage to remorse, and from remorse to fear.   The rough soldier, seeing him so stricken, made light of all except the danger of discovery.   'Come, noble sir,' said he, 'let us bestir ourselves and take him back to the priory, and there bestow him; so shall we ne'er be known in it.'

Thus urged, the knight roused himself, and he and his man brought the body out, and got it as far as the wall that did part the house from the monastery.   Here they were puzzled awhile, but the man remembered a short ladder in the back yard that was high enough for this job.   So they set the ladder, and, with much ado, got the body up it, and then drew the ladder up and set it again on the other side, and so, with infinite trouble, the soldier got him into the priory.

The next thing was to make it appear Friar John had died a natural death.   Accordingly, he set him up on a rickety chair he found in the yard, balanced him, and left him; mounted the wall again, let himself down, and then dropped into the knight's premises.

He found the knight walking in great perturbation, and they went into the house.

'Now, good master,' said this stout soldier, 'go you to bed, and think no more on't.'

'To bed,' groaned the knight, in agony.   'Why should I go there?   I cannot sleep.   Methinks I shall never sleep again!'

'Then give me the cellar-key, good sir. I'll draw a stoup of Canary.'

'Ay, wine!' said the knight; 'for my blood runs cold in my veins.'

The servant lighted a rousing fire in the dining-hall, and warmed and spiced some generous wine, after the fashion of the day, and there sat these two over the fire awaiting daylight and its revelations.

But, meantime, the night was fruitful in events. The prior, informed of Friar Richard's uncharitable interpretations, had condemned him to vigil and prayer on the bare pebbles of the yard, from midnight until three of the clock. But the sly Richard, at dusk, had conveyed a chair into the yard, to keep his knees off the cold, hard stones.

At midnight, when he came to his enforced devotions, lo, there sat a figure in the chair! He started, and took it for the prior, seated there to lecture him for luxury; but peeping, he soon discovered it was Friar John.

He walked round and round him, talking at him. 'Is it Brother John or Brother Richard who is to keep vigil to-night? I know but one friar in all this house would sit star-gazing in his brother's chair, when that brother wants it to pray in,' etc.

Brother John vouchsafed no reply; and this stung Brother Richard, and he burnt for revenge. 'So be it, then,' said he; 'since my place is taken, I will tell the prior, and keep vigil some other night.' With this he retired, and slammed a door. But having thus disarmed, as he conceived, Brother John's suspicions, he took up an enormous pebble, and slipped back on tiptoe, and getting near the angle of a wall, he flung his great pebble at Brother John, and slipped hastily behind the wall; nevertheless, as he hid, he had the satisfaction of seeing his pebble, which weighed about a stone, strike Brother John on the nape of the neck, and then there was a lumping noise and a great clatter, and Friar Richard chuckled with pride and delight at the success of his throw. However, he waited some minutes before he emerged, and then walked briskly out, like a new-comer. There lay John flat, and the chair upset. Brother Richard ran to him, charged with hypocritical sympathy, and found his enemy's face very white. He got alarmed, and felt his heart: he was stone-dead!

The poor monk, whose hatred was of a mere feminine sort, and had never been deadly, was seized with remorse, and he beat his breast, and prayed in earnest, instead of repeating Pater-nosters—' preces sine mente dictas,' as the great Erasmus calls them.

But other feelings soon succeeded: his enmity to the deceased was well known, and this would be called murder, if the body was found in that yard, and his own life would pay the forfeit.

Casting his eyes round for a place where he might hide the body, he saw a ladder standing against the wall. This surprised him; but he was in no condition to puzzle over small riddles. Terror gave him force: he lifted the body, crawled up the ladder, and placed the body on the wall—it was wider than they build now; then he drew up the ladder, set it on the other side, and took his ghastly load down safely. Then, being naturally cunning and having his neck to save, he went and hid the ladder, took up the body, staggered with it as far as the porch of the knight's house, and set it there bolt upright against one of the pillars.

As he carried it out of the yard he heard a window in the knight's house open. He could not see where the window was, nor whether he was watched and recognised; but he feared the worst, and such was his terror, he resolved to fly the place and bury himself in some distant monastery under another name.

But how? He was lame, and could not go ten miles in a day, whereas a hundred miles was little enough to make him secure.

After homicide theft is no great matter: he resolved to borrow the maltster's mare, and turn her adrift when she had carried him beyond the hue and cry. So he went and knocked up the maltster, and told him the convent wanted flour, and he was to go betimes to the miller for a sack thereof. Now the convent was a good customer to the maltster; so he lent Friar Richard the mare at a word, and told him where to find the saddle and bridle.

Richard fed the mare for a journey and saddled her; then he mounted and rode at a foot pace past the convent, meaning to go quietly through the town, making no stir, then away like the wind.

But as he paced by the knight's house he cast a look askance to see if that ghastly object still sat in the porch.

No; the porch was empty!

What might that mean? Had he come to life? Had the murder been discovered? He began to wonder and tremble.

While he was in this mood there was a great clatter

behind him of horses' feet and clashing armour, and he
felt he was pursued.

The knight and his man sat together, drinking hot
spiced wine and awaiting daylight. The knight would
not go to bed, yet he wanted a change. 'Will daylight
never come?' said he.

''Twill be here anon,' said the soldier; 'in half an
hour.'

The knight said no, it would never come.

The soldier said he would go and look at the sky,
and tell him for certain.

'Be not long away,' said the knight, with a shiver,
'or the dead friar will be taking thy place here and
pledging me.'

'Stuff!' said the soldier; 'he'll never trouble you
more.'

With this he marched out to consult the night, and
almost ran against the dead friar seated in the porch,
white and glaring; this was too much even for the iron
soldier; he uttered a sharp yell, staggered back, and
burst into the room, gasping for breath. He got close
to his master, and stammered out, 'The dead man!—
sitting in the porch!'—and crossed himself energetic-
ally, the first time these thirty years.

The knight stared and trembled: and so they drew
close together, with their eyes over their shoulders.

'Wine!' cried the knight.

'Ay,' said the soldier; 'but I go not alone. He'll
be squatting on the cask else.'

So they went together to the cellar, often looking
round, and fetching two bottles.

They drank them out, and the good wine, falling upon more of the sort, made them madder and bolder. They rolled along, holding on by one another, to the porch, and there they stood and looked at the dead friar, and shuddered.

But the soldier swore a great oath, and vowed he should not stay there to get them hanged. Thereupon a furious fit of recklessness succeeded to their terror: they got a suit of rusty armour and fastened it on the body; then they saddled an old war-horse that was kept in the stable only as a reminiscence, and tied the friar's body on to him with many cords; they opened the stable door and so pricked the old war-horse with their daggers that he clattered out into the road with a bound and a great rattling of rusty armour.

Now, as ill luck would have it, Friar Richard and his borrowed mare were pacing demurely through the town scarce fifty yards ahead. The old horse nosed the mare, and, being left to choose his road, took very naturally after her: but when he got near her the monk looked round and saw the ghastly rider. He gave a yell so piercing it waked the whole street, and, for lack of spurs, drove his bare heels into the mare's side: she cantered down the street at an easy pace, the fearful pageant cantered after, the friar kept turning and yelling, and the windows kept opening and heads popped out to see, and by-and-by doors opened and a few early risers joined in the pursuit, wondering and curious.

The cavalcade never cleared the town of Norwich; the friar, in the blindness of despair, turned his mare up what seemed to him an open lane ; but there was no exit; his dead pursuer came up with him, and he threw himself off, and cried, ' Mercy ! mercy ! mea culpa !— I confess it ! I confess it ! only take that horrible face from me !' and in his despair he owned that he had slain Brother John.

Then some led the horse and his ghastly load away, and wondered sore ; but others hauled Friar Richard to justice ; and he, believing it was a miracle, and Heaven's hand upon him, persisted in his confession, and was cast into prison to abide his trial.

He had not to wait long. In those days the law did not tarry for judges of assize to come round the country now and then. Each town had its mayor and its aldermen, any one of whom could try and hang a man if need was. So Friar Richard was tried next week.

By this time he had somewhat recovered his spirits and his love of life : he defended himself, and said that indeed he had slain his brother, but it was by mis-adventure ; he had thrown a stone at him in some anger, but not to do him deadly harm. This he said with many tears. But, on the other hand, it was proved that he had long hated Brother John ; that he had got out of the priory without passing the door, and had borrowed the maltster's mare on a false pre-tence ; and finally, marks of strangulation had been found on the dead man's throat. All this amazed and overpowered the poor friar, and although his terror at the apparition was not easy to be reconciled with his having been the person who tied the body on the horse, and though one alderman, shrewder than the rest, said he thought a great deal lay behind that, yet, upon the whole, it was thought the safest and most usual course to hang him. So he was condemned to die in three days' time.

The friar, seeing his end so near, struggled no more against his fate. He sent for the prior to confess him, and told the truth with deep sorrow and humility. 'Mea culpa! mea culpa!' he cried. 'If I had not hated my brother and broken our rule, then this had not come upon me!'

Then the prior gave him full absolution, and went away exceeding sorrowful, and doubting the wisdom and justice of laymen, and in particular of those who were about to hang Brother Richard for wilful murder. This preyed upon his mind, and he went to Sir Thomas Erpingham to utter his misgivings, and pray the good knight to work upon the sheriff, who was his friend, for a respite until the matter could be looked into more closely.

The knight was not at home, but my lady saw the prior, and learned his errand. 'Alas, good father,' said she, 'Sir Thomas is not here; he is gone to London this two days.'

The prior went home sick at heart.

Even so long ago as this they hung from Norwich Castle. So the rude gallows was put up at seven o'clock, and at eight Brother Richard must hang and turn in the wind like a weather-cock.

But before that fatal hour a King's messenger galloped into the city and spurred into the courtyard of the castle. Very soon the sheriff was reading a parchment signed by the King's own hand: the gallows was taken down, and the people dispersed by degrees. Some felt ill-used. They thought appointments should be kept, or else not made.

At night Friar Richard, not reprieved, but, to the amazement of smaller functionaries, freely pardoned by his sovereign, in a handwriting a housemaid of this day would blush for, but with a glorious seal the size of an apple-fritter, crept forth into the night, and, gliding along the streets with his head down, slipped into the priory, and was lost to the world for many a long day. Indeed, he was confined to his cell for a month by order of the prior, and ordered to pray thrice a day for the soul of Brother John.

When Brother Richard emerged from his cell he was a changed man. He had gathered amid the thorns of tribulation the wholesome fruit of humility and the immortal flower of charity. Henceforth no bitter word ever fell from his lips, though for a time he had many provocations, and 'Honi soit qui mal y pense' was the rule of his heart. He had made himself of little account, and outlived all enmities. He lived much in his cell, and prayed so often for the soul of Brother John that at last he got to love him dead whom he had hated living.

Time rolled on. The knight's hair turned gray, and the good prior died.

Then there was a great commotion in the little priory, and three or four of the leading friars each hoped to be prior.

That appointment lay with Sir Thomas Erpingham. He attended the funeral of the late prior, and then desired the sub-prior to convene the monks. 'Good brothers,' said he, 'your prior is Brother Richard. I pray you to invest him forthwith, and yield him due love and obedience.'

The knight retired, and the monks stared at each other awhile, and then obeyed, since there was no help for it: they invested Brother Richard in due form ; and such is the magic of station that, in one moment, they began to look on him with different eyes.

The new prior bore his dignity so meekly that he disarmed all hostility. His great rule of life was still, ' Honi soit qui mal y pense,' and there is no course more apt to conciliate respect and good-will. The knight showed him favour and esteem; the monks learned to respect and by-and-by to revere him; but he never ceased to reproach himself, and say masses for the soul of Brother John.

The years rolled on. The knight's gray hair turned white; and one day he sent for the prior and said to him, 'Good father, I have grave matter to entertain you withal.'

'Speak, worshipful sir,' said the prior.

The knight looked at him awhile, but seemed ill at ease, and as one that hath resolved to speak, but is loth to begin. At last he said, 'Sir, there be men that waste their goods in sin, or meanly hoard them till their last hour, yet leave them freely to Mother Church after their death, when they can no longer enjoy them. Others there be whose breasts are laden with a secret crime they ought to confess, and clear some worthy man suspected falsely ; yet they will not tell till they come to die. Methinks this is to be charitable too late, and just when justice can neither cost a man aught nor profit his neighbour. Therefore, not to be one of these, I will reveal to you now a deed that sits heavy on my conscience.'

'You would confess to me, my son?'

'As man to man, sir, but not as penitent to his confessor, for that were no merit in me; it would be no more than bury my secret in a fleshly grave. Nay, what I tell to you, you shall tell to all the world, if good may come of it.'

Here the knight sighed, and seemed much distempered, like one who wrestleth with himself. Then he cast about how he should begin, and to conclude he opened the matter thus: 'Sir, please you read that letter; it was writ by Brother John unto my wife.'

The prior read it, but said never a word.

'Sir,' said the knight, 'do you remember a sad time when you lay in Norwich jail accused of murder, and cast for death?'

'I do remember it well, sir, and the uncharitable heart that brought me to that pass.'

'While you lay there, sir, something befell elsewhere, which I will hide no longer from you. The King being at his palace in London, a knight who had fought by his side in France, sought an audience in private. It was granted him at once. Then the knight fell on his knees to the King, and begged that his life and lands might be spared, though he had slain a man in heat of blood. The King was grave but gentle, and then I showed him that letter, and owned the truth, that I and my servant, in our fury, had strangled that hapless monk.'

'Alas! sir, did you take my guilt upon yourself to

save my life, so fully forfeit?   'Twas I who hated him;
'twas I who flung the stone——'

'At a dead body!   I tell thee, man, we strangled
him, and set his body up where you saw it: hand in
his death you had none.'

The prior uttered a strange cry, and was silent.
The knight continued, in a low voice:

'We set him in the yard; and when we found him
in the porch, being half mad with terror and drink
together, we bound him on the horse and launched
him.   All this I told the King, and he, considering the
provocation, and pitying too much his old companion
in arms, gave me my life and lands, and gave me thine,
which, indeed, was but bare justice.   So now, sir, you
know that you are innocent of bloodshed, and 'tis I am
guilty.'

The knight looked at the churchman, and thought
to see him break forth into thanksgivings.   But it was
not so.   The prior was deeply moved, but not exultant.
'Sir,' said he, like a man that is near choking, 'let
me go to my cell and think over these strange tid-
ings.'

'And pray for me, I do implore you,' said the
knight.

'Ay, sir, and with all my heart.'

Some days passed, and the knight looked to hear
his own tale come round again.   But no; the prior was
silent as the grave.   Then after a while the knight sent
for him again, and said, 'Good father, what I told you
was not under seal of confession.'

'I know it, sir,' said the prior.   'Yet will it go no
farther, unless I should outlive you by God's will. Alas!

sir, you have taken from me that which was the health
of my soul, my belief that I had slain him I hated so
unchristian-like. This belief made humility easy to
me, and even charity not difficult. What engine of
wholesome mortification would be left me now, were I
to go a-prating that I slew not the brother I hated?
Nay, I will never tell the truth, but carry my precious
burden of humility all my days.'

'Oh, saint upon earth!' cried the knight. 'Outlive
me, and then tell the truth.'

The monk replied not, but pondered these words.

And it fell out so that the knight died three years
after, and the prior closed his eyes, and said masses for
his soul; and a good while afterward he did, for the
honour of the convent, reveal this true story to two
young monks, but bound them by a solemn vow not to
spread it during his life. After his death the truth
got abroad, and among churchmen the prior was much
revered, for that he had cured himself of an uncharitable heart, and had enforced on himself the penalty of
unjust shame so many years.

Two women, sisters, kept the toll-bar at a village in Yorkshire. It stood apart from the village, and they often felt uneasy at night, being lone women.

One day they received a considerable sum of money, bequeathed them by a relation, and that set the simple souls all in a flutter.

They had a friend in the village, the blacksmith's wife; so they went and told her their fears. She admitted that theirs was a lonesome place, and she would not live there, for one, without a man. Her discourse sent them home downright miserable.

The blacksmith's wife told her husband all about it when he came in for his dinner. 'The fools!' said he; 'how is anybody to know they have got brass in the house?'

'Well,' said the wife, 'they make no secret of it to me; but you need not go for to tell it to all the town —poor souls!'

'Not I,' said the man: 'but they will publish it, never fear; leave women-folk alone for making their own trouble with their tongues.'

There the subject dropped, as man and wife have things to talk about besides their neighbours.

The old women at the toll-bar, what with their own

fears and their Job's comforter, began to shiver with apprehension as night came on. However, at sunset the carrier passed through the gate, and at sight of his friendly face they brightened up. They told him their care, and begged him to sleep in the house that night. 'Why, how can I?' said he 'I'm due at —— ; but I will leave you my dog.' The dog was a powerful mastiff.

The women looked at each other expressively. 'He won't hurt us, will he?' sighed one of them, faintly.

'Not he,' said the carrier cheerfully. Then he called the dog into the house, and told them to lock the door, and went away whistling.

The women were left contemplating the dog with that tender interest apprehension is sure to excite. At first he seemed staggered at this off-hand proceeding of his master; it confused him; then he snuffed at the door; then, as the wheels retreated, he began to see plainly he was an abandoned dog: he delivered a fearful howl, and flew at the door, scratching and barking furiously.

The old women fled the apartment, and were next seen at an upper window, screaming to the carrier, 'Come back! come back, John! He is tearing the house down.'

'Drat the varmint!' said John, and came back. On the road he thought what was best to be done. The good-natured fellow took his great-coat out of the cart and laid it down on the floor. The mastiff instantly laid himself on it. 'Now,' said John, sternly, 'let us have no more nonsense; you take charge of that till I come back, and don't ye let nobody steal that there, nor yet t' wives' brass.   There now,' said he, kindly, to the women, 'I shall be back this way break-fast-time, and he won't budge till then.'

'And he won't hurt *us*, John ?'

'Lord, no !   Bless your heart, he is as sensible as any Christian ; only, Lord-sake woman, don't ye go to take the coat from him, or you'll be wanting a new gown yourself, and maybe a petticoat and all.'

He retired, and the old women kept at a respectful distance from their protector. He never molested them ; and, indeed, when they spoke cajolingly to him, he even wagged his tail in a dubious way ; but still, as they moved about, he squinted at them out of his bloodshot eye in a way that checked all desire on their parts to try on the carrier's coat.

Thus protected, they went to bed earlier than usual, but they did not undress ; they were too much afraid of everything, especially their protector. The night wore on, and presently their sharpened senses let them know that the dog was getting restless : he snuffed, and then he growled, and then he got up and pattered about, muttering to himself. Straightway, with furni-ture, they barricaded the door through which their protector must pass to devour them.

But by-and-by, listening acutely, they heard a scraping and a grating outside the window of the room where the dog was, and he continued growling low. This was enough : they slipped out at the back-door, and left their money to save their lives : they got into the village. It was pitch-dark, and all the houses black but two : one was the public-house, casting a triangular gleam across the road a long way off, and the other was the blacksmith's house. Here was a piece of fortune for the terrified women. They burst into their friend's house. 'Oh, Jane! the thieves are come!' and they told her in a few words all that had happened.

'La!' said she; 'how timorsome you are! ten to one he was only growling at some one that passed by.'

'Nay, Jane, we heard the scraping outside the window. Oh, woman, call your man, and let him go with us.'

'My man—he is not here.'

'Where is he, then?'

'I suppose he is where other working-women's husbands are, at the public-house,' said she, rather bitterly, for she had her experience.

The old women wanted to go to the public-house for him; but the blacksmith's wife was a courageous woman, and, besides, she thought it was most likely a false alarm. 'Nay, nay,' said she, 'last time I went for him there I got a fine affront. I'll come with you,' said she. 'I'll take the poker, and we have got our tongues to raise the town with, I suppose.' So they marched to the toll-bar. When they got near it they saw something that staggered this heroine. There was actually a man half in and half out of the window. This brought the blacksmith's wife to a stand-still, and the timid pair implored her to go back to the village. 'Nay,' said she, 'what for? I see but one—and— hark! it is my belief the dog is holding of him.' However, she thought it safest to be on the same side with the dog, lest the man might turn on her. So she made her way into the kitchen, followed by the other two;

and there a sight met their eyes that changed all their feelings, both toward the robber and toward each other. The great mastiff had pinned a man by the throat, and was pulling at him, to draw him through the window, with fierce but muffled snarls. The man's weight alone prevented it. The window was like a picture-frame, and in that frame there glared, with lolling tongue and starting eyes, the white face of the blacksmith, their courageous friend's villanous husband. She uttered an appalling scream, and flew upon the dog and choked him with her two hands. He held, and growled, and tore till he was all but throttled himself, then he let go, and the man fell. But what struck the ground outside, like a lump of lead, was in truth a lump of clay! the man was quite dead, and fearfully torn about the throat. So did a comedy end in an appalling and most piteous tragedy; not that the scoundrel himself deserved any pity, but his poor, brave, honest wife, to whom he had not dared confide the villany he meditated.

The outlines of this true story were in several journals. I have put the disjointed particulars together as well as I could. I have tried to learn the name of the village, and what became of this poor widow, but have failed hitherto. Should these lines meet the eye of anyone who can tell me, I hope he will, and without delay.

SUSPENDED ANIMATION.

A JOURNAL called the Los Angeles *Star* recorded the following incident at the time it occurred :—

A gentleman in that city had a very large and beautiful tom-cat, which he had reared from a kitten. It was now five years old, and the two animals were mutually attached. Every morning, when the servant brought in the water for his master's tub, Puss used to come in and sit at the side of the bed, and gaze with admiration at his employer, and sometimes mew him out, but retired into a corner during the tubbing, which he thought irrational, and came out again when the biped was clothed and in his right mind. One day the cat was seen in the garden, tumbling over and over in strong convulsions, which ended in its crawling feebly into the house. The master heard, and was very sorry, and searched for the invalid, but could not find him. However, when he went up to bed at night, there was the poor creature stretched upon the floor at the side of the bed, the very place where he used to sit and gaze at his master, and mew him out of bed.

The gentleman was affected to tears by the affectionate creature's death, and his coming there to die. He threw a handkerchief over poor Tom, and passed a downright unhappy night. He determined, however, to bury his humble friend, and no time was to be lost, the weather being hot. So, when his servant came in to fill his tub, he ordered a little grave to be dug directly, and a box found of a suitable size to receive the remains.

Then he got up, and instead of tubbing, as usual, he thought he would wash poor Tom's body for interment, for it was all stained and dirty with the mould of the garden.

He took the body up, and dropped it into the water with a souse.

That souse was soon followed by a furious splashing that sent the water flying in his face and all about the room, and away flew the cat through the open window, as if possessed by a devil! Nor did the poor body forgive this hydropathic treatment, although successful. He took a perverse view, and had never returned to the house 'up to the time of our going to press,' says the Los Angeles *Star*.

The cat is not the only animal subject to suspension of vital power. Many men and women have been buried alive in this condition, especially on the Continent, where the law enforces speedy interment. Even in Britain—where they do not shovel one into the earth quite so fast—live persons have been buried, and others have had a narrow escape. I could give a volume of instances at home and abroad—one of them an archbishop, who was actually being carried in funeral procession on an open bier when he came to, and objected, in what terms I know not; but the Scotch have an excellent formula in similar cases. It runs thus: 'Bide ye yet, mon; I hae a deal mair mischief to do fir-r-r-st!'

Two recent English cases I could certify to be true: one a little girl at Nuneaton, who lay several days without signs of life; another, a young lady, not known to the public, but to me. She was dead—in medicine; but her mother refused to let her be buried, because there was no sign of decomposition, and she did not get so deadly cold as others had whom that mother had lost by death.

This girl remained unburied some days, till another of God's creatures put in his word: a fly thought her worth biting, and blood trickled from the bite. That turned the scale of opinion, and the girl was recovered, and is alive to this day! However, the curious reader who desires to work this vein need go no farther than the index of the *Annual Register* and the *Gentleman's Magazine.* As for me, I must not be tempted outside my immediate subject. The parallel I shall confine a very large theme to is exact.

At the opening of the century the public facilities for anatomy were less than now; so then robbing the church-yards was quite a trade, and an egotist or two did worse—they killed people for the small sum a dead body fetched.

Well, a male body was brought to a certain surgeon by a man he had often employed, and the pair lumped it down on the dissecting-table, and then the vendor received his money and went.

The anatomist set to work to open the body; but, in handling it, he fancied the limbs were not so rigid as usual, and he took another look. Yes, the man was dead! no pulsation either. And yet somehow he was not quite cold about the region of the heart.

The surgeon doubted: he was a humane man; and so, instead of making a fine transverse cut like that at which the unfortunate author of 'Manon Lescaut' started out of his trance with a shriek to die in right earnest, he gave the poor body a chance; applied hartshorn, vinegar, and friction, all without success. Still he had his doubts; though, to be frank, I am not clear why he still doubted.

Be that as it may, he called in his assistant, and they took the body into the yard, turned a high tap on, and discharged a small but hard-hitting column of water on to the patient.

No effect was produced but this, which an unscientific eye might have passed over: the skin turned slightly pink in one or two places under the fall of water.

The surgeon thought this a strong proof life was not extinct; but, not to overdo it, he wrapped the man in blankets for a time, and then drenched him again, letting the water strike him hard on the head and the heart in particular.

He followed this treatment up till at last the man's eyes winked, and then he gasped, and presently he gulped, and by-and-by he groaned, and eventually uttered loud and fearful cries as one battling with death.

In a word, he came to, and the surgeon put him into a warm bed; and as medicine has its fashions, and bleeding was the panacea of that day, he actually took blood from the poor body. This ought to have sent him back to the place from whence he came—the grave, to wit—but somehow it did not; and next day the reviver showed him with pride to several visitors, and prepared an article.

'Resurrectus' was well fed, and, being a pauper, was agreeable to lie in that bed for ever, and eat the bread of science. But, as years rolled on, his preserver got tired of that. However, he had to give him a suit of his own clothes to get rid of him. Did I say years? I must have meant days.

He never did get rid of him; the fellow used to call at intervals and demand charity, urging that the surgeon had taken him out of a condition in which he felt neither hunger, thirst, nor misery, and so was now bound to supply his natural needs.

However, I will not dwell on this painful part of the picture, lest learned and foreseeing men should, from the date of reading this article, confine resuscitation to quadrupeds.

To conclude with the medical view. To resuscitate animals who seem dead, but are secretly alive, drop them into water from—or else drop water on them from —*a sufficient height.*

LAMBERT'S LEAP.

Near Newcastle is Sandyford Bridge, thirty-six feet above the river, which, like many Northern streams, is seldom quite full, but flows in a channel, with the rocky bed bare on each side; an ugly bridge to look up to or to look over, driving by.

In Scotland and the north of England, when our wise ancestors got hold of so dizzy and dangerous a place, they made the most of it; with incredible perversity they led the approach to such a bridge either down a steep or nearly at right angles. They carried Sandyford Lane up to the bridge on the rectangular plan, and thereby secured two events, which were but the natural result of their skill in road-making, yet, taken in conjunction, have other claims to notice.

At a date I hope some day to ascertain precisely, but at present I can only say that it was very early in the present century, a young gentleman called Lambert was run away with by his horse; the animal came tearing down Sandyford Lane, and, thanks to ancestral wisdom aforesaid, charged the bridge with such momentum and impetus that he knocked a slice of the battlement and half a ton of masonry into the air, and went down after it into the river with his rider.

The horse was killed; Mr. Lambert, though shaken,

was not seriously injured by this awful leap. The masonry was repaired; and, to mark the event, these words, *Lambert's Leap,* were engraved on the new coping-stone. The road was allowed to retain its happy angle.

December 5, 1822, about eleven, forenoon, Mr. John Nicholson, of Newcastle, a student in surgery, was riding in Sandyford Lane. His horse ran away with him, and, being unable to take the sharp turn for such cases made and provided, ran against the battlement of the bridge. It resisted this time, and brought the horse to his knees; but the animal, being now thoroughly terrified, rose and actually leaped or scrambled over the battlement, and fell into the rocky bed below, carrying away a single coping-stone, viz., the stone engraved *Lambert's Leap.* That stone was broken to pieces by the fall. The poor young man was so cruelly injured that he never spoke again; he died at seven o'clock that evening; but the horse was so little the worse, and so tamed by the fall, that he was at once ridden into Newcastle for assistance.

The reversed fates of the two animals, and the two incidents happening within an inch of each other, have earned them a place in this collection.

Richardson's ' Local Historian's Table-book ' relates the second leap, and refers to the first, which is also authenticated.

MAN'S LIFE SAVED BY FOWLS, AND WOMAN'S BY A PIG.

MEN'S lives have been sometimes taken, sometimes saved, by other animals, in ways that sound incredible until the details are given.

Here is a list that offers a glimpse into the subject, nothing more:

1. Several ships and crews destroyed by fish.
2. Two ships and crews saved by fish.
3. One crew saved by a dog.
4. Many men killed by dogs, and many saved.
5. Many men killed by horses, and many saved.
6. Men killed (and saved) by rats.
7. Man killed by a dead pig.
8. Man saved by fowls.
9. Woman saved from death by a live pig.
10. Woman saved by a crocodile.
11. Ditto by a lady-bird.
12. One man executed by the act of a horse.
13. Crows leading to the execution of murderers.
14. A man's life saved by an ape.
15. Ditto by a bear.
16. Ditto by a fox.

Some of these sound like riddles, and are at least

as well worth puzzling over as acrostics and conundrums.

I will leave the majority to rankle in my reader and rouse his curiosity. But I feel he is entitled to some immediate proof that the whole list is not a romance ; so I will relate 8 and 9 by way of specimen.

And here let me premise that, as a general rule, I exclude from this collection all those wonderful stories about animals which are found only in books especially devoted to that subject. Those writers are all theorists —men with an amiable bias in favour of the inferior animals. This tempts them to twist and exaggerate facts, and even to repeat stale falsehoods which have gone the round for years, but never rested on the evidence of an eye-witness.

On the other hand, when some plain man, who has no theory, writes down a story at the time and on the spot, and sends it off to a newspaper or other chronicle of current events, where it lies open to immediate contradiction, then we are on the *terra firma* of history.

Example.— Here is a letter written on the spot and at the time to a newspaper, and transferred from that newspaper to the ' Annual Register : '

EXTRACT OF A LETTER FROM NOTTINGHAM.

' January 9, 1761.

'On Tuesday se'nnight Mr. Hall's servant, of Beckingham, returning from market, and finding the boat at Gainsborough putting off from shore full of people, was so rash and imprudent (to say no worse of it) as to leap his horse into the boat, and with the violence of the fall drove the poor people and their horses to the farther side, which instantly carried the boat into the middle of the stream and overset it.

'Imagine you see the unfortunate sufferers all plunging in a deep and rapid river, calling out for help and struggling for life. It was all horror and confusion; and during this situation the first account was despatched, which assured us that out of eighty souls only five or six were saved. By a second account we were told that there were only thirty on board, but that out of these above twenty had been drowned. This was for some time believed to be the truest account, but I have the pleasure to hear by a third account that many of those who were supposed to be lost have been taken up alive, some of them at a great distance from the ferry, and that no more than six are missing, though numbers were brought to life with difficulty. It was happy for them that so many horses were on board, as all who had time to lay hold of a stirrup or a horse's tail were brought safe to shore.

'A poor man who had a basket of fowls upon his arm was providentially buoyed up till assistance could be had, and he, after many fruitless attempts, was at last taken up alive, though senseless, at a distance of four hundred yards from the ferry.

'A poor woman who had bought a pig, and had tied one end of a string round its foot and the other round her own wrist, was dragged safe to land in this providential manner.'

Observe—I am better than my word; for I have thrown you in the circumstance that the horses saved the rest: certainly in this particular business the lord of the creation does not show that vast superiority to the brutes which he assumes in some of his sculptures and nearly all his writings, Butler's 'Analogy' included. The animal that makes the mischief by his folly is a man; the animals that prove incompetent to save their own lives are the men. All the other animals in the boat, down to the very pig, turn to and pull the lords and ladies of the creation out of the mess one of these peerless creatures had plunged them all into.

EXCHANGE OF ANIMALS.

OLD traditions linger in country places long after they have perished in great towns. Were the English provinces to be groped for modern antiquities, and the sum total presented, the general reader would be amazed at the mass of ancient superstition lingering in modern England. Not only do popish practices, popish legends and charms, flourish in our most Puritanical counties, but even Pagan rites and ceremonies. In the North the mummers at Christmas, of all days, dance a sword-dance which belongs to the worship of a Scandinavian god; in Northumberland and parts of Ireland, the young folk still make little bonfires and leap through them on a certain day, though the practice is forbidden in the Old Testament as an abomination, for this is no other thing than 'going through the fire to Baal,' and is one of the many signs that we Celts were an Oriental tribe. Any novice wishing to strike this vein of lore without much trouble has only to read the excellent book of Mr. Henderson, and grope the index to *Notes and Queries*. I strongly recommend the latter course.

> For index-reading turns no student pale,
> Yet takes the eel of science by the tail.

My own reading in such matters has taught me one

thing—to suspect old tradition whenever I encounter any strange practice down in the country. Why, even rustic mispronunciation is often a relic where it passes for an error. Rusticus calls a coroner's inquest 'crowner's quest,' and the educated smile superior. But Rusticus is not wrong; he is only in arrear. 'Crowner's quest' is the true mediæval form, and was once universal. Every English peasant calls a theătre a theătre, and young gentlemen sneer. Yet theătre is the true pronunciation; and fifty years before Shakespeare, nobody, high or low, mispronounced the word into theătre, as he does and we do.

To the tenacity of old tradition I ascribe a prevalent notion, in rude parts of this country, that an Englishman and his wife can divorce themselves under certain conditions. 1st, the parties must consent; 2nd, there must be a public auction; 3rd, the lady must be sold with a halter round her neck. That our rural population ever invented this law is improbable in itself and against evidence : there are examples of the practice as old as any chronicle we have; and I really suspect that in some barbarous age—later, perhaps, than our serious worship of Baal, but anterior to our earliest Saxon laws—this rude divorce by consent was the unwritten law of Britain.

The thing has been done in my day many times, and related in the journals, and I observe that it is always done with similar ceremonies, and that the lower order of people, though they jeer, are not shocked at it, nor does it seem to strike them as utterly and profoundly illegal. It dates, I apprehend, from a time when marriage was a partnership at will ; and the Roman theory

that marriage is a sacrament, and the English theory that marriage is not a sacrament, but half a sacrament, were alike unknown to a primitive people.

My note-book contains numerous examples. I select one with a bit of colour, which was published at the date when it occurred.

Joseph Thompson rented a farm of forty acres in a village three miles from Carlisle. In 1829 he married a spruce, lively girl twenty-two years of age.

They had many disputes, and no children. So after three years they agreed to part.

The bell-man was sent around the village to announce that Joseph Thompson would sell Mary Anne Thompson by auction on April 5, 1832, at noon precisely.

At the appointed hour Joseph Thompson stood on a table, and his wife a little below him on an oak chair, with a halter of straw round her neck. He put her up for sale in terms that a by-stander thought it worth while to take down on the spot:

‘ Gentlemen, I have to offer to your notice my wife, Mary Anne Thompson, otherwise Williamson. It is her wish as well as mine to part for ever, and will be sold without reserve to the highest bidder. Gentlemen, the lot now offered for competition has been to me a bosom serpent. I took it for my comfort and the good of my house; but it became my tormentor, a domestic curse, a night invasion, and a daily devil. The Lord deliver us from termagant wives, and troublesome widows! Gentlemen, avoid them as you would a mad dog, a roaring lion, a loaded pistol, *cholera morbus*, or any other pestilential phenomenon—’

Here it seems to have occurred to Joseph Thompson that he was not going the way to sell his lot at a high figure, so he tried to be more the auctioneer and less the husband.

'However,' said he, 'now I have told you her little defects, I will present the bright and sunny side of her. She can read novels, milk cows, and laugh and weep with the same ease that you could toss off a glass of ale. What the poet says of women in general is true to a hair of this one :

> Heaven gave to women the peculiar grace
> To laugh, to weep, and cheat the human race.

She can make butter and scold the maid ; she can sing Moore's Melodies, and pleat her own frills and caps. She cannot make rum, nor gin, nor whisky ; but she is a good judge of all three from long experience in tasting them. What shall we say for her, with all her perfections and imperfections? — fifty shillings to begin ?'

There was a dead silence. He had better have employed George Robins, Sr. 'Cuilibet in suâ arte credendum.' There was no bidding at all. Then the auctioneer was angry, and threatened to take the lot home.

The company in general sustained this threat with composure; but one Mears conceived hopes, and asked modestly whether an exchange could not be made. 'I have here,' said he, 'a Newfoundland dog—a beauty. He can fetch and carry ; and if you fall in the water, drunk or sober, he'll pull you out.'

Thompson approved the dog, but objected to give a

Christian in even exchange for a quadruped. Each species has a prejudice in its own favour, owing to which the company backed him. So at last Mears agreed to give the dog and twenty shillings to boot.

The bargain was made. Thompson took the halter off the wife and put it round the dog, and Mears led his purchase away by the hand, amid the shouts and huzzas of the multitude, in which they were joined by Thompson.

After a while, however, the latter recollected he had a duty to perform. 'I must drink the new-married couple's health,' said he gravely. Accordingly he adjourned with his dog and his money to the public-house, and toasted his deliverer so zealously that he took nothing home from the sale except the dog. Fortunately for *him*, a man can't drink his superior.

LONDON : PRINTED BY
SPOTTISWOODE AND CO., NEW-STREET SQUARE
AND PARLIAMENT STREET

www.ingramcontent.com/pod-product-compliance
Lightning Source LLC
Chambersburg PA
CBHW020943120726

47905CB00008B/2649